A DANGEROUS ACCUSATION

"Rumor has it that you think I am witless and utterly boring," Gilbey said, and stared into Venetia's eyes, searching for the truth.

"Well, I—" Venetia started to say.

She did not finish. The very air around them seemed charged.

"Tell me if you find this boring, then," Gilbey said softly, his voice husky. He slipped his arms around her and brought her against him. He found her lips and proceeded to kiss her as thoroughly as he knew how.

Lost in that kiss, Venetia felt an almost overwhelming urge to surrender. His mouth was gentle yet demanding, he tasted warm and slightly spicy. She was aware of every inch of her body that pressed against his, of his arms around her.

No, she told herself. This was impossible. Impossible that this perfect gentleman could be doing this. Impossible that she could be letting him.

Impossible, she thought one last time in despair. If only it were. . . .

An Unlikely Hero

by

Gail Eastwood

A SIGNET BOOK

SIGNET
Published by the Penguin Group
Penguin Books USA Inc., 375 Hudson Street,
New York, New York 10014, U.S.A.
Penguin Books Ltd, 27 Wrights Lane,
London W8 5TZ, England
Penguin Books Australia Ltd, Ringwood,
Victoria, Australia
Penguin Books Canada Ltd, 10 Alcorn Avenue,
Toronto, Ontario, Canada M4V 3B2
Penguin Books (N.Z.) Ltd, 182–190 Wairau Road,
Auckland 10, New Zealand

Penguin Books Ltd, Registered Offices:
Harmondsworth, Middlesex, England

First published by Signet, an imprint of Dutton Signet,
a division of Penguin Books USA Inc.

First Printing, August, 1996
10 9 8 7 6 5 4 3 2 1

To my dad, my best PR man!
I love making you proud of me,
and I love you.

Chapter One

"Sorry, old man, but I'm telling you 'no' is simply not an acceptable answer. You can't keep your head buried in books all of the time. I want you to meet my sisters."

The son of the Duke of Roxley, Nicholas St. Aldwyn, Marquess of Edmonton, strode purposefully across the green by the River Cam, trying to keep pace with his longer-legged friend Gilbey Kentwell, Viscount Cranford. The late-afternoon sun cast exaggerated shadows of the young men upon the grass, as if to emphasize that while both were tall, Edmonton still did not quite reach the measure of his companion.

The viscount made no effort to slow his steps, but for a moment he did allow a grin to light up his normally serious face. "My apologies, Nicholas. I should have said, 'No, thank you ever so very much. It is more than kind of you to ask, and I am overwhelmingly honored by the invitation, but I must regretfully decline.'"

Edmonton growled. "Dressing it up won't improve it and neither will groveling."

"Just so! 'No' means 'no' any way it is offered. I have work to finish up here, and obligations to see fulfilled."

The two friends were headed toward the river and the newly built King's Bridge, whose single arch was illuminated by dancing reflections of sunlight from the water beneath it. Beyond it the familiar Gothic spires of King's College Chapel, Cambridge, rose majestically into a clear sky.

The marquess made an extra push to catch up. "You have nothing that can't be put off for two weeks or passed on to someone else. Of course you'll come. You wouldn't want to offend me—I'm far too valuable a friend."

Cranford's laughter bounced off the stone buildings across

the river. "That sounds suspiciously like a threat, my so-called friend."

"At least hear the rest of the guest list, Gilbey. I promise you this affair at my father's will not be like any ordinary house party you have ever been to."

As they reached the bridge Cranford finally slowed and took stock of the determined expression upon his friend's face. Nicholas had obviously forgotten, as he often did, the vast differences in rank, wealth, and experience that separated the two friends. Gilbey had only attended two house parties in his life, both in the past year and then only through Nicholas's connections and in his company. Such meager exposure did not provide much basis for comparison.

"I'm sure the list is most impressive," he began dubiously as they crossed over the river. Only the quacking protest of some ducks and the faint rattle of traffic on King's Parade disturbed the surrounding quiet. "I might be more easily convinced if you can assure me that I would not be on anyone's list of potential husbands. You know I have had enough trouble with women in this past year to last me for the next several."

"You'll get over it."

"I suppose, in time. Nevertheless, I am not in the market for a wife, nor in the mood for a party, and I doubt very much that I would fit in amongst your father's exalted guests. What, pray tell, would be the point of attending?"

"Ah," said Edmonton with a significant lift of his expressive St. Aldwyn eyebrows.

He took hold of Gilbey's elbow and as Gilbey began to head toward the residence halls at one side of the smooth quadrangle lawn, Edmonton gently but firmly turned him to the right and propelled him in an entirely new direction. Their shadows melded into a single long stripe that moved along beside them.

"I say, Nicholas—"

The duke's son shook his head. "For one thing, it is imperative to improve your social cachet. Only a very select group are honored with invitations to parties at Rivington. Trust me, it will do you credit for many seasons to be numbered among the Duke of Roxley's guests."

"But, Nicholas—"

"As for the fair sex, you need not worry. You've learned not to fall passionately in love with opera dancers who neither expect nor desire you to love them, and you've learned how to avoid traps set by simpering young ladies who believe that they are passionately in love with you!"

Gilbey sighed, recognizing a sense of impending doom. "You make it sound so simple. I am still greatly obliged to you for helping me out of both of those unfortunate episodes. But, Nicholas—"

Edmonton shook his head again, still refusing to be interrupted. "I'm taking you for tea." They had entered a narrow lane, deep in shadow at this time of day, and his voice echoed between the buildings as did the sound of their footsteps on the pavement. "There won't be any opera dancers at Rivington and you will be relatively immune to all that will be going on. I'm asking you to come as my own personal guest. You can enjoy some fine fishing. And I promise that you will find my sisters fascinating."

"I'll be immune?"

"The point of the party is, after all, to provide husbands for my troublesome twin siblings. I suspect my father will not settle for anyone ranking lower than an earl. If you'll forgive my speaking frankly, despite your admirable progress in restoring your estates, your fortune and title are too modest to interest either my father or the other marriage-minded guests who will be at this affair."

Gilbey was not even slightly offended. Instead, he felt relieved and he brightened considerably. Perhaps Nicholas had not lost his perspective after all.

"I had not considered that," he replied cautiously. He did not wish to offend Nicholas, certainly, and it did sound as if he could attend the party without complicating his life.

He had heard of Nicholas's sisters, of course. In the two years since their come-out they had become notorious for refusing all offers of marriage and for putting their suitors through all sorts of tests. As the twins were wealthy, titled, and supposedly quite beautiful, this behavior had only made them seem a greater challenge to certain gentlemen among the *ton*. To witness the contest might indeed prove interesting. Certainly, the chance to see Rivington, the duke's famed country estate, would be compensation of sorts for the time spent. Two weeks!

"To tell the truth, I could use your help," Edmonton confided in a more serious tone. "My father does not take a very active part in these things once he has them all arranged to suit his wishes. As a chaperon I will be sadly outnumbered at this affair. My aunt is coming to help, but she is bringing my cousin Adela, and I suspect they will be husband-hunting for themselves. I know I can trust you—you could be an extra pair of eyes for me."

"Huh. You're asking a man who wears spectacles."

"You happen to be extremely observant, my friend, when your head is not in a book. But you simply cannot go through life buried like that all of the time. I think you are wedded to this place."

"I'm not," Gilbey said, but his friend's comment had struck a sore spot. Gilbey's own sister Gillian had just made that accusation in her latest letter to him. Nicholas's invitation was the perfect way to prove her wrong. At any rate, Gilbey saw that he no longer had a choice. He owed Nicholas for so many kindnesses shown in the past three years, to refuse him this favor would be unpardonable.

"All right." He relented at last. "Right or wrong, no one is ever proof against your persuasiveness, Nicholas—as I of all people should know by now. God help our country the day you take your father's seat in the House of Lords! So who are the poor victims on the official suitors list?"

"Save us, you'd think my sisters were harpies with two heads."

"Knowing you, I think I'll reserve judgment on that until after I've met them."

Little more than a week later the viscount found himself ensconced in Lord Edmonton's elegant traveling coach, pondering the butter softness of the leather upholstery and the comfortable difference a fine set of springs could make as the Gloucestershire countryside rolled past the window.

"We are nearly there, now," Edmonton said offhandedly as the carriage turned into a lane. He nodded toward the window. "That's the first entrance."

Gilbey peered out, anxious for his first view of Rivington. A low wall with modest gateposts marked their entry into the Duke of Roxley's domain, but there was nothing else. The drive rose and dipped over several hills of increasing size without any visible hint of a dwelling. As the carriage climbed to the top of each hill, Gilbey could see another patchwork of fields and woodlands laid out below him, yet the road still led on with no apparent end in sight. Impressed anew with the gulf between his own station and that of his friend, Gilbey cleared his throat uneasily.

"I am not convinced that this is the wisest idea that you have ever had, Nicholas," he said.

The young man sitting opposite him chuckled. "You imply that at least some idea of mine in the past has had some merit. I think I am flattered. But you will see. Do you not trust me? Have I not been your social mentor these past three years? You will get on famously with my father once he discovers your genuine interest in his Italian marbles. And I think because you are a twin yourself, you may well understand my sisters better than most people."

Gilbey's uneasiness increased. Did his friend have some hidden expectations? He was not sure how to respond. Nicholas's sisters were reputedly identical, although he had heard that among the *ton* they were irreverently known as "the lamb and the lioness." Apparently they differed dramatically in temperament. Gilbey thought he could relate better to that difference than to the fact that they were twins. His own twin sister Gillian was petite, auburn-haired, and given to trouble, while he was tall, flaxen-haired, and peace-loving above all else.

"I doubt that I can provide any special perspective," he warned Nicholas, shaking his head. "My twin and I are as different from each other as twins can be. It was nothing more than a trick of nature that had us formed and born at the same time. Now that she is comfortably married, my life is certainly calmer." He did not add that he missed her terribly.

"Consider it an experiment," Edmonton said. He edged forward on his seat and directed Gilbey's attention to the window once again. "Here. If you watch carefully you will get a first glimpse of Rivington beyond that stand of trees when we come to the top of the next rise."

The note of anticipation in his voice told Gilbey volumes about his friend's pride in and attachment to his ancestral home. It seemed as if Nicholas's public facade of the polished, bored man of the world had gradually slipped away during the carriage drive from London, where they had gone from Cambridge to procure suitable clothes. Gilbey knew Nicholas well, and was fond of the private man behind the facade. It pleased him to share this small moment with his friend, and he positioned himself close to the window where he could see. He pushed away his concern that the private Nicholas would disappear once they arrived at Rivington among the Duke of Roxley's guests.

"There it is!"

Gilbey peered over the treetops and caught his breath as he made out the impressive outline of crenellated towers and what seemed like countless chimneys, gables, and ornamental roof finials in the distance beyond. Rivington appeared to be the size of an entire village. The sight quickly was lost again behind the trees, and several more minutes passed before the carriage rounded the last of a wide, sweeping curve and the entire massive structure of Rivington came into view, set in its own private valley, with the River Coln at its feet.

Edmonton chuckled. "That first glimpse teases, but nothing can prepare you for the full effect of seeing Rivington from here."

Gilbey could not tear his eyes away from the sight in front of him. Built on a slight rise beyond a decidedly Tudor gatehouse, Rivington sprawled over its site with a majesty that defied convention. From this side it showed some attempt at architectural symmetry, for an imposing facade with a central entrance was balanced by equal numbers of window bays stretching off to either side and a matching pair of towers. But this had clearly been imposed upon an eccentric collection of earlier structures, whose irregular rooflines revealed themselves behind and at either end of the central section.

"The oldest tower and part of the chapel dates to 1380," Nicholas said, the pride in his voice unmistakable. "The tower on the right was added later to provide a bit of balance." He related a short history of the estate and his family's three-hundred-year connection to it while the carriage covered the remaining distance to the bridge over the river and the ornate stone gatehouse.

Gilbey hardly noticed when they were greeted and waved through enthusiastically, so enthralled was he by the majesty of what he saw. Even his doubts and trepidation about being a guest at Rivington were temporarily forgotten.

Meanwhile, Nicholas's twin sisters, Lady Venetia and Lady Vivian St. Aldwyn, were perched on the sofa in the Chinese dressing room between their chambers, their golden heads bent over a piece of paper.

"It's just like being dealt a hand of cards—you don't know what you've got until you sort it all out," Venetia was saying. "Let me see the list."

She scanned the paper and groaned, thrusting it back into her sister's hand. "Aunt Alice did make additions, just as I thought."

"Surely it cannot be as bad an assortment as Papa assembled the last time he did this to us."

"You think not?" Venetia made a face that caused her twin to laugh, although she sobered immediately. "Consider Colonel Hatherwick. He is much too old. We already know that he comes only for the trout fishing. The only reason Papa keeps including him is because they are such good friends. Can you imagine being married to him? He reminds me of a fish!

"Then there is Lord Chesdale, ex-cavalry officer. Do you not recall how he constantly peers through his quizzing glass and talks of nothing but horses? He puts me in mind of an eggcup, with those long, spindly legs and that big barrel chest of his. And they say that Lord Wistowe has a different mistress for each day of the week. I wonder how he keeps track of them!"

"Netia! What a thing to speak of! And I cannot help feeling that we are being uncharitable by judging them so before some have even arrived," Vivian said. "Should we not try to keep an open mind?"

Venetia made a rather unladylike sound, something between

a snort and a growl. "If I thought there was even the remotest chance that any of them would give us the same benefit, I would perhaps return the favor."

Their discussion was interrupted by a discreet knock on the dressing room door. A young footman in splendid black velvet livery and powdered wig presented himself with a formal bow.

"Lady Venetia, Lady Vivian, I am sent to inform you that guests are arriving. There are two carriages at the front entry now—Lord Munslow's and Lord Marchthorpe's and another is approaching along the carriageway."

"Lady Colney is not yet arrived, Martin?"

"No, my lady."

"Thank you. We'll come right away."

The servant withdrew, and the two young women turned to each other.

"Lord Munslow," Venetia said, wrinkling her pert nose. "And Aunt Alice is not here yet to do the greetings."

"Lord Munslow? I don't recall . . ." said Vivian.

"Come, we'll reconnoiter from the gallery before we go down." Venetia caught up her sister's hand as she rose hastily from the settee.

"Oh, Netia, they'll be wondering where we are!"

"Not if we're quick enough, and besides, I don't care if they do. None of this affair was our idea."

Gilbey's anxieties returned to him in full force as Nicholas's carriage pulled up in front of Rivington. The massive scale of the house in such close proximity seemed overwhelming and seemed also to symbolize in a most solid form the very different world of wealth to which Nicholas belonged. So did the two other carriages which were drawn up before the grand entrance of the house. Both, Gilbey noticed, were every bit as elegant as Nicholas's, with gleaming appointments and handsome heraldic arms decorating the doors.

"Nicholas," he said, trying hard to control his voice, "I don't belong here. What could you have been thinking of? This is a mistake, an absurd mistake. If your coachman will take me back as far as Northleach, I will hire a post-chaise to take me back to London."

"Nonsense." The single word was spoken with the finality

and unquestionable authority that proved Nicholas was every inch a duke's son. Further argument was pointless. Gilbey watched helplessly as several servants descended upon their carriage and his friend got out. He had no choice but to follow as one of the footmen continued to hold the door of the carriage open for him.

As he emerged he saw a bevy of footmen flocking about rather like blackbirds, he thought, in their black coats with silver lacings. They paused to pay their respects to Nicholas, and then returned to unloading what seemed to be more luggage than either of the two carriages ahead could possibly have held. The scene reminded Gilbey of a comic routine he had seen Grimaldi perform at Sadler's Wells, and that brought a smile to his lips.

"That's the spirit—smile in place, head up," counseled Nicholas in a low voice. "If you don't own the world, at least try to look as if you do, and half the people will believe it. Shall we go in?"

The vast entry hall had a marble floor and marble columns and a gallery that ran around all four sides of the huge room. The vaulted ceiling must have been forty feet from the floor and was lit by a skylight in the center. There were a number of people in the hall at that moment, including footmen depositing luggage and the guests who had arrived just before Nicholas and Gilbey. More servants entered bearing additional luggage, some of it from Nicholas's carriage.

Nicholas appeared to be looking for someone. "I don't expect my father to—"

Just as he began to speak there was a cry and a sudden commotion behind them. Gilbey had a sinking premonition of disaster as he turned to look.

Until that moment, Lady Venetia and Lady Vivian had been observing the hubbub below them from a relatively unnoticeable position behind the rail of the gallery.

"That is Lord Munslow who just handed his hat to Blaine," Venetia said in a low voice. "I suppose because he is tall he thinks no one will notice that bald spot on the top of his head. And that is the Marquess and Marchioness of Marchthorpe and their daughter, Elizabeth. We met them in London, Vivi—I distinctly remember how shy Elizabeth was. Their son Lord Lindell is on the guest list also."

She paused for a moment, surveying the guests under discussion. "Look, there is Nicholas! And I would say Elizabeth has been miraculously cured of her affliction, would you not agree? She cannot seem to tear her eyes away from that fellow who just came in with him. Who is he, I wonder?"

"He is even taller than Lord Munslow. Is he not on the list?" Vivian peered down curiously, leaning a bit over the railing.

Venetia ran her finger down the paper. "I am quite certain he is not. Unless—perhaps this is he: Gilbey Kentwell, Viscount Cranford. I have no idea who that might be. We have already suffered most of these other people at one time or another."

"Netia, you are incorrigible! My, I do think he is quite handsome. Look! Now he has removed his hat. His hair is so pale it is almost silver."

Venetia did look up and noticed her sister's position at the rail. "Hssst! Don't hang over so, Vivi—someone will notice us! Then we'll have no choice but to go down and do the pretty. We'll be subjected to that soon enough as it is."

As she drew her twin back from the rail she took a good look at the unknown visitor. "Hmph. Too tall, too blond, and too thin by half," she pronounced. "Do you not think his nose rather long? He looks like a schoolmaster with those spectacles. I would hardly count him as a likely prospect!"

"I wonder if he is meant to be a prospect at all—for one thing, he is only a viscount, if indeed he is who we suppose," Vivian answered. "Perhaps he is just a friend Nicholas brought with him from Cambridge."

Venetia's gaze sharpened with interest. "You don't think Aunt Alice put him on the list? He is obviously not as wealthy and connected as Lord Newcroft, or surely we would have met him before now. After all, Lord Newcroft is on the list, and he is only a viscount. But that does put a different cast on things."

It was Vivian's turn to groan. "Nicholas will never forgive you if you get up to tricks with his friend, Netia. And Papa will never forgive you this time if you drive off all the men he's lined up."

"What about you, Vivi? Would you forgive me? Do you

think there is anyone in this batch who could be the husband you need?"

At just that moment the sharp exclamation that claimed everyone's attention broke through the sound of voices in the hall below. Both young women rushed back to the rail to see what was happening.

They were just in time to see a cascade of personal effects spill forth from a heavy portmanteau carried by one hapless footman. It was he who had cried out as the worn straps on the shabby luggage in question let go. A small amount of snowy linen fell into a heap, and books—dozens of books—scattered across the polished floor.

The reactions in the hall were as varied as the number of people standing there. Lady Marchthorpe exclaimed loudly in astonishment while her daughter Elizabeth shrank back as if she feared contamination. Lord Marchthorpe turned his back on the scene and shepherded his ladies to one side of the room as if he shared his daughter's fear. Lord Munslow merely stepped to one side and surveyed the accident disdainfully. The footman turned to Gilbey and Nicholas and began to apologize in frantic tones. The other servants appeared to be frozen in horror.

"Nicholas is laughing," said Vivian in scandalized tones.

"His friend is turning bright red," observed Venetia. Smiling mischievously, she added, "Perhaps now is a good time to go down and join them, after all."

Chapter Two

If only the earth could have opened and swallowed him, his books, and his broken portmanteau, Gilbey would have been eternally grateful. Unfortunately, the stone floor beneath him remained as solid as ever. When he felt the blood rush to his face he mentally cursed for the thousandth time the nearly alabaster skin he had been born with. He groaned and turned to Nicholas, who was laughing rather unhelpfully beside him.

"Confounded baggage! Forgive me, Nicholas. What a scene! You see? I told you—"

The duke's son stopped laughing long enough to draw a breath and punched the young viscount playfully on the shoulder. "I should have known I couldn't separate you from your books for two weeks, Gilbey." Turning to the room at large, he added in a louder voice, "What a splendid joke on me, my friends, don't you agree? You have to admire Lord Cranford's originality."

Quite naturally, no guest would risk being so rude as to disagree with the son of their host. Gilbey watched the others transform their various negative reactions into artful titters of laughter. While most did not appear entirely convinced that they should go so far as to admire Gilbey, at least he would now be spared their immediate scorn. He thought Nicholas was the one who should be admired—he could turn a situation around so easily!

The poor footman who had been carrying the ill-fated portmanteau was still apologizing profusely, obviously afraid that he would be held to blame for the accident. Gilbey hastened to reassure the man, and Nicholas ordered the servants to start gathering together the collection of books.

"We'll find something else to put them in," he said with a chuckle still lurking behind his words.

Gilbey stooped to pick up a volume that had landed by his feet. As he inspected it for creased pages or a cracked spine he happened to glance up and saw a vision he thought he must have dreamed. Two young women, more lovely than any he had ever seen, had entered the room and were walking toward him. They had to be Nicholas's sisters, for although they had dressed their glorious, guinea-gold hair in somewhat different styles, they seemed in every other respect identical. They had the same graceful, slender figures, the same flawless, creamy skin, and the same delicate facial features. They wore matching gowns of apricot muslin. As he watched, transfixed, one of them bent gracefully to retrieve a book from the floor and held it out at arm's length.

"You never told me," Gilbey said accusingly to Nicholas under his breath.

"What?"

"That they were so exquisite!"

His friend shrugged, as if the omission did not signify. Gilbey reflected that perhaps it did not, for certainly he had heard others say that the St. Aldwyn twins were beautiful. Somehow the report had never impressed him, and perhaps the truth from Nicholas would not have made any difference. But a man would have to be made of stone not to feel an attraction to such goddesses, and Gilbey felt more certain than ever that the two weeks looming ahead of him would be miserably difficult. Immune? Ha! How could he have believed that his desire to remain unattached and uninvolved would render him both numb and blind? How could Nicholas have thought so, too? They had only taken into consideration the attitudes of the others at the party, never Gilbey's own feelings.

"*A Defense of Ancient Architecture,* by Morris," read the twin who had picked up Gilbey's book. She quirked an elegantly arched eyebrow in a manner so like her brother's that Gilbey was forced to smile, releasing his momentary paralysis. She was a few steps ahead of her sister and reached the young men first.

"Really, Nicholas, what a unique arrival. We seem to have more underfoot than a mere houseful of guests." She gave

Nicholas a sisterly hug and stepped back to inspect Gilbey
with a frankly appraising stare.

"Hullo, Nicholas. Welcome home." The second twin
hugged her brother as well and then moved next to her sister to
await the introductions. She glanced at Gilbey curiously, but
the look was fleeting and demure.

"Allow me to present my good friend Lord Cranford,"
Nicholas said, bowing to his sisters quite formally. He winked
as he turned toward Gilbey. "My sisters, Lady Venetia and
Lady Vivian St. Aldwyn."

They held out their gloved hands to him in turn, and he dutifully kissed them. He tried very hard to keep his own hand
steady.

Around them the servants had retrieved most of the errant
books and collected them into a pile under the watchful eye of
Blaine, who was apparently in charge. Someone magically appeared with a trunk in which to pack them.

"If I am not mistaken, this volume belongs to you, Lord
Cranford." The twin who had greeted Nicholas first, Lady
Venetia, also addressed Gilbey first. She held out his book. "I
must say, most people do not feel the need to bring such things
to a house party." She treated him to a heart-melting smile that
revealed an enchanting pair of dimples in her cheeks. "Did you
fear that we would not keep you amply entertained?"

For a moment Gilbey felt as tongue-tied as the greenest
schoolboy. Nicholas's sister was flirting with him and trying
to provoke him at the same time, he knew. She had uttered the
last sentence in a most suggestive tone, and when he looked
into her eyes—her gorgeous violet-blue eyes—he saw the
devil dancing there as surely as he had often seen it in his own
sister's eyes. How was he supposed to answer? She clearly
knew the effect she had on a man.

"Netia—," Nicholas began in a warning tone, but Gilbey
was not about to let his friend fight all of his battles. He forced
a cool smile onto his face and accepted the book from Venetia's hand with what he hoped would pass for indifference.

"Thank you, Lady Venetia. As your brother knows, I find it
difficult to be parted from my studies for long. My eccentricity
is no reflection on your family's hospitality, I assure you."

That was the role he would play, he decided—the eccentric

scholar, too devoted to his books to be of interest to anyone. How could he possibly keep his feelings under control if Nicholas's sisters paid any attention to him at all?

"You are far more polite than my sister deserves," Lady Vivian said with a reproving glance toward her twin. "Welcome to Rivington, Lord Cranford. We are pleased to make your acquaintance." Gilbey caught only a sweet smile and a quick flash of her violet eyes before she added, "If you are a friend of Nicholas's, you must be quite an exceptional fellow. I hope you will enjoy your stay with us. Please, will you excuse us while we greet our other newly arrived guests?"

Gilbey nodded and could not help watching in admiration as the twins moved away.

Beside him Nicholas chuckled. "Your 'eccentricity'? I must say, friend, you slipped out of that one quite handily. I do apologize for Venetia's behavior. She has gotten away with it for so long now I fear she cannot change. I trust you do not need me to tell you now which one of my sisters is 'the lioness' and which one 'the lamb'?"

"They are both utterly enchanting, Nicholas. I can see that coming here was an even bigger mistake than I thought."

Nicholas took him by the arm and began to walk. "Oh, nonsense. You're not in love. Every man is bowled over the first time he meets them—why should you be different? Trust me, you'll soon get caught up in the swim of things. There will be a good deal going on to hold your interest."

Gilbey was not altogether pleased with the casual way Nicholas dismissed his reaction, but perhaps his friend was right. Why indeed should he consider himself different? Perhaps as he became a bit more accustomed to the twins, he would find their effect on him less powerful.

"You definitely had an improving effect upon Vivian, I must say," Nicholas added. "She seldom has so much to say to anyone she has just met."

The speculative gaze he turned on Gilbey made the young viscount distinctly uncomfortable. Before Gilbey could reply, however, Nicholas abruptly changed the subject. "Here, let me introduce you to these other guests while we are still here in the hall. There will be many more unfamiliar faces for you when we gather for dinner, and I must greet these people, anyway."

He glanced about once again, as he had done just before the accident with the books. "My father does not condescend to greet guests upon their arrival, but I am surprised that my Aunt Alice is not here to supervise the ritual. She has served as hostess for my father ever since my mother's death. I can't remember her ever arriving later than I have, for anything!"

He steered Gilbey toward Lord Munslow, casting back a grin. "Not to worry, old fellow. Refreshments will be served on the terrace outside the salon very shortly whether Aunt Alice is here or not. Tradition is tradition, after all."

The twins watched the last footman stagger out of the hall carrying several pieces of Lady Marchthorpe's baggage. As they followed him into the grand salon behind the hall, Venetia sighed.

"I hope that is the last of the guests for a while," she said, smoothing an imaginary wrinkle from her skirt. "I have quite completely lost track of who has arrived and who has not, except for Aunt Alice, of course."

"We've nearly everyone, I think," Vivian replied. "Lord Amberton, the Upcotts, Lord Munslow, Lord Lindell, the Whitgreaves—"

"Oh, do stop!" exclaimed her sister, laughing. "You are making my head spin. We had best prepare to feed them all for the first of countless times ahead of us."

She paused and looked at Vivian with concern. "Are you quite certain that you are up to this? We have dinner and the entire evening still to get through. Perhaps you should rest. I can pour tea and make your excuses, if you like."

Vivian shook her head. "I am fine. Besides, what kind of an impression would it make if I am absent so soon? I'll be all right."

Venetia shrugged and opened one of the French windows that gave access to the terrace outside. "I am just concerned that if you don't rest until after you are already tired, you will have a more difficult time for these two weeks, Vivi. Please promise me that you will take some time to rest each day."

"I promise. I am certain that some of our guests will wish to do the same."

Venetia gave an unladylike snort. "Undoubtedly! Father will want every minute to be filled with activity." She sighed again. "If only he would accept that you—"

"Never mind about Father right now," Vivian interrupted, her voice firm. "I shall be fine, and we will get through this. Where shall we have them put the table?" She gestured toward a pair of approaching servants who bore between them a long table already adorned with a snowy linen cover that fluttered in the breeze.

"Under the tree, there, in the shade," Venetia directed, pointing to the ancient beech at one corner of the terrace and shading her eyes from the afternoon sun. Turning back to her sister, she added, "Will you want your parasol? Shall I send someone to fetch it?"

Vivian rolled her eyes heavenward in obvious annoyance, sending a clear message to her sister even before she replied. "Do stop fussing, Netia! I am not a bit tired, I shall sit in the shade under the tree, and if I want my parasol I can certainly send for it myself!"

Venetia knew that she would have to bury her concern for the time being. In the space of an instant she gave her twin a sheepish smile that begged forgiveness and received an answering one that absolved her. As a steady procession of servants began to supply silver platters filled with cakes, fruit, and cold meats to the table along with brightly polished serving trays, steaming pots of tea, and vast quantities of porcelain teacups and plates, the two young women arranged themselves beside the table ready to do the honors for their guests.

"Let me see your smile, Netia," teased Vivian.

"Let me see yours, Vivi."

They made faces at each other and burst into laughter, quite unaware that one of their guests had arrived to join them. Only when Venetia looked up did she notice a thin, somewhat elderly gentleman standing quite still in the doorway.

"Sh-h! Lord Amberton!" Laughter still lurked in her voice as she nudged her sister.

The man came forward with a bow. "Ladies, with all candor I must tell you what a delightful picture you present, with your innocent laughter and beauty and surrounded by such a sumptuous feast. I suspect it might be almost too much for a weaker man's sensibilities."

Venetia avoided her sister's eye, afraid that any exchange between them would free the laughter she suppressed at the man's fulsome flattery. "Quite clearly you are not overwhelmed, Lord Amberton," she replied with perhaps a touch too much sweetness. "I'm so glad."

He reached for Venetia's hand and raised it to his lips. "As am I, my dearest, as am I."

She thought she detected a glint of challenge in his eyes and snatched her hand back quickly. A wary glance about her reassured her that there were plenty of servants about and that several stood in position near the table, ready to serve the food to any who wished it. Even so, she felt the absence of her father, brother, or aunt quite acutely.

Her father, she knew, would remain in his study until close to dinnertime. Only then would the duke emerge to preside over their guests. But where was Nicholas? Where was Aunt Alice? Would they leave her and Vivian so unsupervised for the entire two-week party? Surely her family could not hope that one of the invited suitors would trap her or Vivian into a compromising situation and solve the marriage problem once and for all.

"Some tea, sir?" She did not wish him to see that he discomposed her even slightly. "As you can see, you are the first to descend and join us."

"I did not want to wait," he said in a low, smooth voice that gave his words a suggestive tone.

Venetia managed to pour his tea with a steady hand and to pass him the cup without flinching, even though he very deliberately pressed his gloved fingers over hers as he took the cup from her. What if all the unattached gentlemen behaved this boorishly? How could she and Vivian stand two weeks of it?

"I hope you found your accommodations acceptable, Lord Amberton," Vivian said politely. Twin to the rescue! Venetia shot her a look of gratitude for her obvious attempt to distract the man.

"Indeed, Lady Vivian, I am quite comfortable. I find I have almost everything a man could possibly wish for, thank you."

His words were quite unexceptional in themselves. It was the emphasis he placed on the word "almost" and the look he directed toward Venetia that made her think his reply seemed exceedingly rude. She began to wish that the other guests—indeed, *any* of the other guests—would appear quickly.

"What delights have you ladies in store for us later tonight and tomorrow?" Lord Amberton queried. He took a sip of his tea as if he had only just remembered it was there.

"I don't know about 'delights,'" Venetia replied, fed up with the pretense of courtesy to the fellow. "You'll be treated to the honor of dining with His Grace this evening, and as I am sure you know, he will not suffer any sort of idiocy. I believe there is to be mutton, onion pie, and—oh, what else was on the menu, Vivian? Some more of that stringy venison we had the other night?"

Lord Amberton laughed uneasily. "Your sense of humor is well-known, Lady Venetia, ha ha. Stringy venison indeed."

Venetia summoned her most exquisitely charming smile and turned the full force of her dramatic, dark-lashed eyes upon the poor man. "Oh, but would I jest with you about such a serious matter? Perhaps you were not aware that my father has very simple tastes."

She paused to let her comment take effect. Out of the corner of her eye she saw Nicholas approaching. "Tomorrow I think the gentlemen are invited to go swimming while the ladies tour the park."

"Swimming?" Lord Amberton blanched. "I—I don't swim. Do you not think it is a bit early in the season for swimming? A—a bit cold?"

Vivian joined forces with her sister. "Oh, we do so admire hardy men."

"As they do admire men with a fine sense of humor," said Nicholas as he joined them. He darted a telling look at Venetia. "You may judge for yourself, Lord Amberton, my father's 'simple' tastes." With a broad sweep of his hands he called to their attention the vast expanse of building that bordered the terrace on three sides, and the gardens and park that extended in front of them as far as the eye could see.

"Yes, of course, ha ha," responded Lord Amberton unhappily. "And swimming?"

"Is not among the plans for tomorrow, as far as I am aware. We do not generally count pneumonia as something we wish to send home with our guests."

Venetia gave her brother a dark look as she turned back to reach for the teapot. "Not generally," she muttered under her breath. "Tea, Nicholas? In a cup, I mean."

"That is how I prefer it, yes, thank you." He quirked an eyebrow at her and grinned as he reached for the cup.

As a handful of other guests began to filter out onto the terrace, Lord Amberton retreated to the safety of conversing with them. Watching him go, Venetia shook her head. "This could be the longest two weeks we've ever survived."

It was a thoughtless statement, an exaggeration that she hadn't really meant. Six years ago they had suffered through agonizing weeks that had tested them all and still gave her occasional nightmares. She regretted the words as soon as they slipped out of her mouth, but it was too late to recall them.

"I can remember worse," Nicholas said, glancing pointedly at Vivian.

The mood between them was suddenly somber, and Vivian spoke up as if to break it.

"I am surprised that your friend Lord Cranford did not come down with you, Nicholas."

Nicholas sipped his tea. "He is getting settled in his room. I had him put in one of the tower bedrooms. He is likely to become absorbed in studying the design of the place, but I've no doubt he will appear soon—Cranford is no slacker when it comes to food."

Venetia was relieved to have the conversation move on. "He does not look as if he would have much of an appetite. His interest in architecture is far more obvious."

"Why would you say that, Netia? There is nothing wrong with the way he looks. He is slender but he has lovely broad shoulders."

How quickly Vivian came to Lord Cranford's defense! Venetia looked at her in surprise and noticed that Nicholas was looking at her that way, too.

"Did I say there was anything wrong with him, Vivi? He just looks like an underfed Viking. With spectacles."

"Do not underestimate my friend Cranford, ladies," Nicholas cautioned. "He is likely to surprise you."

As if on cue, Venetia's underfed Viking appeared in the entrance to the terrace, putting an abrupt end to the discussion. Before he could join his hosts, however, he was drawn aside by a matronly woman standing at the edge of a small knot of guests. Venetia noticed that he seemed surprised to be drawn into a conversation.

"Are you pouring, my dear?"

"Oh!" Venetia realized with a start that she had utterly failed to notice the approach of Lady FitzHarris and a few other guests seeking tea. "Yes. Yes, of course, Lady FitzHarris." She busied herself with the task of filling cups. That was easier than asking herself how she could have been so preoccupied with watching Lord Cranford.

The guests seemed to have become unusually thirsty and Venetia doled out countless cups of tea. It amused her to notice how many people failed to address her or Vivian by name, undoubtedly to be safe in case they had gotten the twins mixed up. She lost track of the minutes and was caught by surprise when she looked up into the face of the next person to discover Lord Cranford. He was smiling and observing her over the top of his small spectacles with his striking blue-green eyes—eyes she had noticed immediately when they had first been introduced in the hall. She wondered if Vivian had noticed them. There had been no time to compare impressions.

"You are very gracious to be doing the honors, Lady Venetia," he said politely as she poured for him.

She gave him a demure smile that she thought would rival one of Vivian's. "La, sir, are you certain you are addressing the right twin?"

He studied her for a moment before replying, and she struggled to maintain the look of innocence on her face. Then he leaned over close to her and spoke in the low voice of a conspirator.

"If you wish to pass as your sister, Lady Venetia, you would do well to disguise the look of mischief in your lovely eyes. It must give you away every time."

His closeness and the intimate tone of his voice startled

Venetia as much as his words. She felt her pulse leap and was relieved when he straightened and stepped back.

"I—I will keep that in mind, Lord Cranford." She had to give him credit for being quite certain, even though he was dead wrong about her ability to masquerade. How surprised he would be if he knew how often she was called upon to use it. "Do you take cream? Sugar? Lemon?" She passed his cup to Vivian even though he shook his head. He had no choice but to follow it and move along down the table.

When his plate was fully loaded, Gilbey moved away from the table, prepared to balance his teacup precariously beside his food if anyone approached with whom he must shake hands. However, Nicholas came up to him almost immediately.

"My sister thinks you look like an underfed Viking," the duke's son reported. "She should only see you now."

"Which sister?"

"Venetia."

"I should have known."

"Yes, and Vivian seems to be ready to leap to your defense at the slightest hint of criticism. You seem to have made an impression on both of them."

Gilbey groaned. "That is not good, Nicholas. It would be far better if they had scarcely noticed me at all. What have I done? I've barely met them. I will have to try harder to be invisible. I'll try not to engage in even polite small talk with them."

Nicholas hardly seemed to be listening. "It certainly makes things interesting," he said, almost to himself. He gestured toward the stone balustrade at the edge of the terrace and herded Gilbey in its direction, away from the press of other guests.

"You know, my friend, a great game is afoot." He settled himself against the balustrade, looking out at the gardens laid out below. He waved his teacup back and forth, as if pointing out the opponents in an invisible wrestling match. "On one side is my father, determined that my sisters shall put off becoming betrothed no longer. He has decreed that they shall choose husbands from the lot of suitors at this party or forfeit their right to choose at all. On the other side you have my sisters, who have found fault with every man who has ever tried to woo them and who are highly unlikely to bend to my father's wishes.

"I want you to know that I am not the only St. Aldwyn who can be stubborn. You are likely to witness a great clash of wills before these two weeks are finished. Throw into the balance each one of the suitors here who thinks he will win one of my sisters, and it makes for an interesting mix, don't you think? But I confess that I had not anticipated that you might wind up in the middle of it."

Chapter Three

The task of arranging the dinner seating was a delicate one, fraught with potential disaster. Venetia stood at one end of the vast stretch of table that had been put together in the state dining room, absently tapping the small bundle of name cards she held in one hand against the pages of the guest list she held in the other. She stared at the long rows of elegant, empty chairs in the dwindling daylight and tried to envision the guests seated at dinner.

"Hm, no, I think Lady Upcott next to Lord Whitgreave, instead of Lady Norbridge."

Advancing to a position halfway down the table, she extracted a name card from those in her hand and exchanged the card with one already set in place on the table. "Yes, better, but then where to put Lady Norbridge?" She paced along the length of the table, studying the cards she had already put out.

She was alone. Most of the guests had obligingly gone off with Nicholas for a tour of the house after satisfying their appetites with refreshments on the terrace. She had insisted that Vivian use the opportunity to rest. The room was full of eyes, but all were unseeing, from the heraldic beasts above the chimney mantel to the plaster menagerie permanently lurking among the leaves in the sculptured ceiling cornice. As Venetia weighed matters of protocol and preference under their fixed gaze, she fought the temptation to turn everyone's expectations topsy-turvy.

She paused when she came to the place marked LORD CRANFORD. She had dutifully placed him at the foot of the table, across from the voluble Colonel Hatherwick and the other unmarried viscount, Lord Newcroft. There was no avoiding the awkwardness of seating the lower-ranked men together—the absence of her aunt and cousin created the dreaded "uneven numbers" of men and women guests at the table.

Of course, much would be made of who had the good fortune to partner the twins for dinner. Venetia had changed her mind at least three times already over which of the four marquesses among their guests would have that privilege this first night. *Would it not be fascinating to see the reactions were she to put Lord Cranford beside her instead? Or perhaps beside Vivian?* Her lips quirked into a mischievous smile at the thought. Now there was a test that would quickly reveal a good deal about their guests. Dare she?

"Ah, Venetia, there you are. Blaine said we might find you here." The breathless, high-pitched voice of her Aunt Alice, Countess of Colney, arrested Venetia's hand in midmotion just as it reached for Lord Cranford's place card.

Venetia withdrew her hand quickly. "Aunt Alice!" She fished momentarily for an appropriate reply. "You've no idea how relieved I am to see you." That choice safely did not specify. "Did you—?"

Her question went unfinished. Lady Colney, still slim and attractive in middle age and dressed in a highly fashionable lavender silk pelisse with a bonnet to match, bustled in and quite took charge of the conversation.

"Oh yes, I've a very good idea, my dear. You must have been fretting terribly. Never fear, we are here at last. Never tell me you are only just now arranging your dinner seating? I can imagine you were concerned about our late arrival, but you look to be resetting the places of everyone." Lady Colney nodded critically at the telltale group of name cards in Venetia's hand.

The countess sighed dramatically. "If only your poor mother were here, she would have taught you better. This should have been worked out well in advance, Venetia, for tonight and for all the subsequent nights as well. Let me see the list."

Venetia surrendered the list of names and the place cards along with it, burying her mixed feelings about her aunt's arrival. Fine. Let Aunt Alice take the responsibility for the puzzle of seating everyone appropriately. There shouldn't have been last-minute changes. At least there were even numbers now, not counting her father.

She dutifully bestowed a kiss upon her aunt's cheek. "I hope you did not have a difficult journey." Aunt Alice meant well, she had no doubt. If at times the woman failed to understand that no one could take the place of the twins' mother, and if at times she seemed a bit overeager to play her role as hostess at Rivington, that could at least be understood and forgiven. But her total preoccupation with appearances and her attitude toward Vivian was intolerable as far as Venetia was concerned.

"We simply got off to a late start, and some of the roads were terribly muddy and slow," Lady Colney said mournfully. "I can't imagine what people will think of us, being so tardy! However, I dare say we are not the only latecomers?" She quickly moved on to another topic of concern. "Where is Vivian? I should have thought your sister would at least be here helping you."

Venetia knew how to use her aunt's conversational technique. "Vivian is resting," she replied and then quickly changed the subject. "How is Cousin Adela? I trust she was not too fatigued from your journey? Where is she? Has she gone up to her room?"

Now that they must each make excuses for someone absent, Venetia felt they were at a draw. She doubted her aunt would still make an issue out of Vivian's absence, at least for the moment.

The countess sniffed audibly and made a great show of examining and switching some name cards. "Adela felt she needed to rest after our long journey, which is quite understandable. Certainly she did not wish to be fatigued at dinner."

"No, of course," Venetia agreed graciously. "Are you not weary as well, Aunt? I can finish this, if you would prefer to be resting."

Venetia supposed she should have known that her attempt to be civil was doomed.

"Someone has to be certain you don't make a botch of this, Venetia. Of course I would prefer to be resting, but obviously it will have to wait until we are finished here. Where is the card for Lord Amberton? I don't see it on the table or in the pile. His name is most definitely on the list."

"And he is most definitely here," Venetia replied regretfully. "Let me see. I thought I had seated him between Lady Duncross and Lady Sibbingham, to tell the truth."

"Between two countesses? You have not seated everyone according to rank, Venetia." Lady Colney's cluck of disapproval was too breathless to sound very much like a hen's.

Venetia and her aunt were too busy hunting for the missing name card to notice when Vivian slipped into the room.

"Aunt Alice, you're here! Is that my sister under the table? What in heaven's name are you two doing?"

"Ouch! Dash it!" Startled by her twin's voice, Venetia forgot where she was for just long enough to crack her head against the underside of the table as she attempted to straighten up. More annoyed than hurt, she backed out and rubbed the stricken spot as she held out the missing name card. "Here, he was on the floor."

"Who?"

"Good afternoon, Vivian. Your sister somehow misplaced Lord Amberton," Lady Colney said without any welcoming warmth in her voice. "I can just imagine how the poor man would have felt at dinner."

"We're so glad you arrived safely, Aunt. We were beginning to worry!" Vivian replied.

"Were you?" The countess softened visibly. "Well, ahem, we were just a bit delayed, that is all. I'm glad I arrived just in time to sort this all out." She waved a hand vaguely at the table.

Venetia and Vivian exchanged a glance.

"I trust you are not ill, Vivian?"

"Not at all, Aunt Alice. I was only resting. Shall I help?"

Lady Colney looked from one twin to the other as if weighing the question carefully. Finally she said, "I suppose it will save me from walking miles up and down and around this table if you two would get on the other side and help to place the cards where I tell you. To start with, I think Lord Amberton should sit next to you, Venetia."

It was only when they had finally arranged all the seating to their aunt's satisfaction that the twins had a moment to themselves. As the countess departed with a rustling of silk, Vivian whispered, "Did you lose Lord Amberton on purpose, Netia?"

"No, I swear I did not." Peeking out of the doorway to make sure her aunt was gone, she added, "But I'll tell you, I am not sitting next to him at dinner." She returned to the table and deftly switched his name card with that of her brother two seats away.

"I would much rather suffer Nicholas for my partner, to tell the truth!"

"I am partnered with Lord Ashurst," Vivian said. "I know nothing at all about him."

"Well, that means you shall have something to talk about during dinner, at least."

"I noticed that Lord Cranford is near the end, next to Cousin Adela, and across from Georgina Whitgreave." Vivian did not try to mask her disappointment.

"Aunt Alice switched things about so that he is partnering Lady FitzHarris," Venetia said with a sigh. They would have to try out other arrangements on another night. "Come, let us escape upstairs before Nicholas's touring group comes upon us here. I don't want to hear him pontificate about the ceiling paintings or the 'original carved chimneypiece dating from 1590.'"

"It might be enlightening to see if the members of the group are interested. We know so little about most of them. Although 'tis clear one of them considers himself a poet." Vivian fumbled for a moment at her belt. Smiling, she withdrew a small folded piece of paper and handed it to her sister. "I found this slipped under the door of our sitting room."

Venetia held it up to the pale light still coming in the window. "'N'er did Venus shine so fair / As two stars here residing / Twin suns whose shining golden hair / Lights hearts with love abiding,'" she read, wrinkling her nose. "'Would that Venus had her twin! / What double glory might have been! / Love's own beauteous face as two / But still no fairer than are you.' Good heavens! It goes on for four verses! Who could have written this?" She turned it over. "It isn't signed."

"Yes, I noticed," Vivian answered. "It seems we have a mystery to solve during dinner."

The St. Aldwyns gathered with all their guests in the long drawing room before proceeding in to dinner. The Duke of

Roxley finally appeared to greet everyone, and all seemed to be going smoothly. Quite improperly Venetia managed at the last minute to go in on her brother's arm, and it was only when they reached the table that she discovered she had been outmaneuvered. Lord Amberton's name card sat at the place just to her left, and Nicholas's was once again two seats away.

Unfortunately, there was nothing she could do about it now. When could Aunt Alice have switched the cards back? As Venetia took her place, she noticed that although Nicholas was partnering the Countess of Sibbingham, he was across the table from Lord and Lady Marchthorpe's daughter, Lady Elizabeth. She had a sudden suspicion that the culprit might not have been her aunt at all.

The twins' father sat at the head, looking distinguished in a splendid dinner coat of darkest maroon velvet set off by his snowy linen and a waistcoat of embroidered ivory satin jacquard. He was a handsome man, with deeply etched features and a thick crop of white hair. He surveyed the table and his guests with the air of a benign ruler.

Venetia surveyed the guests as well, wondering who among them might be the anonymous poet. Her feelings were undoubtedly less benign than her father's, but she hoped that her fixed smile hid them. She noticed with some small sense of satisfaction that even Aunt Alice had not followed the rules of rank to perfection.

The amiable Duke and Duchess of Brancaster quite properly flanked her father, with the duchess seated on his right as the highest-ranking lady present. Below them Lady Elizabeth's parents, the very proper Lord and Lady Marchthorpe, sat across from each other, but this meant that the marquess and marchioness were placed above the proud Duke of Thornborough. Then Aunt Alice had risked offending the other countesses in the group by seating Lady Duncross, an elderly Scottish countess who was friendly with the duke, above her station across from him.

As a widower, His Grace was a potential suitor for the twins. Would the old duke dabble in anonymous poetry? Venetia doubted it. Thornborough was notoriously high in the instep. He would never fail to put his name on some creation of his, and he probably thought writing poetry quite beneath him.

The Marquess of Ashurst, Vivian's partner, was seated below Lady Duncross and directly across from Venetia. She studied him with surreptitious glances as the meal began. He was undeniably handsome, with dark hair and shaggy dark brows over deep-set eyes, but he said little and did not seem to smile easily. He was reputed to be cynical and unsociable. Would such a man indulge in poetry?

The warm, mouth-watering scent of shrimp bisque penetrated to Venetia's brain and she paused to take a spoonful of her soup before continuing her scrutiny of the guests. So far, none had made any comments that might link them to the poem, either in the drawing room or at the table.

On Vivian's right was Lord Wistowe, whose notorious reputation as a rake made Venetia wonder what her father had been thinking to include him on the list. He had the kind of roguish good looks and angelic smile that she could imagine many ladies found irresistible. He was behaving quite charmingly to his partner, Lady Elizabeth. Nicholas seemed to be watching them rather carefully, although he was not noticeably neglectful of his own partner.

Venetia let her gaze wander past the many other guests until it came to rest on Lord Cranford at the far end of the table. He was dutifully assisting their neighbor Lady FitzHarris, a widowed baroness who had been invited to help make up the numbers. The viscount turned his attention to the twins' cousin Adela on his other side whenever she made a remark, and appeared to listen politely to Lord and Lady Whitgreave's daughter Georgina opposite him, but Venetia thought she could discern a lack of enthusiasm. Colonel Hatherwick seemed to be carrying the conversation. Most of the time Lord Cranford appeared to be busily studying either the dishes in front of him or the splendid mural panels that covered the walls and ceiling.

Could the viscount have written the anonymous poem? Judging by his arrival, he was the bookish sort, but the author of the poem was also clearly a romantic. Was he? He certainly did not impress her as being so. If the poet was not Lord Cranford, then who? She allowed her glance to stray from one guest to another, weighing what she knew of each of them, hoping that her speculations did not show on her face.

Beside her, Lord Amberton consumed his soup with noisy enthusiasm.

"I had no doubt His Grace would set an excellent table, Lady Venetia, despite your attempts to tease me," he said in between mouthfuls.

"The rest of the meal is yet to come, sir," Venetia replied coolly. She watched Vivian converse quietly with Lord Ashurst. Despite his reputation, the marquess was doing a reasonably good job of holding Vivian's attention at their own end of the table. Only occasionally did Venetia see her sister's gaze slip to the far end where Lord Cranford sat. It never occurred to her that her own glances returned there far more often than Vivian's.

Gilbey was studying the group assembled at the duke's table almost as thoroughly as Venetia. Nicholas had been right about the guest list—the diners seated at this table represented the highest levels of British society. Three dukes and a duchess, five marquesses if you included Nicholas, one marchioness, four earls, and no less than five—five!—countesses. . . . It was enough to make one wonder who was left in London to carry on with the remainder of the Season.

The very fact that all these people had been willing to come attested as much to the Duke of Roxley's prestige and power as to the beauty of the six younger ladies who brightened the table like the candles in the crystal chandeliers over their heads. All were turned out in their most elegant finery, the ladies in white or in luminous colors with fine jewels setting off their pale skin, the men in more somber colors but every bit as flawless.

If the company glittered, the table itself nearly equaled them. Gilbey had always been proud of his own family's display of plate in the dining room at Cliffcombe, his home in Devonshire, but he had never seen anything like the silver that gleamed in the candlelight on the St. Aldwyns' table. Fabulous ten-branched candlesticks that featured the figures of stags and hunters in their bases towered like small trees planted on the dining table. The brightly polished covers of huge serving dishes waiting to reveal their steaming contents reflected the faces of the diners as well as the flames of the candles. Two large silver epergnes with dolphin figures as supporters graced the table as well, holding towers of fruit for later consumption.

Certainly it was all most impressive, as Nicholas had promised, and Gilbey felt rather surprised to find himself there. Even the room was spectacular. He was glad to have a further chance to admire the special features Nicholas had pointed out during the tour. But nothing captured his attention quite the way Nicholas's sisters did, not even the attractive young women beside and across from him.

How could two such beautiful women be so truly identical and yet so different? He did not seem to have any trouble telling the twins apart, although apparently other people did. Lady Venetia held her head at an altogether different angle than did Lady Vivian, and she moved with a smooth, natural fluidity that contrasted sharply with the hesitant, rather deliberate way her sister moved. Too, Venetia was restless and moved often, while Vivian was calm and only moved for a purpose.

Were others simply less observant? He had been quietly studying the twins in the drawing room before dinner. He saw no reason to stop studying them simply because dinner had begun, although he now sat a good deal farther away from them. He did his best to appear attentive to those around him. Fortunately Colonel Hatherwick was an avid talker who easily relieved him of the burden of making conversation at their end of the table.

What surprised him was how often he had to turn his gaze elsewhere lest Lady Venetia catch him watching her. She spoke very little to her partner, Lord Amberton, and appeared to be studying the other guests almost as avidly as Gilbey was studying her. It did seem as though her gaze strayed to his end of the table with disconcerting frequency, however.

It is not very likely she is looking at you, he counseled himself. Upon consideration it seemed much more likely that she might be casting glances at the young Earl of Lindell, who was sitting just on the other side of Lady Adela. Still, it was safer to become absorbed in the play of light bouncing off the silver on the table or in the formation of the clouds in the painting on the ceiling at those moments when her head turned in his direction.

Lady Vivian, on the other hand, seemed quite absorbed in her own dinner partner, Lord Ashurst. In an interesting turnabout, the quiet twin appeared to be talking considerably more than her sister. Gilbey could not see her quite as readily as he could see Lady Venetia, for Lady Vivian was seated on the same side of the table as himself, with eight places between them.

"The glacéed carrots *vont très bien* with the salmon, don't you think?" Lady FitzHarris said, interrupting his thoughts. "Could I ask you to pass the dill sauce, Lord Cranford, *s'il vous plaît?*"

Gilbey located and obtained the sauce for her, spooning some onto her plate with a gallant smile. He wondered if the plump baroness felt ill at ease among the other guests or if she always sprinkled French phrases into her speech to seem fashionable. Was he the only one who was uncomfortable? But then, these people would have been trained for these roles since birth, not left to their own devices from the tender age of eight, as he and his sister had been.

He glanced at Nicholas, seven places up from him on Lady Venetia's side of the table. Nicholas's father had not succumbed to grief at the loss of his wife, although the place at the foot of the table had been left vacant in her memory. Quite without meaning to, Gilbey happened to catch his friend's eye. The duke's son winked and raised his wineglass in a salute. He had taught Gilbey the custom of "taking wine," and Gilbey answered with his own glass. Just as he took a sip, however, there was motion beyond Lady Venetia near the far end of the table. The elderly Duke of Thornborough struggled to his feet to offer the first toast of the evening.

"To the King, God bless him and grant him peace."

"To the King!" And so it went, through all the traditional toasts from the Prince Regent and the nation on down to the host and his fair daughters, the health of the company, and the skill of the cooks. The glasses were charged and recharged several times, keeping the servants busy.

"La! I shall be quite giddy by the time I drink another glass," declared Lady Adela when her glass was filled once again. Unfortunately she accompanied this pronouncement with a dramatic fluttering of her hand that caught the poor footman's arm just as he was refilling Gilbey's glass. Glass, bottle, and footman all lurched at the same moment, sending the wine quite where it did not belong.

"Oh, heavens!" cried Adela, leaping up in alarm even as the horrified footman began to beg Gilbey's forgiveness. The dark red wine splashed down Gilbey's arm, soaking into his coat-sleeve, pooling on his trousers, and finally running down his leg.

"Never mind, never mind. It was purely an accident," Gilbey mumbled, rising slowly to test whether the wine had quite finished its travels. He was certain the carpet beneath his feet was worth a hundred times the value of his modest cloth-ing. When he looked up he realized that all the eyes around the table were turned toward him.

So much for not attracting attention, he thought with a sigh. The sooner he retreated from the dining room the sooner the rest of them would return to their meal and forget him. Cer-tainly he was not needed to help chaperon anyone in such a structured setting as dinner. Perhaps he could even escape the inevitable evening of cards that was bound to follow.

"Oh, my dear sir! Your poor coat!"

"How terribly clumsy! That footman should be turned off."

The fuss was beginning and would only escalate. It would be ungentlemanly to point out that Lady Adela was most at fault, but Gilbey did not want to see the poor footman lose his position.

"My fault, all my fault," he murmured. "No one to blame but myself, please—just what comes of making a wrong move at the wrong moment." He would make certain to speak to Nicholas and the duke later. With polite apologies to his host and the gathering in general, Gilbey turned tail and fled.

Much later, after hours of whist and six-handed loo with various partners including Lord Cranford, the twins had finally begged leave to retire to their rooms. They had changed into the night rails carefully laid out for them and, after dismissing their maids, were reviewing their evening while they took turns brushing each other's hair.

"Netia, you were positively wild this evening!" Vivian said wonderingly, submitting to her sister's ministrations. "What did you think you were about? Such deep play, for casual card play among our guests. I thought Father would have apoplexy."

Venetia laughed, although she did not miss the note of mild reproval in her sister's voice. "He was not the only one who was disturbed. But did you not think it a good way to discover which of our suitors does not mind dipping into his pockets? It does little good to marry a rich husband if the man is tight-fisted."

"I suppose you are right. It is also wise to discover which of them is bitten with the gamester's habit."

"Lord Munslow and Lord Chesdale seemed a bit inclined that way, I thought. We will have to test that out some more." She paused, working the brush carefully through a tangled bit of Vivian's hair. "Of course, I like a man with some spirit of adventure. It doesn't do to be afraid of taking risks."

"I think Lord Cranford was relieved not to be at your table."

"Do you? Hm. I wonder about him." Venetia gave Vivian's hair a final stroke and the twins exchanged places. "You do realize of course that Lord Cranford was not the one who spilled his wine at dinner," Venetia said, settling herself on the sofa. She handed the hairbrush to her sister.

"I could not see what happened at all from where I was sitting."

"It was all Adela's fault, but you know she would never admit to it. I saw the whole thing happen."

Vivian gave her sister's hair a mischievous tweak. "Yes, you did seem to be paying attention to that end of the table."

"I was trying to guess which of our guests was the secret poet. Or did you forget about that in your efforts to draw out the taciturn Lord Ashurst?"

Venetia's back was turned to her sister so she could not see if this sally was met with a blush. "You did seem quite occupied with him, Vivi, or am I mistaken?"

For a moment the strokes of the brush stopped. "He did not seem so bad as his reputation," Vivian said noncommittally. "I do not recall that he made any disrespectful remarks, and al-

though he seemed rather solemn, he responded well enough
when I asked him intelligent questions."

"Well, that is better than it might have been. All of our
guests must have been on their best behavior. Lord Wistowe
seemed quite charming, although I suppose that comes naturally to a rake."

"Did you come to any conclusion about our poet?"

"No. The only conclusion I have made after the entire
evening is that it must not be Lord Amberton. I don't believe
he has the wit to put two rhyming lines together and have them
make sense."

"Oh, Netia!"

The two young women lapsed into giggles. Just as they qui-
eted, however, they heard a small sound at the door of their
chamber and turned to see that a slip of paper had appeared
under it.

"Oh, no, not another poem," groaned Venetia.

Vivian moved to retrieve the folded note. She broke the wax
seal and stood by the door scanning the contents.

"Don't read it now, Vivi—open the door and see if anyone
is still in the passage!"

But Vivian did not open the door. Instead she sagged
against it, all color drained from her face.

Venetia was on her feet in an instant. "Oh, Vivi, not a
seizure. You've been doing so well!"

Before she reached her sister's side, however, Vivian shook
her head. "No, I am all right. But 'tis not a poem, this time."

Chapter Four

With a mixture of alarm and curiosity curling through her, Venetia took the paper from her sister's trembling fingers and read.

Lady Venetia,

I will save you the great trouble of choosing a husband by casting myself in that role. If you do not agree, I will inform the entire world that your sister has the falling sickness, and the name of St. Aldwyn will become synonymous with scandal and deceit. I will reveal myself on the day of the betrothal ball. Looking forward to our future together, I remain for now your Secret Admirer.

Anger boiled out of her. "This is blackmail, Vivi! We can't give in to this. Who could have written this? Who could know? It isn't even right. You don't have the falling sickness. You've never lost consciousness during a seizure and you've never fallen. It's not even a sickness. What do they know about it? How could they know?"

Thoroughly distraught, Venetia paced in front of the door, turning each time her words reached a new crescendo. She shook the paper in her hands as if somehow the words written on it could be forced off into oblivion where they belonged.

Placing gentle hands on her shoulders, Vivian steered her twin to the sofa and made her sit down.

"You begin to sound like Father, Netia. Don't. You know 'tis true I have epilepsy. Denying it as he has will never make it go away."

Venetia had tears in her eyes. "Oh, Vivi, I know." She swallowed and could not go on. There was so much shared pain that she could never express, and so much grief. Until six years ago their lives had been so trouble-free, and then in one night so much had changed!

"I hate that name for it, and I hate how ignorant people are about it. I hate the fact that we have to hide it from everyone. If we didn't have to hide it, if people were not so afraid and so unreasonable, no one could write us a hateful note like this!"

"Shh, Netia. We cannot change the way things are," Vivian hugged her sister and removed the blackmail note, now badly crumpled, from her fingers.

Venetia jumped up from the sofa. "How can you remain so calm? Does it not make you angry? It is all so unfair!" She began to pace about the room again.

Vivian sighed. "Of course I get angry! But most of the time I consider it a gift that I am alive at all. 'Tis a gift that Mother was not granted, and mine is a conditional gift—I must accept the circumstances. I have come to terms with it better than you have, but perhaps that is just my nature. No one knows better than you how angry I was in those first months after the accident, when the seizures began."

Vivian smoothed out the note, her calm motion at odds with her words. "I do still feel angry when Father tries to gloss things over with some reference to my 'delicate nerves,' or when Aunt Alice insists I do it purposely for attention. But if I have to live with this, as I must, there is just one thing I would change, Netia, and that is Father's insistence that I marry."

"That is but another thing that makes me angry, Vivi. How can he be so blind? Does he not see the possible jeopardy in which that places you? But do not fear. No blackmailer will make me break my vow. I will not marry until we have found the right husband for you."

Vivian went to her and they clasped hands silently, allies against an uncertain future.

After a moment Venetia managed to smile. "If such a paragon does not exist, then poor Nicholas will simply have two spinster sisters on his hands in the future."

They moved back to the sofa and Vivian picked up the note. "I wish I had opened the door," she said ruefully.

"It does not matter," Venetia reassured her. "In such a mat-

ter as this, I doubt the writer was also the bearer. He probably
paid one of the servants to deliver it."

"What shall we do?"

"We must find him out, Vivi. Only by discovering who he is
can we then find some way to stop him. We cannot allow him
to carry out his threat."

"Nor can you marry such a blackguard! I would rather be
exposed than see you meet such a fate. But how will we discover him? We have shown little enough talent in that line.
We could not even discover our anonymous poet."

"We will not go to Father, that much is certain. We will
question the servants and pay more attention to our guests, and
we'll try to discover some clues. To begin, let me see that
note."

Down in the yellow drawing room many of the Rivington
guests clearly intended to continue their card play into the
morning hours. Like the twins, however, Gilbey had retired for
the night. Ensconced in a huge, old, heavily carved oak bed
with simple hangings of crimson worsted, he watched the
flickering light from the dying fire dance over the substantial
stone walls of his room.

In the four hundred and thirty-nine years preceding his arrival, how many other people had lain here doing the same
thing? He tried to distract himself by imagining those people,
and failing that, tried to perform a numbers game to determine
how many nights that had been, allowing for leap years and
the change in the calendar.

Nothing successfully kept his thoughts away from the
events of this particular evening. After the fiasco at the dinner
table, he had escaped to his room, thoroughly dismayed by his
apparent inability to avoid attracting attention. Twice in one
day! It was as if the Fates had decreed some other plan for
him. Was he destined to play the fool? Invisibility was a far
more comfortable way to ensure he attracted no romantic en-
tanglements here.

He had barely begun to consider the disastrous effect the
wine stains were going to have on his limited wardrobe when
one of the many chamber servants employed by the duke appeared, ready to assist him and take charge of the damaged

clothing. Gilbey was more than a little impressed. His brother-in-law's estates were well run, but this palatial residence tended by scores of servants ran so smoothly it seemed as if the very walls must have eyes and ears.

He had hoped to stay in his room for the remainder of the evening, certain that the portion of dinner he had eaten would be sufficient. But the valet's arrival had been followed by a tray laden with delicacies, and a short while after that a note had arrived from the duke himself, summoning Gilbey to the great man's study.

Escorted by a footman, Gilbey had traversed endless echoing corridors and passed through many rooms he recognized from Nicholas's tour. He had yet to formulate an accurate plan of Rivington in his mind—it seemed to defy logic with its many additions and odd changes in levels. He thought moving through the house was almost like a journey through time, so many centuries were represented there.

When he finally arrived at the duke's study, Gilbey was not at all surprised to find the room far grander than its name implied. Although the light from a number of handsome multibranched candlestands illuminated the room, much of its magnificence was still lost in shadows. Within its cavernous depths Gilbey made out several sculptures set on pedestals, including a few that looked genuinely antique to his educated eye.

Seated behind a massive flat-topped mahogany desk ornamented with ormolu, Nicholas's father was dwarfed by the proportions of his surroundings. For a fleeting moment, Gilbey was struck by the thought that His Grace, the Duke of Roxley, for all his wealth and power, was after all no more than a man, and an aging one at that.

"Please sit down, Lord Cranford."

The duke indicated a chair with a nod of his head, and Gilbey realized that he had already been discreetly deserted by the footman. He knew he should have felt honored to be summoned for a private audience with the duke, but given the way his visit had been going so far, he felt somewhat uneasy. It helped that the duke's voice and even his tone of unmistakable authority sounded so much like Nicholas's.

He was mistaken, however, about the footman. The servant

had merely disappeared into the shadows; he reappeared instantly when the duke offered Gilbey a glass of port.

"I was concerned when you did not rejoin us at dinner by the time the ladies withdrew," the duke said. It was clear that he expected an explanation.

"I apologize if I caused any concern or offense, Your Grace," Gilbey replied carefully, accepting a glass from the footman. "None was intended. I did not think I would be missed."

"I am responsible for the welfare of all my guests. I must apologize for the accident that befell you at dinner. If your garments cannot be cleaned, they will be replaced, of course."

"That is most generous of you, sir, but altogether unnecessary. I've no wish to be any trouble to you."

"Hmph, no doubt." The duke set down his own glass and leaned back in his chair, interlacing all but his index fingers and tapping those thoughtfully against his pursed lips. His face had been shadowed before but now light from the candles nearest him shone upon his face, revealing an expression Gilbey could think of only as calculating.

"At the risk of being offensively candid, I would like to ask what it is that you do wish to accomplish here, Lord Cranford. As we are not at all acquainted, I trust you will forgive my bluntness." He smiled a lopsided smile and arched an eyebrow exactly the way Nicholas did. Gilbey knew he really was not being offered any choice.

"As a duke I am granted amazing license in polite company," His Grace continued. "You must realize that you are here merely by the request of my son, suddenly thrust among a very carefully selected group of guests who have been assembled for a particular purpose. What exactly, sir, is your own business at Rivington?"

So that was it. Gilbey smiled in a way he hoped the duke would find reassuring. Reading people was a talent the viscount had discovered he possessed at an early age, and he understood very well what the duke, despite his declared frankness, had left unsaid. His Grace wanted to know if Gilbey posed any threat to his well-laid plans to marry off his daughters, or if Gilbey had come seeking political favors or hoping to ingratiate himself with the powerful elite gathered here. He wanted to know Gilbey's credentials as well as his intentions.

Gilbey didn't blame the man one bit. After all, Gilbey was a stranger. By confronting him, the duke could test his personality and social skills. The choice of strategy impressed him. He hadn't the slightest doubt that it had been quite deliberate.

"Your Grace, allow me to reassure you—I hope without seeming unappreciative of your hospitality—that I have come here for no purpose of my own at all. I promise you I have no wish to attract the attention of your daughters, or anyone else for that matter, and I seek nothing. I had no intention of coming here, even after Nicholas—uh, Lord Edmonton—invited me. However, your son has rather admirable powers of persuasion, as I am sure you are aware."

"You do not find my daughters attractive?"

Now, that was a sticky question. Gilbey took a gulp of his port. Wouldn't do to offend his host, or to give him a wrong idea, either. "My first impression of your daughters is that they are both beautiful and charming, Your Grace. If I were seeking a wife, I would be sorry indeed that my station is so far below what they deserve. But as Nicholas—uh, your son—is well aware, I have only just finished my stint at Cambridge and am newly named a Fellow of my college."

"Don't wish to give up the stipend before you've even begun to collect, eh?"

Gilbey felt the cursed tingling of a blush start in his face. "No, sir—that is, it's not the stipend. I have studies I wish to complete and traveling I wish to accomplish before I am tied down to a wife and family. I am rather young yet to be married."

"Yes, you are." The duke leaned forward. "Perhaps you can enlighten me as to why my son was so keen to have you here?"

Gilbey set down his glass. "That, Your Grace, is a question you would do well to ask Nicholas." Gilbey was not about to risk offending the duke by telling him his son thought he would not adequately supervise his daughters. But the sooner Gilbey could extricate himself from these treacherous waters, the better. "I must say that I am delighted to have the opportunity to see Rivington, Your Grace. It is even more magnificent than I expected from the descriptions I have read."

"Have an interest in architecture, have you? What was your field of study at Cambridge?"

"History. Roman civilization in particular."

"Ah. Perhaps you might recognize this, then." The duke picked up a small object from his desk. Quite unexpectedly, he tossed it in Gilbey's direction.

With his heart in his throat Gilbey leaned forward and caught the object. Opening his hands slowly, he examined what lay there. It appeared to be a miniature axe, made out of bronze, somewhat oxidized and eaten away by time.

"It appears to be a votive object, sir. May I ask where it came from?"

"A few miles up the road," the duke answered. He rose from his chair and picked up the branch of candles that stood by his desk. Walking off into the shadows behind him, he summoned Gilbey to follow. "This was found there, also," he said, setting the candles where they threw light upon a head and torso carved in stone.

Gilbey sucked in his breath. "Minerva. Made from local stone?"

The duke nodded.

The atmosphere in the room was changing, thawing. Gilbey felt as if he had been plucked out of the treacherous water and put into a rescue boat.

"Have you heard of Lysons, over there at Cambridge?" the duke asked. "Excavated a huge Roman villa at Woodchester some twenty-five years ago."

It was Gilbey's turn to nod.

"It is thought that this entire area had a number of villas. Several years ago he dug up another near Withington," the duke continued. "I was interested in his work, struck up an acquaintance. He presented me with these." Roxley moved again, and Gilbey followed.

"This is my favorite. Perfect little figure of Diana, wouldn't you say?"

The duke had stopped in front of a fluted marble column on which was perched a small bronze statuette. It was indeed quite perfect: a semiclad female with a bow in her hand and a dog—or was it a lion?—at her feet. Gilbey reached up to adjust his spectacles so that he might improve his admiration and nearly knocked them off his face when the duke said, "Reminds me of my daughter Venetia."

Gilbey rocked back as if the statue had kicked him. What the devil was that supposed to mean? The duke was smiling and Gilbey thought he had better say something to cover his involuntary reaction. "Lady Venetia, Your Grace?"

"Yes, my daughter the huntress. She will find herself a husband and one for her sister, too, I don't doubt." The smile disappeared suddenly and was replaced by a level stare. "I would be most displeased if she chose someone unsuitable, Lord Cranford. I'm certain that you understand my position."

Fresh from this interview Gilbey had been obliged to join the party playing cards in the yellow drawing room. His attempts to catch Nicholas's eye or have a word with him failed utterly, perhaps because he had to devote so much of his attention to keeping away from the twins. Periodically the groups would break up and regroup, specifically so that no one would play with the same partner all evening. Gilbey worked very hard to avoid being paired with any of the younger ladies.

Unfortunately, this strategy appeared to have given both Lady Norbridge and Lady Sibbingham the idea that he preferred the company of older women, specifically that of widowed countesses. They had flirted with him outrageously all evening. Lady Norbridge was no more than thirty-five and did have certain charms—large green eyes and an admirable figure, if only she would not flaunt it quite so openly. He had been unfailingly polite without encouraging them, he hoped. He doubted either of them had meant anything serious by their actions.

No, the biggest problem had been himself. Despite Lady Norbridge's distracting green eyes, he had not been able to stop thinking about two pairs of violet blue ones that belonged to the golden-haired twins. He had not been able to stop watching them during the evening, even from across the room. He hoped that no one had noticed.

The contrast in their personalities was remarkable. Vivian had been determinedly modest, insisting that she had no skill at cards and warning all her partners of their handicap. Whenever she played well, a look of genuine surprise lit her sweet face quite delightfully in the warm glow of the candles. Gilbey was certain she had no idea that she had utterly charmed several of the gentlemen present. It struck him as odd that her father had barely mentioned her during the after-dinner interview in the duke's study. Shouldn't such a daughter, the very model of modesty and decorum, be the apple of her father's eye?

Venetia, on the other hand, had challenged her partners to match her skill and had played with a reckless aggressiveness much like a man's. Gilbey had been astonished at the size of the wagers she placed, encouraging others to follow her lead, quite careless of the results. She seemed vibrant—full of energy and passion. Gilbey was not surprised by the number of men who had been ready to worship at her temple.

Lying in bed now, he indulged in an dangerous fantasy. If he wanted a wife, if he were an eligible suitor, if he could have his choice—which sister would he prefer? He wrestled with the dilemma and finally gave up. How did one choose between a pearl and a diamond?

Poor Nicholas! Small wonder he was concerned about keeping an eye on the twins for two weeks! There were nine suitors, and only two of them could win. In the days ahead the competition among them was likely to become the very devil.

Chapter Five

Venetia and Vivian were up early the next morning and had already been out walking in the garden terraces and the nearby woodland paths before most of the house was awake. Morning mist clung to their bonnets and wool cloaks as they reentered the house.

"It will be interesting to see which of our guests come to breakfast this morning," Venetia said, handing her red cloak to the footman who stood ready to receive it. "Some of them may have barely been to bed."

"You do not think the prospect of attending church with us this morning will be enough to rouse them again?" Vivian answered Venetia's sly grin with one of her own.

"We shall see."

Breakfast had been set up in the tapestry room under the fixed gazes of medieval lords and maidens woven in cloth. The muted colors of the wall hangings and rich oak paneling gave the room a warm feel despite the coolness of the misty morning outside the casement windows. When the twins entered they were surprised to find Nicholas and Lord Cranford already seated at one of the several tables, happily munching on sliced smoked ham, a variety of breads, fresh honey, and early strawberries from the Rivington hothouses. A pained expression came across Lord Cranford's face as soon as the twins approached, however. Indeed, as he and Nicholas arose from their chairs, he began to choke on the tea he had just attempted to swallow.

"Oh, heavens. Bones in the tea, sir? If so we must really speak to our cook," Venetia teased him. "Good morning, Nicholas. And may I wish you a good morning also, Lord Cranford?"

Cranford was blushing bright red and still coughing. Nicholas moved to pound him on the back.

"Poor Lord Cranford. Are you quite all right?" asked Vivian with a good deal more sympathy.

The viscount nodded, but he remained standing even after the ladies were seated and Nicholas had returned to his chair.

"I do beg your pardon!" he finally managed to sputter once he had found his breath. "My appetite is apparently more awake this morning than the rest of me. Lady Venetia and Lady Vivian, good morning."

Unfailingly polite, thought Venetia. She was not sure she found that such a great virtue. She smiled sweetly. "We have been up and awake for hours, sir. Are you prone to city habits, staying up far into the night? I'm afraid we follow country ways here at Rivington. Perhaps you should try the coffee."

At least he had the grace to laugh. He made no move to join them at the table, however. "I think I am quite finished trying anything this morning. I've already consumed a most generous breakfast. I hope you will excuse me. I was not up late last night—in fact, I retired just after you ladies. However, I have a few things to do to get ready this morning before attending church . . ."

Venetia arched an eyebrow and gave her sister a significant look. If Lord Cranford had retired just after they had, he could have delivered the blackmail note. She saw that some sense of the idea reached Vivian, for a small frown suddenly creased her pale forehead.

"What nonsense, Gilbey," Nicholas said. "You've no need to be ready any sooner than we are. We won't be leaving for St. Michael's until just before ten o'clock." He smiled wickedly. "One might almost get the impression you wish to avoid our company."

Venetia thought Lord Cranford looked as if he would like to strangle Nicholas. *Interesting.* Perhaps he truly was trying to avoid them. Why? Could it be because he had secrets to hide from them? Didn't want them to guess he was really a blackmailer? Didn't feel the need to court them because he already had another way to win one of them as a wife?

Now that she stopped to consider it, he had managed very neatly to keep apart from both her and Vivian last night. He had even been absent for a good part of the dinner. *He could have been writing the note then,* said the little voice in her head.

"One might not be surprised if I wished to avoid *your* company, Nicholas, since you are ungracious enough to make the suggestion," Cranford said. "I can't imagine that anyone would not wish to remain in the company of your delightful sisters, however."

Bravo. It was an admirable reply, one her brother richly deserved. Venetia studied Lord Cranford's face with renewed interest. Telltale color still washed across his cheekbones, but a smile was lurking around his mouth. The light from the windows reflected off the lenses of his spectacles, effectively screening his eyes from her view. Something her brother had said the day before came back to her as she looked at the viscount: *Do not underestimate my friend Cranford, ladies.* Now she wondered exactly what he had meant.

"Surely you don't mean to abandon us, Lord Cranford?" she said. "Why, you haven't even finished what was on your plate."

As he turned toward her the reflction disappeared from his spectacles, revealing his breathtaking blue-green eyes. She could read indecision there and in the way his smile wavered for a moment.

"No, not at all, of course not," he said, fidgeting with his watch fob. "But you really must excuse me . . ."

"We have been out walking in the gardens, Lord Cranford. You might find a quick turn along some of the paths quite delightful at this time of day," Vivian commented suddenly.

What in heaven's name was she about? Venetia tried to kick her twin under the table but couldn't quite reach without making an obvious effort. If they were going to investigate Lord Cranford as a suspected blackmailer, they would have to spend some time with him. Offering him reasons to absent himself was not the way to go about it!

Cranford looked relieved. "I truly do have a few things I must see to before we go off this morning. If I have a chance, Lady Vivian, perhaps I will try to steal a few moments to walk in the garden. Thank you for suggesting it. If not this morning, then perhaps tomorrow." He bowed. "Ladies, Nicholas. Until later."

Venetia watched him leave. He actually was a handsomely built man—she wasn't certain why she had not noticed it before. Perhaps the chocolate brown coat he was wearing this morning was cut better than the one he had worn yesterday. She had to admit that she felt a little begrudging admiration for him. He had clearly meant to quit the table from the moment she and Vivian walked in, and despite her protests he had achieved his object without even being rude.

He paused in front of the carved and columned doorway to allow a small knot of guests coming into the room to pass him. The group included Lord and Lady Whitgreave with their daughter Georgina, Lord Lindell, Lord Newcroft, and Lady Duncross tottering along behind them on the arm of Lord Chesdale. Cranford greeted them quietly and went out.

Lord Chesdale lifted his quizzing glass and peered at the viscount's retreating figure. When he turned back to the trio seated at the table he did not look at all pleased. "Good morning, Lady Venetia, Lady Vivian, Edmonton," he said. "I see that Lord Cranford has already been here, well ahead of the rest of the pack."

A string of carriages wound their way out of the park at Rivington later that morning, headed for the ancient little church at Yanworth. Gilbey remembered passing through the tiny hamlet with Nicholas. It amounted to no more than a handful of small estate cottages, but the church was older than even the oldest parts of Nicholas's home, dating back to the twelfth century.

Nicholas had told him the church was decorated with interesting wall paintings, and Gilbey was looking forward to viewing them. All he had to do was keep to his own company and keep an eye on Lady Venetia and Lady Vivian from a distance. Since he had to share the drive to church with someone, however, he had sought out Lady FitzHarris. The plump, cheerful baroness had been a harmless enough dinner partner and Gilbey did not think anyone, male or female, could possibly misread his motives in accompanying her. They rode in Nicholas's carriage, listening to Colonel Hatherwick rhapsodize about the fabulous trout fishing to be found just a short distance downriver. Venetia and Vivian rode in their father's carriage up ahead along with the Duke of Thornborough.

The expedition proved blessedly uneventful. The wall paintings were indeed interesting, and Gilbey managed to evade the twins without losing sight of them. No one in particular tried to engage him in conversation. Few of the Rivington guests had failed to come along—Gilbey guessed that none of the suitors wanted to risk missing opportunities that could be used to advantage by their rivals. The Marquess of Ashurst was the only one of the single male guests who had not come.

Venetia and Vivian also noted Lord Ashurst's absence, and his defection from the ranks sparked a discussion once they returned from church. They took refuge in the gardens for a few minutes of privacy.

"You see, Netia, you cannot say that Lord Cranford is the only one making no attempt to court us," Vivian said in a low voice, leading the way down a flagstone path between huge evergreen topiaries. "Lord Ashurst was pleasant enough at dinner last night, but he was not very attentive during the evening, and this morning he did not even come. It is quite probable that he took a dislike to me because I pestered him with so many questions. But according to your logic, he is just as likely to be the blackmailer as Lord Cranford."

"Oh, heavens, Vivi! I'm certain that Lord Ashurst has not taken you in particular dislike. They say he dislikes everyone. And his case is considerably different than Lord Cranford's."

Venetia glanced about quickly to make sure no one else was in this part of the garden. "What possible reason could the marquess have for resorting to blackmail to make me his wife? He is high-placed, handsome and wealthy. Plenty of women would willingly wed a reclusive misanthrope like him for those other qualities. That reputation is less damaging than Lord Wistowe's, and I doubt many women would balk at marrying him, either, even if he is such a rake."

The path ended at a short flight of steps leading up to the next terrace. This was a rectangular rose garden enclosed by sheltering walls of yews. The scent of the early blooms washed over the twins as they entered. Vivian went to the fountain at its center and sat down on the edge, gazing at the bronze figure of a woman captured forever pouring water from an urn into the pool. The sound of the trickling water was comforting.

"Netia," she said, "you are assuming that Lord Cranford has an interest in marrying you. Do you not remember what we said of him when he first arrived?"

Venetia patroled restlessly around the borders.

"I know, we said he was probably not meant for the list. But I have learned a little bit about him from Nicholas. He had an uncle who gambled away most of his inheritance before he came of age. He needs money to restore his estates." Venetia stopped and looked directly at her twin. "Why would he not be interested in marrying me?"

She went on before Vivian could reply. "The best way to determine whether or not he could be the blackmailer is to spend more time with him, Vivi. That is what I was trying to set up at breakfast. Why did you help him by offering him an excuse to be elsewhere? I could have kicked you—I tried, to be honest."

"Well, I like that! My own twin. But truly, Netia, I do not believe he could be the blackmailer."

"You are blinded by the paleness of his hair, or mesmerized by the sea color of his eyes."

"So, you have noticed his eyes, too, have you?" Vivian got up again and moved toward her sister. "Well, I am not blinded. I know you were thinking after breakfast that because he retired just after we did last night he had the opportunity to deliver the blackmail note. But you said yourself that the blackmailer probably had one of the servants deliver it. The fact that none we questioned this morning had done so does not mean it is not true. Whether he did or not, don't you think that the blackmailer would make certain his time was accounted for all evening, to avoid our suspicion? I think the fact that Lord Cranford has no alibi, as they call it, is a sign of his innocence."

It was a long speech for Vivian. That alone told Venetia how deep her sister's feelings ran.

"If it isn't Lord Cranford, Vivi, then who can it be? He has a motive, and surely he must be aware that he has no chance of winning one of us any other way. If nothing else, Father would never approve of him. Why would it be anyone else?"

"That is what we must try to find out, Netia. If we determine to focus our efforts only on Lord Cranford, the real culprit may be completely overlooked."

Venetia had been toying with a pink blossom she'd plucked from the border and now she threw it into the fountain. It swirled about for a moment and then the petals began to separate. "All right. I agree we must look closely at everyone, not just Lord Cranford. We cannot afford to fail in this—we have far too much at stake. But I do not agree that he should not be a suspect."

Vivian turned toward the steps at the foot of the garden. "Come. If we do not go in, we will not have enough time to get changed for the picnic." With a mischievous smile she added, "Netia, I think you simply can't accept that Lord Cranford might be immune to your charms."

The Duke of Roxley's idea of a picnic was quite different from anything Gilbey imagined. Wagonloads of servants had been sent ahead to prepare the site, and as the guests who had chosen to walk there set off through the garden, more servants were leaving with what looked like supplies for an entire army. The rest of the guests would arrive by carriage.

The walkers constituted a sizable group, including all the young guests and a few who could not bear to be classified as anything else, such as Lord Amberton and the intrepid Lady Norbridge. Eight ladies and nine gentlemen in all made up the group. Lady Elizabeth, Lord and Lady Upcott's daughter Lady Caroline, and Miss Whitgreave had successfully won permission to join the walking party without their parents, so there was a spirit of joyful rebellion in the ranks. The twins' Aunt Alice, Lady Colney, had promised to serve as chaperon.

Nicholas led the way up the central path through the gardens, pointing out the branching paths and walkways that led to individual terraces designed with their own themes. He raised his voice to reach the ears of his audience, who had quickly become a disorderly line strung out behind him.

Following along at the rear, Gilbey spotted a peacock feather lying on the grass beside the flagstones and picked it up, absently twirling it in his fingers. He had been observing the members of the party as they chose companions and jock-eyed for position in the line, but now the thought of peacocks in the garden distracted him. He had always admired the beautiful birds. Hoping for a glimpse of one strolling on the side paths, he failed to notice that ahead of him Lady Norbridge had stopped to let the others in the group pass by her. The next thing he knew she had fallen into step beside him.

"I was very disappointed that you chose to abandon us so early last night," she said in a low voice, casting a sidelong glance at him that quickened his pulse despite his sense of dismay. She took the feather from his hand, brushing her fingers against his quite deliberately, he was certain.

Botheration! This was not what he needed. It did not help that her choice of words was so similar to Lady Venetia's at breakfast. Twice in one day he was being accused of abandoning an attractive woman. How much self-control was a man expected to have?

With relief he noticed that the twins' cousin, Lady Adela, had stepped aside from the line and was waiting for him and Lady Norbridge to catch up to her. Talking to her should be safe enough. At least there was no wine anywhere about.

"La, there you are, Lord Cranford," she gushed, tipping her chin up and looking directly at Lady Norbridge instead of at him. "I felt so terrible about what happened at dinner last night, I just had to speak with you."

The line of walkers had progressed through a gate at the back of the garden and had begun to ascend a fairly steep hill following a path through the ancient beech woods. Just after Adela spoke, she slipped on some leaves on the path. Gilbey reached out and steadied her by her elbow. Had she done it deliberately?

He risked a glance at Lady Norbridge and could have sworn that she bristled. There were certainly sparks in her eyes. She looked very beautiful and quite displeased.

Botheration. Now what was he supposed to do?

"You mustn't concern yourself about last night," he told Lady Adela gallantly. "Accidents happen. I hope you escaped the reach of the wine? That was an exquisite gown you were wearing."

Lady Adela positively beamed, and beside him Lady Norbridge glowered. Perhaps he had gone a little overboard?

"Naturally, both of you looked splendid last night, as you do this minute. I'm sure I have the envy of all the other gentlemen, walking here with the two most handsome ladies in the group."

Of course, it was a lie. Lovely as they were, neither lady could compare to the twins. Probably all three of them knew it. Whatever made Nicholas think that he, Gilbey, had learned how to handle women? He was saved from further conversation however, as they came down the other side of the hill to find the rest of the group standing about in the hollow. A somewhat winded Lord Amberton was seated on a stone bench, puffing and blowing between complaints.

"Bless me, but no one said we were going mountain climbing! I thought this was meant to be a pleasant stroll to the picnic site." The path ahead led up another steep, wooded hill.

While the twins and Nicholas endeavored to reassure him, the other members of the party were using the opportunity to regroup. Gilbey desperately looked for someone else to walk with, and finally discovered Lord Ashurst, who appeared to be keeping apart from the group.

"Lady Vivian and her sister are stuck with Amberton, now," the marquess observed bluntly. "He is like a bulldog they will have trouble shaking loose."

Gilbey nodded. "He is not the only one." The twins were surrounded by Lord Amberton, Lord Wistowe, Lord Newcroft, and Lord Chesdale. Georgina Whitgreave and Lady Caroline walked together behind them, looking neglected, while Lady Elizabeth was keeping very close to Nicholas. Gilbey noted with relief that Lady Norbridge had sought out Lord Munslow and that Lady Adela had been reined in by her mother and now walked dutifully between that good lady and the very young Earl of Lindell.

Their route wound through the woods, up and down hill, until finally it descended a long slope to an open meadow beside the River Coln. There the intrepid foot travelers found long tables set out, clad in snowy linen and laden with all kinds of dishes. Rugs had been spread upon the grass, and soft pillows offered comfortable seating. The guests who had come by carriage were settled and already eating.

With appetites sharpened by exercise, the new arrivals clustered around the tables, waiting to be served, and then joined their cohorts. Gilbey and Lord Ashurst were the last to be served. They took their loaded plates and slipped off to one side, where they could observe the scene before them.

The twins had, with applaudable tact, plunked themselves down in the midst of the group of young ladies, forcing their admirers to dance attendance on all of them. Gilbey noticed that Venetia was the one who kept the gentlemen hopping, sending one back to the table for one thing and directing another to the carriages to fetch something else.

"Not one of them is worth so much as the littlest toe of either of the twins," Lord Ashurst muttered.

Surprised by this comment, Gilbey smiled. "Perhaps we should be in there offering our own services, sir?"

The marquess shook his head. "I wouldn't be so presumptuous."

"Presumptuous?"

"Certainly. Do you think we are any better qualified to attend them than the rest?" He shook his head again. "I would not wish to inflict myself upon them. I cannot fathom what Roxley thinks he is about. If this sorry group of suitors is the best he can do for his daughters, then he is a fool."

Gilbey could hardly believe his ears. Cynical the marquess might be, but that comment did not come from a man who was cold or aloof. It appeared that Lord Ashurst was exceedingly modest, perhaps even to the point of being shy. He clearly held Nicholas's sisters in high esteem.

Gilbey decided that he rather liked the marquess. "We may cause more offense by staying away than if we join the throng, I regret to say," he replied. "I see that we are observed, and I suspect we are judged neglectful."

Ashurst looked around. "By whom?"

"Lady Venetia. She has cast several dark looks in our direction."

"Has she? I didn't notice." Ashurst sighed. "I suppose we have no choice, then. It simply won't do to offend our hostesses."

* * *

Later, after all the guests were fully sated, the company prepared to scatter about the meadow to enjoy the fine afternoon.
Equipment for quoits, battledore and shuttlecocks, ninepins
and trap-ball had been brought along for any who wished to
play, and sketching materials were available. For a little while,
however, Venetia insisted that the men compete in the games,
while the ladies watched. It seemed to Gilbey that she singled
him out particularly, perhaps in retribution for his earlier inat-
tention.

He allowed Lord Amberton to beat him at trap-ball, and the
Viscount Newcroft, a small, agile fellow, beat him handily at
battledore and shuttlecocks. Despite his dandyish ways and the
affectation of constantly using his quizzing glass, Lord Chesdale had the competitive spirit to be expected from an ex-cavalry officer, and he was clearly disappointed with his easy
victory at quoits. Gilbey, however, was quite pleased with his
own undistinguished performance.

Eventually Venetia relented and allowed the guests to do as
they wished. Many simply strolled or lounged upon the pillows, indulging in relaxed conversation. Gilbey wandered
down to the river's edge, intent upon investigating its potential
for fishing. Everyone else seemed contentedly occupied. The
twins had gathered up pads and paint boxes, so he had re-
strained his own impulse to sketch or paint. Nicholas was
caught up in a game of tag that Lady Norbridge had started by
tickling people with Gilbey's peacock feather. Their muted
squeals and laughter made a pleasant counterpoint to the gentle murmurs of the river, which was slow enough here to sport
masses of water crowfoot in the center of the stream.

Gilbey admired the turquoise bands on a damselfly that hov-
ered near some yellow flag at the water's edge. The sun was
warm and brought out the insect's jewel colors. The mild
breeze was fresh and sweet—in fact, the day was idyllic, all
trace of the morning's mist vanished. Why then did he feel so
at odds?

He asked himself all the obvious questions. Was it because he
would rather be back at Cambridge with his nose in a book? Or
was it because he did not fit in here at Rivington among the

duke's guests? The answer was always no. Still, he could not seem to banish the restlessness and discontent that plagued him.

He was lost in thought, still watching the damselfly above the surface of the water, when the sound of voices near him intruded upon his consciousness.

"Netia, you have already made them wait upon us like servants, and the games provided ample opportunities for us to observe their fitness and physical skills. Why is that not enough for one day?"

"I want to see how far they will go. Courtesy is a fine quality, but do you want to marry a man with no backbone?" There was a brief pause, and then Gilbey heard Venetia say, "I expect the river is still quite cold."

Gilbey knew he should not be shamelessly eavesdropping. A clump of brush and a willow tree with its roots reaching right into the water stood between him and the twins, effectively screening him from their view. But what the devil were they up to?

"What if the current takes your hat too quickly, or what if none of them will go after it?" Vivian asked quite rationally.

Venetia sighed. "Well, it is only a hat, after all. I think it would still be worth the price to see if any of them will go after it."

So, it was all a plot. Was everything the twins did so calculated? Gilbey did not like the feeling that gave him. He stepped back behind the bushes and the tree trunk and emerged on the other side.

"Lord Cranford!"

"Oh dear."

Surprise and displeasure registered on their faces. Vivian was properly bonneted and she held a parasol to protect her from the sun as well. Venetia stood bareheaded with her wide-brimmed cork hat in her hands. The sun shone gloriously on her golden hair, which must have come partially unpinned when she removed the hat.

The sight of her fanned Gilbey's disapproval into anger. How could she be so unbearably beautiful and yet so cold, so self-serving?

"I know Nicholas can be manipulative at times, but I have never known him to be so utterly calculating and heartless," he said, venting his feelings without the slightest preamble. "I overheard what you are planning to do and I'll be damned if I'll stand by and say nothing while you trick your own guests into a cold bath for your own amusement."

"Oh, please, Lord Cranford, it is not quite as you think!"

"Never mind, Vivi. I shall do it anyway." Venetia looked at Gilbey defiantly.

In the split second before she drew back her arm and sailed the hat through the air to land in the river, Gilbey realized several things. One was that he had been unpardonably rude to his hostess. It did not matter how justified he might have been. Another was that it had felt good to speak his mind honestly for once, even if he was rude. A third was a sudden revelation that his anger was out of proportion to her mischief and that he would do well to examine it further when he calmed down. But the fourth thing overpowered all the others in that instant, and it was a flash of *déjà-vu* that took him all the way back to Devonshire.

The defiant look. The hat sailing through the air. It was as if his sister Gillian stood there on the riverbank. Gillian, who always got into mischief. Gillian, who so often needed to be bailed out of trouble.

Only it was Venetia who needed to be bailed out of trouble now. Intent on defiance and mischief, she had not paid attention to her footing. At the moment she released the hat she slipped and with a genuine cry of distress tumbled into the river.

Chapter Six

Venetia was not in the water for more than a minute, but to her those seconds seemed like a lifetime. The shock of the cold water quite took her breath away. She struggled to find air and panicked when she discovered that she could barely move. One of her hands was tangled in the tendrils of the crowfoot weeds and her feet could not seem to get clear of the weight of her soaked skirts.

What a horribly embarrassing way to die, she thought just before she felt strong arms close around her. As her head emerged from the water, she gulped in a huge breath. Relief and gratitude surged through her. For a moment she just savored the secure, wonderful feeling of being held. It hardly mattered that the body she rested against was just as wet as she was or that water from her hair was still streaming down her face and neck. Then she opened her eyes.

Blue-green eyes stared down into hers, the anger she had seen in them just before she slipped now replaced by concern. Lord Cranford. Of course.

"Are you all right?" he asked. His voice was deep and had a rough edge to it that she did not remember.

He helped her to stand. The water was still swirling around them, knee-deep, tugging gently at her skirts. She opened her mouth to reply, but what came out was a gurgling, spluttering cough. Gracious! She had not realized she had swallowed half the river.

"Best get it up, if you can," he said gently, turning her away from him.

She coughed out what she could. Then she began to shiver, and she felt him slip an arm behind her knees and scoop her up

into his arms. He carried her out of the river as if she weighed
nothing.

There was a crowd awaiting them on the bank, drawn there
by Vivian's cries of alarm, but Venetia had only one thought
in the moment before she and Cranford arrived there. *How can
he be so warm when he has been in the cold river?* Instinc-
tively she huddled against him, pressing closer to the heat that
radiated through his wet clothes and hers.

"What happened?"

"Yes, what happened?"

"By Joseph! Is she all right?"

She heard all the questions, and she heard Cranford answer.
"She slipped and fell into the water. She is all right, just frightened, wet, and chilled."

He forgot to say embarrassed to death, she thought. Perhaps
it would have been better to have drowned. At least he did not
say that she had deserved it, although she was certain that he
thought so.

"Have you anything to wrap around her?"

He set her on her feet and immediately she was enveloped
in a soft pink silk shawl she recognized as the Duchess of
Brancaster's, and a warm red plaid one that could belong to no
one but Lady Duncross. Even so, she missed Lord Cranford's
warmth. She had no chance to turn back to him, however; Vivian was fussing about her and suddenly Aunt Alice was there,
too, and then Nicholas was there, steering her through the
crowd of guests, heading for the carriages.

She did not consider her appearance at all until she saw
Lady Elizabeth shrink back as she passed by. Then with a
sinking feeling she recognized the awful truth. *No doubt I look
like a half-drowned rat. Mayhap Elizabeth fears I will bite her.
Or drip on her, even worse!*

Behind her she heard shouts and a commotion, but she kept
moving steadily toward the carriages. Her teeth were chatter-
ing and she had finally realized how thoroughly revealing her
wet garments must be. She drew the two shawls closer around
her.

After a moment she heard Nicholas laugh. "So that's what
the noise is all about. Colonel Hatherwick has rescued your

hat, Netia. He hooked it out with his fishing gear when he saw it come floating downstream."

Venetia didn't know whether to laugh, scream, or cry.

Gilbey had flung his spectacles on the bank before he entered the water, but once he had found them again, he followed along behind Lady Venetia and her entourage. He had, of course, noticed the coldness of the water when he had first plunged in after her, but it was peculiar that he had never noticed it again until the moment he released her. Now he felt somehow bereft as well as wet and chilled. His wet clothes were sticking to him like a plaster. His hair was dripping water onto his spectacles and more droplets trickled down his neck. He imagined he cut quite a miserable figure. But worse than that, once again he was at the center of everyone's attention.

Lord Whitgreave shook his hand, sending drops of water in every direction. "Well done, sir, I say."

Someone else slapped him on the back. "Jolly good show."

Gilbey noticed a few less-than-congratulatory glances directed his way. Then Lord Wistowe fell into step beside him and gave him a knowing leer. "You sly dog, Cranford. Didn't know we ought to be keeping an eye on you. Got a good armful, eh? Just how did you manage to be right there when it happened?"

His tone was not particularly friendly. In fact, there was an underlying implication to his words that Gilbey did not like at all. He clenched his jaw to hold in his anger and merely said, "Stroke of fate, I suppose."

By rescuing Lady Venetia, how many enemies had he made? Had his prompt action compromised her reputation? What else could he have done? Was he supposed to stand back and do nothing while they waited for one of her suitors to play the hero? The water was not dangerously deep, but he had seen right away that she had been in difficulties.

Gad, she had felt wonderful in his arms. How beautiful she was when she had opened her eyes and stared up into his. Would the memory of those moments torment him forever? How much better for him if he had never touched her!

Up ahead he saw her bundled into the Duke of Roxley's landau. Lady Vivian climbed in beside her, but not before she touched Nicholas on the shoulder and pointed back toward Gilbey. As the carriage set off, Nicholas trotted back to join him.

"Bit cold for swimming, old man?" he said with a huge, lop-sided grin. "Remind me to thank you properly when we've gotten you warmed and dried. You look like something the dog dragged in. What the devil happened, anyway?"

How to answer? Nicholas would likely be insulted on his sister's behalf if Gilbey explained things just the way he saw them. On the other hand, Gilbey was getting very tired of being perfectly polite to everyone, especially when so many of the people around him did not seem to play by the same rules.

"It seems your sister likes to play games," he said in a clipped tone, choosing his words carefully. "She had some idea of tossing her hat into the river to see who would retrieve it, but she accidentally threw in more than she intended."

Nicholas laughed, not just a cursory chuckle but a heartfelt belly laugh that lasted at least a full minute. He clapped an arm across Gilbey's wet shoulders and steered him toward a carriage, signaling to the coachman at the same time. He was still laughing as they climbed in.

"You find that humorous?" Gilbey said stiffly.

Nicholas wiped his eyes with the back of his hand. "I know Venetia, and I know you, my friend. I think I am able to fill in all the blanks you have left in the story. I only wish you knew each other as well as I do! Of course, I can go to Vivian for a full accounting." He lapsed back into laughter which Gilbey could not share.

Gilbey stared out the carriage window. He saw nothing funny about the situation. He was in danger of falling in love with a woman he was not sure he even liked or approved of. But the woman was not even the worst part! Falling in love at all was unthinkable—utterly ruinous, a disaster of major proportions. He was not a man who could afford to love. Thank God Venetia could never be his. If only he could get her out of his mind. From there it was only a short way to his heart.

The remaining guests returned to Rivington from the picnic in small bunches, drifting in almost randomly as they saw fit. The St. Aldwyn carriages made several trips to the picnic site and back, for it seemed that no one felt moved to walk back. As there was no further entertainment planned until dinner, the guests filled the time by wandering through the picture rooms and galleries of Rivington, writing letters in the salons, or wandering in the gardens.

Venetia had chosen to remain in her room, for although she was quite recovered from her dip in the river, she was not in the best of moods. To Vivian, this was an ideal opportunity to slip off and attend to a matter that she knew her sister would disapprove.

Assuming that Lord Cranford was also fully recovered from his unintended bath, where would he spend the hours until dinner? Vivian suspected the library was the most likely place, for his interest in old architecture and his predilection for books would both lead him there.

The library occupied the original hall of the old manor house that formed part of the north wing of Rivington. With its great vaulted ceiling of wooden beams, the room was one of her own favorites. Many times she had curled up in a chair there, imagining the medieval lord of the manor dining with his family and guests on the dais at the far end of the room, proudly showing off the great oriel window he had installed there. His massive carved fireplace with its heraldic motifs seemed to fit comfortably among the much newer wall cases filled with books.

Vivian did not see Lord Cranford in the library when she arrived there, but neither had she seen him in any of the other rooms she had passed through on her way there. Had she guessed wrong? What if he and Nicholas had devised some other amusement for themselves? She decided to settle in the alcove of the oriel window to continue with one of Miss Austen's novels and wait for a bit.

Anne Elliot had just come to realize her error in sacrificing her romance with Captain Wentworth when Vivian heard voices and looked up to see Lady Norbridge and Lord Munslow enter from the screen passage. She was surprised to see them—they seemed to her the most unlikely among the guests to be interested in books. They looked equally surprised to see her.

"Why, Lady Venetia, we did not expect—we did not mean

to disturb you," Lady Norbridge faltered. Her heavy scent of lilac clashed with the room's musty scent of old leather. "I hope you are quite recovered . . . ?"

"I am Lady Vivian, and it is quite all right. We are happy to have our guests make use of the library."

Lord Munslow cleared his throat. "No, no, wouldn't think of disturbing you. Didn't think there'd be anyone here." He paused as if uncertain what to do or say next.

Finally it dawned on Vivian that they might have come seeking privacy rather than books. Well, they would have to go elsewhere if they wanted a private tête-à-tête. She had gotten there first and she was not about to relinquish her post. At least she was reading. She lifted her chin and smiled at them sweetly.

Lady Norbridge appeared to have recovered her composure. "I do beg your pardon. It is so difficult to tell you apart. How does your sister do now, Lady Vivian? We were all quite concerned over her mishap."

Ah, polite conversation. Of course they couldn't just leave. "She says it was nothing. She is fine now, thank you." Vivian wondered if she should suggest that they try the solarium upstairs, but she realized they would likely be shocked at her forwardness. Shouldn't she be the one who was shocked? They seemed to have gotten this backward.

Just as she came to the conclusion that at least Lord Munslow could be removed from the list of interested suitors, Lord Cranford appeared in the arched passage doorway.

"This seems to be a popular spot. Am I intruding?"

Lady Norbridge replied before Vivian could say a word. "Ah, Lord Cranford, the hero of the day. Not at all—do join us." With a rather exaggerated swaying of her hips and provocative swishing of her soft green silk skirt, the older woman went to him and put her hand on his arm. "Lord Munslow and I were just leaving, but I have something that belongs to you. I would like very much to return it—sometime."

Lord Cranford looked as if he did not know what to say, and Vivian could not blame him. Now she *was* shocked. The invitation in Lady Norbridge's tone was quite blatant.

When Lord Munslow and the countess had left the room,

Lord Cranford turned to Vivian. "The worst thing is, I cannot even call to mind anything of mine that she might have."

Vivian could not find a reply. She had wanted to speak with him. Her hunch about the library had proven right, and her opportunity was at hand. But what had seemed so easy in her mind was not so easy to carry out. Finally she blurted, "I hope you suffered no ill effects from the river? We owe you many thanks."

"No thanks are due. It was but a moment's work, and I am perfectly fine." With an odd expression on his face he added. "An early season swim is hardly the worst thing that could happen."

He began to stroll casually about the room, looking around him. "This makes a magnificent library. What a splendid idea to install it in here."

She swallowed and nodded. "Yes, I have always loved it." She wanted to talk to him about Venetia. But how was she to bring up the subject? She felt very stupid.

"I'm sorry, Lady Vivian," he said, "I can see I have interrupted your reading. I shall be quiet and let you get back to it."

No! That was the last thing she wanted. " 'Tis only *Persuasion,* a novel that came out this past year. Really, I do not mind."

"May I ask how your sister is faring now after her ordeal?"

Yes, oh yes. That was better. "She is fine now, thanks to you. I am certain she will wish to thank you herself."

"As I said, no thanks are necessary. I was simply the nearest. Anyone would have done the same."

They might not be so modest about it. That was another thing she liked about him, beside the fact that he never had difficulty distinguishing between her and her sister. She really did not believe he could be the blackmailer.

"About this afternoon—there was one thing . . ." Oh, why was this so hard to do?

"I know. You have every right to upbraid me. I owe you an apology for this afternoon. I was unspeakably rude."

"Oh, no. I mean, that isn't it at all . . ." She set her book down and stood up. Perhaps she would do a better job if she walked around the way Venetia would have.

"The thing is, of course, you do not know my sister very

well. If you did, you would see her actions in a very different
light. I cannot blame you for protesting her behavior towards
our guests; I am sure it must seem both callous and—and
somewhat capricious. But she is not like that at all. Perhaps
her idea about the hat *was* ill-advised—certainly it turned out
to be so, did it not?"

She had circled away from where he was standing and now
she turned back to face him. "Truly, she is sweet and generous, quite different from what people think. If only you could
understand . . ."

But of course, how could he, when she could not tell him
the whole truth? "Venetia does not do such things for amusement. How else are we to know which man would make a
good husband? It is not merely our own happiness and future
at stake, but a matter of the family fortune and lineage as
well . . ."

"Do you not trust your father's judgment?"

Ah, now how was she to answer that? Naturally a man
would see it in such simple terms. But she could not expose
her father's failings any more than she could reveal her own
affliction. What would Venetia say? She was so much better
with words.

"Our father has allowed us a certain measure of choice. We
take these steps precisely for that reason. There are many men
who would, uh, take advantage of our situation. Venetia is
only trying to make certain that we know what we are getting.
She means no harm by it."

"I see," said Lord Cranford.

Vivian could not tell if he understood even slightly. At least
she had tried. So much of Venetia's behavior was for her sake,
she could not bear to have him think ill of her twin.

The viscount came up to her and took her right hand. "I
think you are the one who is sweet and generous to attempt to
defend your sister. I will try to remember what you've said. I
only hope you two are not looking for perfection to match
your own, for you will never find it." He raised her hand and
kissed it.

Vivian sighed. "You are very kind." *And so handsome, too.*
If only he were eligible! He would make a fine husband for
anyone. Well, anyone except for her. Any man who was pa-

tient, kind, and understanding enough to live with her infirmity should be spared from such a fate. Marriage was not the right future for her, no matter what her father or even Venetia believed. If only she knew how to convince them.

Chapter Seven

Venetia slept badly that night and was still out of sorts when she awoke the following morning. Breakfast in her room and the prospect of the day's planned activities did nothing to improve her state of mind. Later, as she surveyed the simple blue walking dress her maid had laid out for her to wear to the morning's archery competition, she wished she could spend the entire day alone.

Her bad mood had everything to do with the Viscount Cranford and very little to do with her own folly, at least in her own view. If Cranford had not happened along when he did, she thought, she most certainly would not have slipped when she threw her hat into the river, and she would not have needed rescuing. Perhaps Colonel Hatherwick would still have fished the hat out with his fishing pole, but perhaps not. If one of the other gentlemen had gone into the river after it, it would never have floated downstream to where the colonel was indulging his passion. She and Vivian might still have learned something of value about their suitors.

What made it so much worse was the indignity of having fallen in. What a foolish predicament to have gotten into! She felt grateful to Lord Cranford for rescuing her, and at the same time she resented him.

The fact was, she could not put the rescue out of her mind. The image of Lord Cranford's striking eyes and the feeling of being in his arms invaded all her thoughts. Her inability to banish them was ridiculous!

She had actually caught herself thinking that if he was indeed the blackmailer, perhaps marriage to him would not be so terrible. A harebrained notion! Only a heartless, unscrupulous blackguard would resort to such a tactic as blackmail. The man had to be morally bankrupt, not to mention avaricious and cruel! The fact that she considered such a marriage for even a moment proved how thoroughly Lord Cranford had confused her. She was sorry to think that Nicholas was such a poor judge of friends, but who else could be the villain? Lord Cranford was the only stranger among them. All the other guests had been handpicked by her father and Aunt Alice and were well-known among the *haut ton*.

A light rap on her door brought her back to the present. Vivian entered, her face showing a perfect mixture of surprise, concern, and reproval.

"Netia! You are not even dressed. Aunt Alice is already gathering everyone. Are you feeling unwell? I hardly knew what to think when you did not wish any company for breakfast."

How can I explain? Venetia thought. She had never held anything back from her twin before now, but Vivian did not share her suspicions about Lord Cranford. Vivian had not felt the viscount's arms around her, or looked up into those eyes at a moment when time seemed to stand still. How could Vivi possibly understand the confusion that was tormenting her?

"Where is Millie? Did you send her out? Shall I help you to dress instead?" Vivian asked. "I guess I had better. You are standing there as if you have forgotten how to move."

Venetia sighed. Not sharing her trouble with her sister made her feel even worse. "I wish we could swap places, Vivi. You could be me and I could suffer an attack of 'delicate nerves,' as father calls it, and stay in my room all day."

Of course she didn't mean it. She said it unthinkingly, more to herself than to her sister, but Vivian looked stricken. "Oh, Netia. What a terrible thing to wish for! Anyway, I wouldn't dare to take your place. What if I had a seizure?"

Venetia rushed across to hug her sister, her own frustrations swept aside. "I wasn't serious, Vivi! You know I'll always stand by you. If I could wish for anything, it would be that you could be cured. Or that the accident never happened, so we could have Mama back, too."

If she was utterly, ruthlessly honest, Venetia had to admit that a tiny spark of envy did lurk somewhere in her dark side—a horrible, unattractive reality. Just occasionally she did wish she could have an excuse to get away from everything the way Vivian could when she suffered a seizure. Venetia had cast herself in the role of caretaker, but sometimes she grew weary of the part—indeed, sometimes she felt as though the weight of it might actually break her. When she was tempted to throw off that mantle, she would think of the burden that Vivian carried and knew that her own would never be so heavy.

"Here, do help me to dress," she said to break the awkward moment. "I don't know what is the matter with me this morning. This gown is a good choice for today, is it not? Just the right color—blue for 'blue-deviled.' Perhaps I am just discouraged that we have made so little progress in our investigations. We are no closer to discovering either our poet or our blackmailer than when we started."

Vivian gathered up the walking dress and held it up at arm's length. "Is that what was bothering you last night? You were very quiet again at dinner, and you were paying very little attention while we played charades and anagrams. Why, Netia, you did not even thank Lord Cranford for rescuing you from the river—I noticed that you did not go near him once all evening. 'Tis not like you to be so thoughtless."

Was Vivian testing for a reaction? Did she suspect something? She was fishing very near the truth. "Did I not thank him?" Venetia said innocently, tying the ribbon closure of her chemisette and straightening the ruff at her neck. "Oh dear. I must make certain to do that—I never meant to slight him. Did he seem offended?"

"No," Vivian answered thoughtfully. "He seemed preoccupied, although I'd say he seemed content to stay away from you."

Venetia only paused for half a heartbeat. "Perhaps he was afraid I would need to be rescued again. Seriously, perhaps he is afraid to get close for fear we'll discover he is the blackmailer. I wish we knew how to find out for certain. If only the servants had known something, or the note had yielded some usable clue. I wish we could discover something—anything." She held out her arms to receive the dress.

"I wish that you would discover Lord Cranford is not the blackmailer, so we could begin to look for someone else."

What Venetia really longed for at that moment was for Lord Cranford and the rest of the guests as well to disappear out of Rivington and her life altogether. She knew the chance of that, however. "If only we had some magic wishes," she said. "I'd give anything for these two weeks to be over, or better yet, to have never begun."

Venetia's was not the only bad mood to be found in Rivington that morning. Gilbey, too, had spent a tormented evening and a restless night. He was certain that if even a hint of how he was feeling showed on his face, no one would dare to come near him or speak to him. He got through breakfast civilly, but now as he joined the other guests for the archery tournament, he wondered if putting a weapon into his hands would be wise. Suppose he just happened to mistake Lord Wistowe for one of the targets?

He had to admire the arrangements for the competition, despite his black mood. The range had been set up on a south-facing lawn at the far end of the walled garden, with targets at measured intervals at the bottom of the slope. Instead of the standard round targets, the figures of medieval knights in armor had been painted on canvas and attached to hay bales. Gilbey liked that—it suited his state of mind perfectly. If he wished he could even attach names to the figures; he would likely name one as Nicholas, who deserved a few shots for bringing him to Rivington in the first place. At the top of the slope a gaily striped canopy offered shade for the ladies, and bright pennants on poles fluttered in the breeze.

"Care to make a wager? Highest score, lowest score, most lost arrows, whatever you wish." Lord Munslow's voice penetrated Gilbey's thoughts.

Gilbey turned around and saw Lord Chesdale gesturing at the other earl with his quizzing glass in hand. "Five pounds says you'll lose your money no matter what you wager." That could be nearly half a year's pay for one of their servants, Gilbey reflected. Behind the two earls several other guests laughed.

Gilbey stepped away before they could try to include him in their wagering. Not to join in would be considered unsporting, but he hated to squander his resources. An altogether different

danger was that Lady Norbridge might notice him standing
alone, a fate he wished to avoid. Finding Nicholas seemed like
a good idea until he saw him standing by the rack of bows
waiting for the archers, with Lady Elizabeth close beside him.

"Are you skilled at archery, Lord Cranford?" Lady Caroline
Sainsberry, the daughter of the Earl and Countess of Upcott,
had quietly come up behind him. Gilbey rather liked Lady
Caroline—although she looked fragile with her curly blond
hair and porcelain skin, her conversation focused primarily on
horses and sport. She was not loud and did not put on airs like
the twins' cousin Adela.

"I'm afraid not," he said, feeling rather guilty at the lie. He
had won his college archery cup for two years in a row, but he
was determined to excel at mediocrity on this day. There
would be no accidents, no dramatic rescues, nothing to draw
attention or rile the legitimate suitors.

"A pity," said the young woman. "It would be so lovely to
see someone best that gaggle of popinjays." She inclined her
head toward the wagering gentlemen. "I thought you might be
just the one to do it." Forced to reconsider, she surveyed the
other guests. "Hm, perhaps Lord Newcroft. He acquitted himself rather well in the games yesterday . . ."

She wandered away, leaving Gilbey a clear view of the
twins as they arrived. They stopped for a moment, framed by
the green archway of clipped yews that opened onto the lawn.
One sister was clad in blue and the other in a deep rose color,
but Gilbey had to think and observe them for an instant before
he could tell which twin was which. Then he smiled.

Venetia was in blue. He could tell by the elegant way she
stood, and by the way she held her head. Vivian tended to
keep her hands behind her back and spent a good deal more of
her time looking at the ground than her sister. Venetia could
be counted upon to toss her head every so often in a way that
reminded him of a spirited mare. He almost laughed when she
did so just at the moment he thought of it.

Then there was something new, he had realized. Venetia
preferred hats. Not for her the demurely closed bonnets that
Vivian favored. The one she had thrown into the river yesterday had been a simple confection of cork and silver gray
crepe, and this one, though narrower in the brim, was trimmed

primarily with blue ribbons to match her dress. No foolish fantasies of flowers, fruit, or feathers for her. There was a single large feather, but it curled around the side of the crown quite sensibly, instead of sticking up like a weather vane ready to catch the slightest breeze. He suddenly realized that he was smiling in approval, and turned away.

What was he doing? Was this the way to get Lady Venetia off his mind? He didn't want to admire her, like her, or be around her—he didn't even want to see her. *And that is as much a lie as what you told Lady Caroline,* said a little voice in his head.

The call went up for the archers to prepare to shoot. Gilbey, his black mood restored, went over and snatched up arrows and a bow at random. Nicholas had gotten him into this coil, but he had only himself to blame for agreeing to help. If only he hadn't! He would not now feel honorbound to stay. How much simpler just to leave! From what he had seen so far, there was no lack of supervision over the young ladies. Nicholas seemed so taken up by Lady Elizabeth he did not appear to be in any way concerned.

The archers took their places along a line marked in the grass and listened while the Duke of Roxley's gamekeeper gave them instructions. Gilbey was intrigued in spite of himself. They were to shoot at each of the targets in succession, beginning with the farthest one, as if an enemy were advancing upon them. They would have six seconds to shoot at each target.

How does one defeat an enemy who is advancing from within? Gilbey thought as he nocked his first arrow and positioned himself to shoot. A powerful force was at work in him, and he did not know how to stop it. His heart and mind refused to follow the course he had set for his life—to avoid the mistake his father had made.

Gilbey closed one eye and sighted along the shaft of his arrow, waiting for the command to begin. He had always liked the pressure of timed shooting—it added an element of excitement to an activity that sometimes seemed closer to science than sport.

When the command came, he reacted reflexively. In that initial instant, nothing existed but the bow, the arrow, the target, and himself. Inside his head a clock began to tick off the six seconds. With the smooth ease of long practice, he pulled and released.

"By Jove, you've nailed the fellow right through the heart," Lord Amberton exclaimed.

Most of the first shower of arrows had missed widely.

"Who do you think you are, Cupid?"

More like that mythical cherub's victim, Gilbey reflected as he prepared his next shot. Surely he was the one who had taken a direct hit to the heart. The love arrow's poison was spreading through his system even as he stood there trying not to think of Venetia watching him. He released again, and this time his arrow had no difficulty in missing the target altogether.

The competition continued until nearly noon, lasting through several rounds of standard target shooting, distance shooting, and even a novelty round using apples for targets. Gilbey shot erratically, as if his arrows followed the ebb and flow of his turbulent emotions. That suited his purposes, however, and he was in good company.

"The only thing I hit all morning was the topiary peacock just over the wall," Lord Marchthorpe observed.

"Should have tried for one of the live ones," said Lord Munslow. "Then at least you would've contributed some meat to the dinner table."

"Fowl shot by foul shot, eh?" quipped someone.

"The birds were certainly at more risk from us than the targets," Lord Whitgreave commented. "Given the skill we have exhibited this morning, it is a miracle the ladies were safe while watching from behind us!"

As the group dispersed and began to mingle with the miraculously spared ladies, the Marquess of Ashurst approached Gilbey.

"You have excellent form, Lord Cranford," he said, a hint of puzzlement in his voice. "You are obviously not a novice. I was surprised that your aim seemed so frequently to be off."

Gilbey liked the marquess. He hated lying to him, but what other choice did he have? "Yes, well, uh, I suppose if I practiced regularly, I might learn to fix that." At least he could be truthful about Ashurst's skill. "You shot splendidly—I expect you'll win the prize for highest overall score."

"Hm, yes, so I suppose. Archery is a fine sport for a hermit like me—one can compete against oneself, and no other players are required. I enjoy it."

Gilbey usually enjoyed it, too. He might have enjoyed the competition if he could have put the entire St. Aldwyn family out of his mind and shot with honest skill.

The Duke of Brancaster came to them, smiling. "Lord Ashurst, you have easily won the prize for the highest score. You appear to be the only archer among us."

"What is my prize?"

"You shall escort whichever of the Duke of Roxley's daughters you choose for the rest of the day."

Ashurst looked dumbfounded.

The duke turned to Gilbey, his smile wavering so slightly Gilbey was not certain if he imagined it.

"Quite astonishingly, Lord Cranford, it seems you, too, have won a prize."

Gilbey's heart sank. How was this possible? he had tried so hard.

"It has been determined that you scored the only perfect bull's-eye of the day. It was your very first shot."

Fate was playing with him, there was no question about it, Gilbey decided. "That was only pure luck," he muttered, although he knew full well it wasn't true.

Lord Ashurst clapped him on the shoulder. "And what is his prize?" he asked the duke.

"He is to escort whichever twin you do not choose. Congratulations, gentlemen."

The two younger men stared at each other as the Duke of Brancaster walked away. Then Lord Ashurst chuckled. "This is a fine turn of events. I cannot think of two less likely candidates, can you?" After a thoughtful pause he asked, "Have you any preference as to which of the twins I should choose, Lord Cranford?"

Gilbey was quite certain that Ashurst had a preference of his own, and that it was not Venetia. "No, no, you should choose as you see fit. You earned your prize and should enjoy it. My congratulations. I think I must see what can be done about my own situation, however. I did not come here to court Edmonton's sisters. Someone else most assuredly should have the advantage of my prize."

So saying, he moved off in search of Nicholas, leaving a puzzled Lord Ashurst staring after him.

Nicholas was easy to find. He came up to Gilbey moments later in a state of agitation. "My father has done it again," he said, glancing about.

There was no one within earshot. "What?" Gilbey asked.

"He never told my sisters that their charming company was to be the prize for the competition. Venetia is in a state."

"I can understand that," Gilbey said wryly. "I wanted to speak to you about that, actually . . ."

Nicholas hurried on. "I don't really understand why she is so upset, except that she likes to be consulted. It seems to me that you and Lord Ashurst are perfectly acceptable escorts. As far as I am concerned, in fact, it works out quite well—what better way for you to keep an eye on them for me?

"Congratulations, by the way. What the devil was wrong with your aim? I couldn't believe that you did not win for the highest score. Ashurst was good, but you should have beaten him easily. Instead you won the prize for best shot with the only good one you fired all morning. Is this the man who earned the school's archery cup two years running?"

"Shhh, Nicholas! All I need is for someone to hear you." Gilbey would have liked to have a bow in his hand right then. He would have used it to knock sense into his friend. "Did it ever occur to you that the other gentlemen might not appreciate having to compete with a champion? Or that they might even now resent losing the opportunity to be with your sisters that I have stolen away from them with this prize? I want you to fix this, Nicholas. You can say there was a mistake, and award the prize to someone else."

"How can I do that? No one else had as good a shot, other than Ashurst, and he can't claim both prizes."

"Think up some other prize, then."

"One might think my sisters were two-headed gorgons, you are so eager to stay out of their company, old man."

* * *

Venetia sucked in her breath as if she had been hit in the stomach. She had not meant to eavesdrop on her brother and Lord Cranford—she had walked over to them in good faith, intent on discussing the problem of her father's Machiavellian choice of prizes. They had failed to notice her and now she retreated hastily.

Vivian looked up expectantly as Venetia approached. "So, did you finally thank Lord Cranford for rescuing you yesterday?"

Venetia shook her head silently. Grabbing her sister by the hand, she pulled her along as she ducked through the evergreen arch and hurried up the path. She sought refuge in the garden they called the sundial court.

"Netia! Whatever is the matter? Gracious, you whisked me away in the middle of a conversation with Lady Marchthorpe."

"That woman? She might as well be a match for Father, the way she's plotting with Elizabeth to get their hooks into Nicholas. Right now I wouldn't care if they succeeded."

She led Vivian to a stone bench in the center of the garden and sat down. The delicious scent of the wallflowers growing against it failed to soothe her.

"You are upset with Father, I know," Vivian said. "He should have told us beforehand, I agree, but—"

"Vivi, listen. I overheard Nicholas and Lord Cranford talking. Cranford is a champion archer. He did not want to win the prize—he purposely contrived his poor marksmanship on the archery range."

"Why would he do that? No one knew ahead of time what the prizes were to be, did they?"

"The very idea of being in our company was so hateful to him, he went to Nicholas and asked him to reward the prize to someone else!"

"Well, that is certainly not very flattering."

Venetia felt the pressure of her churning emotions building up to tears, making her chest tight and creating a huge lump in her throat. She had never felt so confused in her life. She had no wish to be with Lord Cranford, yet his rejection hurt like the very devil. She was convinced his dishonesty about his archery skills was just what one might expect from a blackmailer. And why would he have any interest in being in their company? It meant only an extra risk of premature discovery for him. She and her sister were nothing more than a means to an end for him—he cared only for their money.

Sometimes her sister could be hopelessly blind. "Don't you see how it is? He did not need to know the prize to wish to avoid winning. A blackmailer would want to keep attention away from himself. He would not care about any little prize he might win during the party—he is focused entirely on winning the grand prize at the end."

"Netia, you are determined to cast the worst possible light on everything he does. Suppose he did not wish to attract attention simply because he is modest? Perhaps he felt it was not fair to the other gentlemen if his skill was so far above theirs. You know, not every man is as insensitive as Father. Someday you will have to trust one."

"You make Lord Cranford seem such a paragon. Well, he is certainly not the man I will choose to trust. He is altogether too polite, too proper, and too utterly conventional to be true. You'll see. This business about the archery only proves that he is not honest."

"I think he is quite attractive," countered Vivian. Her gentle smile softened the note of reproval in her voice.

"Fine. Let us only hope that Lord Ashurst chooses to spend the afternoon with me. That way you may enjoy the questionable pleasure of Lord Cranford's company."

Chapter Eight

The afternoon arrived all too soon.

"Are you certain you will be all right?" Venetia looked at her sister with concern as she positioned her hat on her carefully arranged hair and tied the lavender ribbons under her chin.

They were preparing for the afternoon's outing, a visit to Sandler's Hill, an ancient chambered long barrow a few miles from Rivington. Normally Venetia would have enjoyed such an excursion, but she was dreading the coming hours to be spent in Lord Cranford's company. However, her concern for her sister overshadowed all else.

"If you were to choose an activity to pass, this would be a good one," she continued. "You have not spent much time resting, Vivi, and remember the climb up the hill is not an easy one."

"I had no trouble yesterday. Anyway, my afternoon has been promised to Lord Ashurst. How can I not go?"

"That was Father's doing and can be undone. You could promise Lord Ashurst that he may escort you tomorrow instead."

Vivian picked up a pair of lilac-colored gloves that exactly matched the shade of both her dress and Venetia's. "No, it is too late to cry off. We are all ready now! And besides, I want to go."

The expression on Vivian's face was quite earnest, and Venetia knew she had best let the subject drop. She smiled. Looking at her sister was often like viewing her own reflection in a looking glass. She did not know how she would have managed to go on if her beloved twin had died in the accident that had claimed their mother's life. At this moment they were more alike than ever, for they had decided to dress identically to spite their father and their aunt.

Aunt Alice was the one who had insisted they change clothes, "to show your advantage in having a vast collection to choose from." Aunt Alice deplored the confusion that was inevitable when the twins dressed alike, so they had promptly selected a pair of matching lilac carriage dresses trimmed with white satin and ribbon in a deeper shade of lavender. Since their father had seen to it that the archery prize winners had to choose between the twins, it occurred to them that his plan could be thwarted neatly by this same bit of mischief.

"If I do not go, what will you do, Netia? You would have to face the gentlemen alone." Vivian grinned and that reassured Venetia more than words.

"All right, then let us go down. You are certain?"

Vivian nodded, and her hat slipped a little.

"A hatpin will fix that. Here." Venetia took a long ornamented pin from the vanity table and helped her sister adjust the hat. "Retie the ribbons and there you go. Perhaps this day will not be so bad."

Lord Ashurst was waiting for them in the huge entry hall, looking splendid in a deep burgundy riding coat and fawn breeches. The polish on his boots reflected light like a looking glass. There was no sign of Lord Cranford. The marquess started toward them and then stopped.

Venetia and Vivian exchanged a wary glance, wondering what his reaction would be. Their joke was aimed at their aunt and their father, but how could Lord Ashurst know that?

Then he began to laugh. Walking toward them he said, "Ladies, my heartiest congratulations. What a brilliant solution to a most awkward conundrum, one that was none of our making. I did not know how I could make a choice between you without inflicting offense or disappointment in some direction, whether you welcomed my company or not, and I did not see how to refuse the prize without causing even more offense!"

"Why would you refuse the prize?" Venetia asked tersely, still stung by the conversation she had overheard earlier.

"Why, simply because it was so unfair to you to have no

choice in the matter. I realize there are others with whom you might prefer to spend your afternoon."

Venetia was surprised to hear such a courteous reply from him. "Why, not at all, my lord."

"If it is agreeable to you, I shall simply have to choose you both, for I admit I cannot tell which of you is which when you are done up so identically. Ahem, exquisitely and delightfully, too." He added the last almost as an afterthought, as if he were not used to making compliments. "I shall simply have to share your company with Lord Cranford."

"Where is Lord Cranford?" Venetia asked, her tone a bit sharper than she intended. *Perhaps he will not go through with it,* she thought, but somewhere inside her that hope met an aggravating echo of disappointment.

"He is waiting outside for us. Shall we join him?" Lord Ashurst extended his elbows to accept a lady on either side.

The carriage drive in front of the house was full of vehicles as the expedition prepared to get underway. Lord Cranford stood by the Duke of Roxley's gleaming landau, pushing gravel about with the toe of his boot.

Why, he looks like a little boy, was the first thought that popped into Venetia's head. His hat was pushed back and he appeared to be studying the effect of the dust on his boots. There was something about his absentminded action combined with the way his pale hair fell forward over his downturned face that held all the charm and innocence of a very young man.

A moment later when he raised his head and saw her approaching with the others she reacted quite differently, however. Oh, she was doomed. The intent look he leveled in her direction might not have been meant for her at all, but it made her pulse leap and turned her knees to jelly nonetheless. Heavens, he was tall! He looked extremely handsome in a superbly tailored blue coat and biscuit breeches. Despite his spectacles she could see that his eyes looked very dark as she came to a stop just a few feet from him. He was not smiling.

"As you may see, Lord Cranford, I was unable to choose which lady should be mine for the day," Lord Ashurst said with a chuckle. "Would you be agreeable to sharing our escort duty?"

Venetia steeled herself to hear Cranford say no. How much easier to simply spend the day with Lord Ashurst! He seemed much more pleasant than she had expected. But Lord Cranford did not say no.

"Clever ladies," he said. "And I suppose you have given poor Ashurst here no clue as to which of you is which."

Venetia raised her chin. "No, we have not. Do you suppose you can help him?"

Cranford laughed then, a laugh with a note of triumph in it. "If I had not already been quite sure, I am now, Lady Venetia."

Vivian would never have challenged him, she realized, recognizing her mistake. Yet she was surprised that he was perceptive enough to know that. *Is there anything he does not know about us?*

Lord Ashurst appeared to be duly impressed. "Confounded if I know how you did that, Cranford! All the same, in deference to the ladies, I would prefer not to have to choose between them. Shall we not simply go along together? We make a fine pair of escorts, the hermit and the scholar. Poor ladies, we will do our very best to entertain you."

The twins could not help laughing at the marquess's self-deprecating comments, and Venetia felt somewhat more charitable as she climbed into the carriage. Lord Cranford took the seat beside her, which she thought was preferable to having him seated across from her for the entire trip to Sandler's Hill. At least she would not have to fight the feelings she might get from looking at him.

What she did not realize was that his close proximity beside her engendered other physical sensations that were perhaps even stronger. Struggling to ignore them, she tried to keep the conversation flowing during the drive. She discovered that Lord Cranford was quite knowledgeable about both the chambered long barrows and the round barrows found in the Cotswold hills. He knew more about them than she or Vivian did, although she was not about to let on that either twin had read about or studied such a subject at all.

Most of the carriages were left with their attendants at the foot of Sandler's Hill, and the small party prepared to begin

the trek along the winding footpath that led to the summit of
the hill. The climb through the woods was steep and required
some attention. The Duke and Duchess of Brancaster, who had
gamely come along to help Lady Colney chaperon, soon
lagged behind. The ladies who had not left their parasols with
the carriages quickly consigned these items to the gentlemen
accompanying them as they made their way up.

There was, however, another way up the hill: a narrow cart
track that gave access to the field at the top. Venetia instructed
the coachman to take the twins' carriage as far up this track as
he thought he could get.

"I am concerned about Vivian," she told the gentlemen, ignoring the black look her sister gave her. "She never will
admit when she is tired." She looked back apologetically as
they left the rest of their group behind. "Oh dear, perhaps I
should have told Their Graces the duke and duchess about this
way up."

The track snaked through the woods less steeply than the
footpath. The horses strained and pulled and the carriage jolted
its way almost to the top of the hill. The coachman halted at a
gate that opened onto the open field and bid his passengers to
alight. Beyond the field the tump, or mound, could be seen at
the summit, crowned by a grove of young trees and surrounded by a ditch and a grass-covered bank. The view from
the hilltop was magnificent, encompassing Cotswold hills and
valleys in several directions.

Venetia pulled Vivian aside for a moment as the gentlemen
opened the gate.

"You are not going to go into the barrow, are you, Vivi?"

"Do not worry. I shall be fine. When are you going to thank
Lord Cranford for rescuing you? You had the perfect opportunity while we were in the carriage."

"I know." Venetia had not wished to bring up the subject
while she and the viscount were so close to each other. She
had battled enough distressing feelings without bringing to
mind the ones she had felt in his arms the day before. She suspected the intimate subject might make him uncomfortable,
too, in front of others. "I promise I will find a time."

Vivian started toward the gate before she could say anything more. Venetia followed, more worried now than before.

The rest of their party was just coming up from the footpath as the twins arrived. In the open field the parasols reappeared, sprouting like flowers although a light cloud cover veiled the sun.

"A shame someone let those trees grow up there," said young Lord Lindell, Lady Elizabeth's brother. He nodded at the mound. "Over time those roots will work in and destroy something that's been here for thousands of years."

For a moment there was no sound or movement except the breeze as a hushed reverence fell over the little group. Then the duke and duchess came huffing up to the company, quite unaware of breaking the spell.

"Well then, are we going in?" asked the duke between gasps. His face was quite red, but he appeared to be recovering. "Have we lanterns?"

"Wistowe and I have them," Nicholas answered, holding them up. "Just let us get them lit, and we'll see who wishes to go in first. There's really only room for two or three inside at a time."

"How do we get in?" asked Lord Newcroft, who had already climbed up onto the banking and examined what appeared to be the entrance to the barrow. "This way is blocked up with a huge stone."

"That is a false entrance," Nicholas explained. "There is a smaller, less obvious one at the back."

The group crowded around, stepping back when the lanterns flared to life. Venetia looked at her sister nervously, but Vivian appeared to be all right.

Two by two, the more adventurous members of the party went into the barrow with Nicholas and Lord Wistowe. As they came out again, they gathered in little knots to discuss what they had seen and to wait for the others. Venetia thought it was interesting to see who paired off with whom. Elizabeth went in with her own brother—probably because Nicholas was busy. The duke and duchess went together, of course. She was surprised to see Cousin Adela go in with Lord Chesdale, while Georgina Whitgreave went with Lord Newcroft. Aunt Alice never went in at all, and neither did Lady Caroline, who said she didn't like enclosed spaces and preferred to admire the view.

Venetia tried again to dissuade Vivian from going into the barrow but she could not insist with so many people around them to hear. The only concession she won from her twin was an agreement to go in together instead of with Lords Ashurst and Cranford.

The barrow was interesting, Venetia had to acknowledge when the twins finally had their turn. The scent of smoke from the lanterns and the smell of damp stone and earth assailed them when they got inside. They had to step carefully to avoid some patches of mud and a puddle from the recent rains. Several tombs opened off a central passageway with walls made from large slabs of stone mixed with sections of neatly fashioned dry-stone work. But only two of the tombs were open, it was dark and a bit spooky, and Lord Wistowe kept positioning himself where she and Vivian had to brush up against him. The lanterns flickered and threw shifting patches of light and shadow on the walls. She felt relieved to crouch down and make her way back out into daylight—until she turned and looked at Vivian coming out behind her.

Vivian was shielding her eyes from the bright daylight and she had turned very pale. When Venetia saw her licking her lips, she recognized it as a warning sign that a seizure might be starting. *What do I do now?* she thought in momentary panic. The unsteady lantern light and the abrupt change from darkness to daylight were more than enough to trigger a seizure—it was just what she had feared. Vivian's eyes met hers, and she knew by the misery she saw in them that her twin was feeling the onset of the other initial symptoms they had come to know in six years: dizziness, nausea, buzzing in her ears, and the beginning of trembling that would soon overtake her.

I have to get her away from these people. Venetia thrust her head back into the barrow entrance and called to Nicholas in a low, urgent voice. She could not say anything that Lord Wistowe might hear. However, her brother appeared in an instant, almost as if he, too, had expected trouble. "Vivi's starting a seizure," she whispered. "You must keep Ashurst and Cran-

ford in here to give me time to get her away. I don't think the
others will notice us."

She took Vivian by the hand and began to lead her away
down the hill, hoping to get her to their carriage. What if she
could not get there in time? When the seizure took hold, Vivian would curl up into a ball and try to hide from the terrible
fear that came with it. She would fight anyone who tried to
touch her, even her own sister. How would Venetia get her
into the carriage then?

Cranford, came the thought. *If he is the blackmailer he already knows about this.* Could she ask him to help? Would he?
Revealing that she knew his identity might mean accepting his
scheme, forfeiting all chance to investigate and stop him.

What if he was not the blackmailer? Did she truly believe
that he was? Did she believe it enough to risk exposing Vivian's secret?

With a sense of defeat she realized the answer was no. What
that meant about her own feelings she must examine later. For
now she must struggle alone. She gave Cranford and Lord
Ashurst an especially brilliant smile as she came to them.
"Nicholas is waiting for you—'tis your turn. I think you'll find
it fascinating."

Perhaps her tone was just a little too bright, too enthusiastic.
Perhaps Vivian just looked too pale and tremulous. Cranford
immediately asked if something was amiss.

"No, no, no, not at all. My sister is tired and we thought we
would wait in the carriage."

Vivian managed to nod even though Venetia could feel that
the trembling was getting worse. She squeezed her sister's
hand in encouragement. At least the seizure had not yet fully
taken hold. As soon as the two men started up toward the barrow entrance, the twins hurried on.

"Hold on, Vivi, hold on," Venetia said, as if her sister had
any control over what happened. She knew full well that that
was not the case, but it still made her feel better to pretend.

"Unh—nixtx mumph." Vivian began making unintelligible
sounds and tried to pull away from her, a sign that the seizure
had entered the next stage. *Only a little farther,* Venetia
thought, tightening her hold. Her sister was trembling all over,
making jerky movements with her free arm. They were almost

to the carriage, but Venetia could not carry her twin. In another moment she would not even be able to keep a grip on her.

"John Coachman!" she called in desperation. Most of the stablehands were aware of Vivian's trouble. Their knowledge was a matter of her safety, and they were well paid for their loyalty. Venetia nearly cried from relief when she saw that he had heard her. She hoped no one else had. Together they half dragged and half carried Vivian to the landau and bundled her in, where she crouched shaking in one corner trying to hide.

Venetia leaned against the side of the carriage, wiping the tears out of her eyes and trying to regain her composure. Vivian's seizures never lasted more than a few minutes. She would be disoriented and confused for a short time when it was over, and then she would be back to normal except for the deep mortification she always felt afterward. Venetia needed to keep the gentlemen busy that long, unless she could convince them to go back with the others.

That was the solution! She would walk down and take the men with her. It might give Vivian just enough time.

Gilbey's mind was not on the construction of the long barrow even as he put his hand on the stones that other hands had placed there in ancient times. He was quite certain something was wrong between the twins, but they obviously did not want it known.

He looked up at Nicholas, holding the lantern a few feet away. Should he say something to him about it? Perhaps he already knew. The twins had just been with him in the barrow before they came by Gilbey and the marquess.

Ashurst was asking lots of questions about the tombs. Under other circumstances Gilbey would have been pleased to see someone show such interest, so similar to his own. But the man kept asking and Nicholas was encouraging him, explaining as many things as he could in great detail. The space was uncomfortably cramped for someone of Gilbey's height, and he found he was quite eager to get out again.

When finally they were finished and had emerged into the natural light, Lady Venetia was waiting for them. At least, he was quite certain it was Venetia. Vivian was the one who had been tired and unwell, but the twin who stood before them looking off at the view seemed too subdued to be Venetia. For the first time since meeting them he was not certain which twin was which. At that moment he realized that he did not know them nearly as well as he had assumed.

"Netia?" The question was Nicholas's.

As she turned to them, Gilbey saw that she almost literally pulled herself together—the shoulders straightened, the head came up, the haughty smile reappeared. *It is all an act*, he thought in astonishment, *performed for our benefit.* Was the lioness actually a fraud? Was that what Lady Vivian had been trying to tell him in the library? The possibility stunned and intrigued him.

"Nicholas, is that Chedworth Beacon over there? You can see so many hills! Truly this is a beautiful spot."

She came to them with a light, careless step, as if nothing in the world was the matter. Did she not care that her twin was unwell? Gilbey narrowed his eyes as he considered. Until this moment that was exactly the interpretation he would have put on her behavior. Now he thought his blindfold had been removed. Yet why go to such lengths if Lady Vivian was merely tired? Certainly that was a common enough malady among delicate ladies.

"I told Vivian to go ahead down in the carriage, since she was weary," Venetia explained, interrupting his thoughts. "The afternoon is so glorious, I did not think you gentlemen would mind at all if we walked. You see? I think the sun is even trying to break through for us."

"Is Lady Vivian all right?" asked Lord Ashurst. "I was looking forward to hearing her impressions of the barrow."

"Oh, yes, she will be fine. Sometimes she just tires before the rest of us. She finds that very frustrating. Does she not, Nicholas?"

"Yes. Yes, that she does."

There was nothing obviously strange about the conversation, Gilbey decided—it was merely his new perspective that made it sound that way. Nicholas beckoned to the others scattered about the field and suggested that it was time to start down.

Lady Elizabeth came over to join them. "Really, Lord Edmonton—Nicholas—what a charming place this is! Perhaps we could come back here for a picnic later in the week?" She was all but purring and Gilbey was surprised that she did not brazenly commandeer Nicholas's arm before he offered it.

Venetia interrupted in sudden excitement. "Oh, Nicholas, my reticule! I don't seem to have it. I wonder if I lost it inside the barrow?"

Nicholas looked caught between the two women, and Gilbey sympathized with him. Now what was Venetia up to? Was this another of her tests?

"See here, Lady Venetia, I'll go with you to look for it," Lord Wistowe volunteered. "My lantern is still lit."

"I don't believe his lantern ever goes out," Lord Ashurst commented softly to Gilbey.

Gilbey did not laugh. The idea of Lord Wistowe alone in the barrow with Venetia actually made him bristle with anger. Surely Nicholas would not allow it?

But Nicholas did not need to say anything. Gilbey realized he should have known Venetia would handle Lord Wistowe.

"Why, you are so kind, sir," she said sweetly. "My shoes are so muddy from going in the first time, perhaps you would just go in and look for me? The reticule is purple silk—I do hope I didn't drop it in a puddle."

Gilbey did not believe for a minute that she had left her reticule behind, nor did he think that her appeal for help was a failed ploy to get a moment alone with any of the gentlemen. But if it was a test, why had she waited until several suitors in the group had already started down? It felt more as if she might be playing for time, delaying them from starting down the hill. But why? Why?

He would have liked to have a moment alone with her in the barrow himself. He would have asked her exactly how much time she wanted to spend pretending to hunt for her reticule, and then he would have demanded to know the reason. *Then you would have liked to show her a pleasant way to pass that time,* came an unbidden thought, shocking him.

Gad, he was no better than Wistowe. No, he was worse, for he wasn't even honest about his feelings, pretending to himself that he wanted nothing to do with her. He wanted everything to do with her, and it was that fact that scared him the most.

The marquess came back from searching the barrow, looking frustrated. Of course he had not found the reticule.

"Oh dear," said a crestfallen Venetia. "Where could I have lost it, then?"

"Perhaps you left it in your carriage all along," Gilbey said sharply before he could stop himself.

Her eyes met his and he saw the wariness in them. *Fool!* he berated himself. *If you set her on her guard you will never solve the mystery.* But he was already a fool for even wanting to.

Chapter Nine

Aunt Alice looked thoroughly flustered by the time the delayed members of the party rejoined the others at the bottom of Sandler's Hill.

"I wondered what had become of you, Venetia. Er, Vivian? And, where is your sister, whichever one of you I am talking to? Ooh, I do hate it when you girls dress alike! Do you enjoy confusing all of us?"

"Now, Aunt Alice, do calm down," Venetia said soothingly, hiding a smile. "All is well. I simply thought I had lost my reticule, and we were delayed while Lord Wistowe very kindly looked for it. Unfortunately we did not find it."

"Your reticule? Lord Wistowe?" It amazed Venetia how quickly her aunt could recover from being upset. Suddenly the countess looked immensely pleased instead.

Oh, Lord help me if now she thinks I've set my cap for Lord Wistowe! Venetia thought. However, she did not disabuse her aunt of that notion. She also did not identify herself.

"As for my sister, she was tired and decided to come down in our carriage instead of walking down with us. I am certain that they will be arriving at any moment." With concern she glanced toward the cart track, but saw no sign of the landau as yet. She prayed that Vivian's seizure would be a short one.

"Well! At least that tells me which twin is standing before me, Venetia, no thanks to you. I know it would be Vivian and not you who would think she lacked the strength to complete the walk with the rest of us."

Realizing, perhaps, that her comment might not be just what potential suitors cared to hear, Lady Colney laughed suddenly. "Of course the girl is perfectly healthy, just a little delicate.

Too used to being pampered, I expect—nothing that a proper husband couldn't put right."

It took every ounce of Venetia's self-restraint not to throttle her aunt. She moved away and was dismayed when Lord Wistowe came with her.

"I would be happy to help you look further for your reticule, Lady Venetia. Have you any other thoughts as to where you might have left it?"

Truly, the man was incorrigible. She knew better than to suppose he really wanted to help. He couldn't abandon the possible opportunity to get her somewhere alone. Obviously, he thought seduction was the way to court a wife—or perhaps he simply knew no other way, she thought with a sudden and surprising spurt of sympathy.

"Frankly, Lord Wistowe, I believe Lord Cranford was right. I must have left it in my carriage. I will look as soon as my sister arrives." She looked the rake right in the eye and hoped that he would understand her unspoken message. She took it as a hopeful sign when barely minutes later she heard him offer to escort Lady Elizabeth on her requested picnic later in the week—no doubt planning to omit invitations to anyone else.

The landau arrived moments after that. Venetia hurried over in relief, hoping she would not have to invent any explanations about what had delayed it.

She could see in an instant that Vivian was not yet fully alert, although the seizure itself was over.

"I thought there'd be questions if we waited too long, my lady," said the coachman apologetically.

"No, no, you did just right," Venetia reassured him. "I will handle things from here." She climbed into the carriage and sat opposite her sister.

"Netia?"

"Yes, Vivi. I'm right here. Everything is all right. Just sit." She took her sister's hands. "Listen to me. I am going to go back out and pretend to be you. That should reassure everyone that you are really all right. You don't have to do anything. Just try to pull yourself together. Do you know where you are?"

Vivian nodded. "The carriage."

"We must let Lord Cranford and Lord Ashurst drive back

with us, or they might suspect something is wrong. Do you understand what I am saying?"

Vivian nodded again, biting her lip. "I'm sorry," she said in an agonized whisper.

Venetia just squeezed her hands encouragingly and then let herself out of the carriage. *I must play a tired Vivian,* she reminded herself, adjusting her posture and slowing her steps. She headed for Aunt Alice.

"How is Vivian feeling now, Venetia? Or is that you, Vivi?" asked Cousin Adela, intercepting her.

Venetia smiled sweetly. She could not count the number of times she and her twin had fooled their cousin over the years. "I am Vivian, Adela, and I am feeling better, thank you. Netia is waiting for me in the carriage, but I thought I should just reassure Aunt Alice before we set off, since she was worried."

"Oh, yes, of course."

Fooling Aunt Alice was not difficult, either. All Venetia had to do was control the exasperation she usually felt when talking to her aunt. "I never meant to worry you, Aunt Alice. I just thought that with the dancing instruction planned for this evening, I would be wise to save some of my strength. Do you not think so?"

Of course, Lady Colney could not disagree, and by now Venetia thought enough people had overheard her to scuttle any speculation about Vivian's health. The real hurdle, she knew, would be the gentlemen. She really could not return to the carriage without having "Vivian" speak to Lord Ashurst and Lord Cranford. They were standing with Nicholas, debating some obscure point about the religious practices of the ancient Mound Builders.

"Nicholas," she said, touching her brother's arm, "Venetia thought I had worried people, and that I should reassure them that I was all right." She turned to the other two men. "Sirs, I apologize for leaving you so abruptly. It suddenly seemed to be such a good idea to save what strength I had left for the dancing this evening."

"Dancing?" Both the marquess and the viscount seemed less than enthused.

Venetia could not imagine that they did not dance! But somehow she felt vaguely disappointed. "Yes, there is to be instruction this evening. My father has brought in a dancing master just for the occasion, to prepare us all for the ball next week." She remembered to keep her eyes downcast, the way Vivian would.

"Well, we are glad you are feeling up to it, Lady Vivian," said Lord Ashurst gallantly. "You show great wisdom by reserving your energy."

She had half expected some biting comment from the marquess, but once again he surprised her.

"Are we ready to head home?" Nicholas asked her.

She knew what he really wanted to know—if they needed to delay any longer. But she was not sure. Lord Cranford had yet to say anything more than the one word he had uttered, and he was the one she was most wary of. If he was the blackmailer, he was the most likely to guess what had happened, although presumably he would say nothing. If he was not the blackmailer, she thought, he was still the most likely to sense that something was wrong—and to guess that she was not Vivian. He seemed to have an uncanny and unsettling ability to distinguish between them.

She had to give Nicholas some answer, and give it the way Vivian would. She blinked and looked uncertain. "Why, I don't know, Nicholas. Are all the others ready?" She made a show of glancing around. Would Vivian be recovered and ready for them? "If everyone else is ready, I suppose we should go. Netia is already waiting in the landau."

Lord Cranford fell into step beside her as they walked toward the carriage.

"Have you had any opportunity to finish reading your book?" he asked.

What book? She was instantly on her guard. "Which one?"

"Oh, the one you were reading in the library," he said very offhandedly. "Your father has kept us all very well occupied with planned activities, it seems to me."

"Yes, he does that, although he never joins in." *That was safe enough to say.* "And no, I have not finished that book." *When had he seen Vivian in the library?*

"Perhaps we will run across each other there again, in that case. I will say I have given the things you told me a good deal of thought."

What things? She would have a few questions to ask Vivian. "Uh, good. Good. I was certain you would."

"Are you not curious to know what conclusions I may have come to?"

"Conclusions? Why, yes, of course. What conclusions have you come to?"

They had arrived at the carriage. "I think perhaps now is not the best time to go into them, all things considered," he said, stepping back. "Perhaps later?"

Did he think he was setting up a secret assignation with her sister? Was there something going on that she had not known about? She could not, did not, believe it. But she would get to the bottom of it. "Later, then," she whispered as she turned away from him.

It was Lord Ashurst who opened the door for her and handed her up the steps. As she climbed in she saw with relief that Vivian looked reasonably restored.

There, Gilbey thought as he watched Venetia disappear through the door of the landau, *that should rattle her a bit.* He had concluded, of course, that she was not who she pretended to be, and that he was an even bigger fool than he already knew for getting involved with the St. Aldwyns at all. What had become of all his firm resolutions?

Venetia was a very talented actress, he'd grant her that. She had imitated her sister almost exactly, even to the softer voice and the demure demeanor. But she had not fooled him for long. Earlier he had noticed that Vivian had secured her hat with a hatpin, and he thought it rather typical that Venetia had not bothered to do the same. His second clue had been the wary look in her eyes whenever she glanced at him. Why was he the one she seemed to particularly distrust? What was she afraid of? Of all the men there, surely he was the least likely to present any kind of threat?

Not all the twins' suitors might have agreed with that, he knew. Comments he had overheard after the archery tournament and even before it told him some of the other men suspected he was somehow arranging for all of the things that had happened. Was that what Lady Venetia suspected, too? Or was it something else? Whatever it was, he was getting tired of being so nice about it. If he was going to be suspected of something, he damn well wanted to know what!

He climbed into the carriage after Lord Ashurst, and for a moment went right back to not knowing which twin was which. Across from him were blue-violet eyes with dramatic dark lashes, skin like porcelain, and lips the color of rose petals. Beside him he knew he would see the same—a second shapely smile set off by dimples, set in a second delicately sculptured face. Looking at the two young women sitting opposite each other was like gazing upon a reflection so perfect you could not tell which image was real.

I don't know what is real, he reminded himself. Certainly there was much more going on here than what appeared on the surface. If he stirred the waters around him, would both lovely images ripple and disappear? Every instinct screamed that he was placing his heart in danger, but he no longer seemed to care. At the end of the following week he would be leaving, no matter what piece of himself he left behind.

He knew one thing—no force on earth was going to get him to dance that evening. He was a creditable dancer and he enjoyed it. But even now he recognized limits, and the thought of dancing with Venetia—touching her, exchanging flirtatious glances, moving with her to the rhythm of the music—was more than he could stand.

He could sacrifice his heart; he had never planned to love. Losing his heart here would make his life simpler in the future. But he did not wish to lose his sanity as well. Just sitting in the carriage beside this woman he could not have was torment enough. He had no doubt that touching her would drive him mad.

Vivian was so despondent after her seizure Venetia could not bring herself to upset her twin more by questioning her about Lord Cranford. Vivi had managed to affect a cheerful facade during dinner, but the strain had been clear. The questions would have to wait. Venetia was actually grateful when another poem appeared under their door while they were preparing for the dancing that evening after the meal. Vivian needed an additional distraction to help get her mind off what had happened.

"At least 'tis not another note from the blackmailer," Vivian said, delivering the paper to Venetia. "I cannot help thinking that if I had had the seizure in front of everyone, whoever it is would no longer have anything to hold over you. Perhaps we should just stop hiding my trouble and accept the consequences."

"Could we do that to Father, and to Nicholas? And I swear that is the one thing Aunt Alice fears most. Think of the scandal! Not to mention that we'd be throwing away your chance of finding happiness with a man who could love you. No, Vivi. There has to be another way out of this coil. We will find it."

To close the subject, Venetia looked down at the poem and read. "'Twice the beauty, twice the worth / Twice the joy, twice the mirth / But twice the heartbreak, twice the sorrow / If love be scorned upon the morrow.' I cannot say that the poetry has improved."

"What does it mean, do you think, Netia? Have we scorned anybody?"

"Only everybody, I suppose."

"Whose heartbreak and sorrow is he talking about? His own, or ours? You could almost take that as a threat, depending upon your reading."

"Well," said Venetia with a small chuckle, "if he means ours, I interpret that to mean he has a monstrously overblown opinion of his own worth and the depth of our distress when we discover he has given up on us. If he means his own sorrow, I'd say that was a much more flattering message." She purposely did not address the possibility that the note was intended as a threat; she did not think it likely, and she also did not wish to upset Vivian any more on this day. "I consider the ambiguity to be a result of poor skill—he has sacrificed clarity of meaning for the sake of the rhythm and the rhyme."

"I hope you are right. I would hate to believe anyone was so impatient that he would give up by the third day of the party, or even would expect us to make a choice by then!"

I would hate to believe we had more than one enemy among these guests, Venetia added to herself. "We will have to make a concentrated effort to unmask the poet this evening during the dancing. Try to draw out any interest in poetry among our partners."

Maybe somehow they would also get some hint of who might indulge in blackmail. Venetia had been forced to recognize the need to look harder at the other guests when she realized on Sandler's Hill that she had doubts about Lord Cranford's guilt. When she had found a moment to consider that revelation, she had uncovered some rather unsettling truths. She did fear and distrust him, partly because he did not seem to be dealing honestly with anyone, but also in large part because he stirred up feelings that she feared and distrusted in herself. She really did not know what to do about Lord Cranford.

"Perhaps we have been mistaken to stay quiet about the poems," Vivian suggested, unwittingly jerking her sister back to the subject at hand.

"About the poems?" *Confound the viscount, anyway, for taking up so much of her thoughts!*

"Perhaps if we showed them around in front of everyone, we might catch some hint of a reaction from the author."

"Yes, I see what you mean, Vivi—he might betray a flicker of pride or embarrassment or annoyance, even. I think that is a fine idea."

The twins showed the two poems to their guests a short while later as everyone gathered in the south drawing room, a spacious room in the newer part of the house, with windows to the floor, elegant gold-and-white paneling, and intricately carved decorations gracing mantels, doorways, walls, and ceiling. Scores of candles in each of the three chandeliers festooned with crystals bathed the room in brilliant light.

"How exciting." gushed Georgina Whitgreave, her brown eyes glowing. "Oh, I would love to have someone write poems to me. Don't you think that is romantic?"

"You have made a conquest without even knowing it." Aunt Alice nodded her head in breathless approval.

"But of course, we have no way of knowing who it is," Venetia said, looking about with a deliberate air of wide-eyed puzzlement. "I suppose it is quite romantic, isn't it?"

She hoped Vivian was looking about with a more discerning eye, trying to catch some reactions among the gentlemen. She noticed that Lord Cranford was not among them. Neither was Nicholas.

"I thought we might be ready to begin the dancing," she said, turning to her aunt, "but we seem to be short a few gentlemen as yet."

Aunt Alice lowered her voice. "I sent Nicholas to fetch his friend Lord Cranford. It simply won't do if we haven't even numbers. And that seemed a more likely solution than getting your father to dance."

"Indeed." *So, Cranford had thought to escape the dancing session.* Venetia wondered why. *I should be glad if he did,* she told herself. *The less I have to do with him, the better.* But she knew she did not really believe it.

She watched her aunt join the dancing instructor who had been brought in for the event. Like Lord Newcroft, he was short and slightly built, but looked agile. Clapping her hands, Aunt Alice said, "Everyone, may I have your attention? I would like to introduce Monsieur Gervais, a most excellent master of dance, who has taught in some of the most exalted circles in Europe—he has even instructed the royal princesses. We are fortunate indeed to have him with us this evening."

During the scattered applause that followed, Venetia saw her brother and Cranford slip into the room. Nicholas was holding the viscount by the elbow as if he feared the fellow would flee. She could not help smiling.

"We will begin with the first set, or French quadrille, which I am certain you must know," the Frenchman announced in a heavily accented and surprisingly resonant voice.

Unlike the "longways" country dances, quadrilles were danced in squares of four couples. Venetia quickly realized that with fifteen couples on hand, six people would have to sit out. Would Cranford try to be one of them? Amid laughing protests, the Duke of Thornborough, Colonel Hatherwick, and the Marquess and Marchioness of Marchthorpe bowed out, along with the Countess of Duncross and Lady FitzHarris.

Too late! Venetia thought with perverse satisfaction. Now Cranford would have to dance, and he could not choose Lady FitzHarris as his partner, either. She watched as he chose Lady Caroline. She noticed that Lady Norbridge was watching him, too.

Well, it is rather difficult not to notice him, she thought. *He is taller than anyone else in the room.* He looked particularly handsome in his dark blue dress coat—the deep color made his hair look almost silver in the light of the chandeliers.

Lord Chesdale presented himself to her and as he led her out, she noticed Cranford leading Caroline to the set forming farthest from her own. *Did he think he would avoid her?* She tapped the earl playfully on the arm with her fan. "Let us join the set on the end, sir, shall we not? I see my sister and Lord Lindell coming—they can take our place here."

Of course, Cranford probably did not know which twin she was, having come in late. After their afternoon's mischief, she and Vivian had decided to wear vividly different evening ensembles. She had chosen a favorite gown of lace net over magnificent apricot satin, while Vivi was resplendent in violet silk gauze embroidered with silver and tiny spangles. Could Cranford tell them apart merely by sight? Was he concerned about his conversation that afternoon with one of them? Did he suspect that he had talked with the wrong one?

That might explain his reluctance, Venetia thought. *If he is suffering uncomfortable second thoughts, it only serves him right.* But she could not pretend to be Vivian now, for the rest of the guests knew she was not. Nor could she betray the ruse she had practiced that afternoon by any reference to the conversation he had shared with her.

She and Lord Chesdale took places opposite Cranford and Lady Caroline and she relished the startled look on the viscount's face. The very first steps of the dance would put them together. She lavished her most brilliant smile upon him as the musicians at the far end of the room struck up the tune of the dance. On the appropriate beat she and Lord Chesdale advanced into the center, meeting Cranford and Lady Caroline there.

"You glow like the fairest pearl, Lady Venetia," Cranford said as he joined right hands with her and she went past him to turn.

Coming back, she simply nodded. She had not been at all prepared for her reaction to him. Her hands and arms tingled from his touch and she felt her face must be flaming. Even her shoulder burned where she had accidentally brushed against him. She had convinced herself that the sensations she had felt from his touch in the river had come from the excitement of the rescue, but now she knew she had beguiled herself with a lie. The truth burned like fire inside her. Oh, she had made a grave mistake in deliberately choosing to dance with him. She hardly noticed when her partner reclaimed her hand.

"I had taken you for a diamond and your sister for a pearl," Cranford said when the dance next brought them together. "I see tonight that I had you reversed."

What in heaven's name did he mean by that? Was it merely a compliment, or did his words conceal a hidden meaning? How could his perfectly polite conversation be making her feel so uneasy?

She risked a glance at him as the side couples took their turns going through the first figure. He was politely conversing with Lady Caroline and watching the others. He looked in every way calm and proper, quite unaffected by Venetia's proximity. Two spots of color showed over the cheekbones in his pale face, but those were easily explained by the exertion required for the dance.

There were four more figures to get through; she had no choice but to continue, all the while struggling to conceal her reactions to the viscount. She was immensely relieved when it was finally over and Lord Chesdale returned her to the spot where he had found her.

Vivian was waiting there. "Netia, I think Lord Lindell might be our poet," she said in a hushed, excited tone.

"Heavens, what makes you say so?"

"Let me tell you what he said. He said, 'Your beauty outshines the brightest star tonight, Lady Vivian.' Is that not poetic? It is very similar to the words in the first poem."

"Yes, it is," Venetia answered distractedly. *Cranford's compliments had been rather poetic, too.* "Of course, the words might have come to Lord Lindell's mind simply because we had been showing the poems and reading from them earlier."

"That's true." Vivian was obviously crestfallen.

"We must try to find out if he has any interest in reading poetry, or if he is known to write at all. Perhaps ask Lady Elizabeth. After all, she is his sister." Venetia did her best to restore her sister's interest. *Perhaps Lord Lindell would suit Vivian,*

*although he is a bit young. He is kind, and most certainly he is
not the blackmailer.*

The tiny diamonds at Vivi's throat sparkled in the light as
she turned to look for Elizabeth, reminding Venetia of Cranford's words. Their grandmother's necklace complemented
Vivian's dress perfectly. Venetia fingered her own pearl necklace and told herself to relax. Perhaps it was only her own
guilty conscience that made her read meanings into the man's
comments.

"I saw you dash off to be in Lord Cranford's set, Netia," Vivian said, as if she could read her twin's thoughts. "Have you
finally changed your mind about him? I thought you danced
together very nicely."

"We hardly 'danced together,' and I did not 'dash' over
there. I was dancing with Lord Chesdale," Venetia said
sharply. *I won't make the same mistake with Cranford again.*
"I have indeed changed my mind about him—I've decided he
is too witless and utterly boring to be what we thought."

Chapter Ten

Like Venetia, Gilbey had thought the first quadrille would never end. He had been in agony trying to hide his reaction to her each time the dance brought them together, and he had no doubt that Lady Caroline would tell others that he danced like an automaton, for he had been as stiff as his fixed, polite smile.

He was quite aware that Venetia had intentionally positioned herself so that she and he would dance together. He blamed himself; no doubt he had stirred up her interest with his provoking remarks that afternoon when he pretended to believe she was Vivian. But he had found one redeeming, surprising source of satisfaction as they danced. The spark of challenge he had seen in Venetia's eyes when she first joined the set with her partner had disappeared very quickly, to be replaced by something much more difficult to read.

When the dance ended, the set broke up, the dancers drifting off to other locations about the room. Gilbey returned the charming and amiable Lady Caroline to her mother and retreated to a position near the fireplace at one end of the room, where he could watch the twins in safety.

Lord Chesdale stopped beside him and began to survey the room through his quizzing glass. "Lord Upcott did not appear to appreciate your attentions to his daughter, Lord Cranford." The comment was delivered as a flat statement, without expression.

"You think not?" Lady Caroline's father had been part of Gilbey's set and had spent most of the dance observing the couple instead of attending his own partner.

"Indeed. And if I might add a word of friendly advice, I

might mention that there are few here who appreciate your interest in Lady Venetia and Lady Vivian."

"I see." *In other words, clear off and let the big boys play.* "Well, I thank you for those words of advice, but allow me to assure you that they are not necessary. Perhaps you were not aware that I am merely a family friend—I have no special ambitions towards the young ladies."

"Indeed? Odd. That is not at all the impression I have received." The earl was at least polite enough to nod in acknowledgment of their conversation before he walked away. He left Gilbey pondering his words, as no doubt he quite intended.

After a moment, Gilbey shook his head in bafflement. If he were pursuing the twins, no mere words from Lord Chesdale would stop him. But he was *not.* Marriage was something to contemplate years from now, and love was not among his goals. He might admit to himself that he desired Venetia, but he was certain he had not betrayed that to anyone. He had done his best to show disinterest without being rude. Could he help it if Venetia *would* fall in the river right at his feet, or that his arrow had struck truer than anyone else's?"

They are judging me by themselves, he concluded, *projecting their own hopes and designs upon me.* It surprised him that the suitors seemed to have set their sights on the twins so exclusively—the other four young women were lovely, and while he thought Lady Norbridge was the most tempting of the older widowed countesses, both Lady Colney and Lady Sibbingham were elegant, attractive women.

Ironically, Lady Norbridge chose that moment to approach him. Certainly no one had objected to his "attentions" to her, not that he had paid her any.

"Lord Cranford, there you are," she said with a playful flutter of her fan. "I was just noting how warm it has become in here, but it is quite dark in the garden to be going out alone." She had arrived in a cloud of lilac scent.

Gilbey stifled his urge to ask how she could be warm when her dress exposed such quantities of bare skin. Instead he smiled politely. "It is quite dark to be going out there at all, I'm afraid, Lady Norbridge, although I am flattered that you would seek me out to protect you." He had almost said, "to be your protector," and only caught himself at the last second. Who knew how she might have interpreted that remark!

"Surely you are not afraid of the dark, sir?" She closed her fan and tapped his chest with it, staring up at him with eyes like dark emeralds.

He felt his resolve softening. "You never know what you might find there."

"Ah-h. My point exactly." She took his arm, but when he would not move, she affected an exaggerated pout. "Perhaps it is just me. I imagine you would go readily enough if Lady Venetia were to ask you."

Another comment! Had they really noticed something, or was she, like Lord Chesdale, simply assuming?

Before he could respond, she said, "You might grow old waiting for that to happen, for I heard her say that she finds you witless and utterly boring."

"Did she!" Gilbey felt as if he had just been slapped, but he struggled not to show it. Lady Norbridge had paused, undoubtedly to see how he would take this news. He did not fail to notice the hint of a tilt at the corners of her mouth. Perhaps it wasn't even true. Heat flushed his cheeks despite his effort.

The countess laughed. "She is obviously not a good judge of men. You are better off with me, sir. I am an expert."

Still smarting but somewhat recovered now, Gilbey laughed, too, hoping the sound did not come out as hollow and artificial as it felt. "While I cannot attest to that, Lady Norbridge, I can say that you are beautiful and charming." *And wicked.* "Perhaps you would honor me with the next dance, instead, if you are not too warm to continue?"

"If it is not a dance that I simply abhor."

The French master called next for a minuet, however, and Lady Norbridge declined Gilbey's offer.

"That old dance! When is he going to teach us something new? I thought that was the purpose of his coming, silly me." She cast a sidelong glance at Gilbey and toyed with the top button on his waistcoat, flirting with him quite brazenly. "Ask me again when he calls for a waltz—I'd like to dance that with you. But you may have to hunt for me in the garden."

Damn but she was talented. Gilbey felt the familiar tingling in his face as she gave him a dazzling smile and swept away.

Maybe he would dance a waltz with her later. It might be the highlight of his entire two-week visit, although he thought he would generally be better off to dance as little as possible. Glancing down, he discovered that the minx had actually unfastened his waistcoat button. He fixed it quickly, hoping no one noticed.

Without Lady Norbridge's distraction, Gilbey's thoughts returned to Venetia. He watched her dance the minuet with the others, wondering if what the countess had told him was true. Had Venetia truly called him witless and boring in front of everyone? By God, that was going a bit far. He was torn between his urge to confront her and his wish to avoid repeating the torture of dancing with her.

Eventually, he was required to dance again so that no lady would go partnerless. The dance master taught the group a new quadrille, "Duval of Dublin's Second Set," and a new country dance called "The Persian Waltz," which was not a waltz at all but which did have some interesting figures. Inevitably, as he and his partner Lady Sibbingham became active in the dance, he came into contact with Venetia.

"I hope you are enjoying your evening," he said innocently.

She tossed her head and turned away without replying—the cut direct! The motion of the dance made it less than obvious, but there it was, nonetheless, for all to see.

What had he done to deserve such treatment? Apparently Lady Norbridge's report was true. Despite his embarrassment, Gilbey realized that he ought to be glad. This should cure him of falling under Venetia's spell; the lioness had showed her claws at last. This should also lay to rest the other suitors' fears of his competition.

Other suitors? He did not count himself as one of them. He did not need or even want Venetia's respect. But why then did he feel so angry? By God, he wanted to take Venetia by the shoulders and shake her.

Gilbey took a long walk by himself the next morning and came in to breakfast determined to enjoy the day ahead of him and to ignore the events of the previous evening. Snatches of conversations reached his ears as he loaded his plate at the buffet, wreathed in the mouth-watering smells of ham, herb-seasoned eggs, and fruit from the hothouses. One of the tables was empty and he chose a seat there, relieved to find the talk among the guests focused on the cross-country race planned for the day rather than on what had transpired between him and Venetia. The glorious weather was still holding, and everyone was looking forward to some good, hard riding along the trails among the wooded hills. He did not see either of the twins.

A vigorous ride is just what I need to purge some of these feelings from my system, he thought, munching on toast spread with fresh honey butter. If the Duke of Roxley's stable compared at all to the rest of Rivington, his guests would be mounted on some prime bits of blood. Gilbey reflected that he had rather forgotten how much he loved to ride, immersed as he was in his quiet life at Cambridge. Was his sister right? Had he buried himself there? Was he retreating from life as their father had done? Nicholas had told him nearly the same thing, but he had refused to see the similarity.

He smiled as he heard Lord Munslow at the table behind him laying wagers on the day's race.

"I'll put my money on Lord Newcroft, this time," the earl said. "He's built like a jockey and he's always out to prove himself."

"What about you, Munslow? Have you plans to make a showing? What odds should we figure?" That sounded like Nicholas, playing devil's advocate.

Lord Ashurst's voice answered with a cynical chuckle. "I wouldn't throw away money on him, Edmonton. He's too lazy to do anything more strenuous than lay odds on what someone else is going to do."

Apparently Lord Munslow agreed with this assessment, or else he was too lazy to take offense. The rest of the little group laughed.

Gilbey had no intention of trying to win the race himself—he had more to lose by such an effort than he had to gain. *Look at what happened with the archery competition.* However, it did seem to him that Lord Chesdale had the advantage over the other contenders—the man had been trained to hard riding as an officer in the hussars. Usually frugal with his money, Gilbey found this contest tempting.

Go ahead, place a wager, he told himself. The visit to Rivington had so far proved quite hard on his clothes, and winning a tidy sum could help to cover the needed replacements. Before the riders all adjourned to the stables he quietly put in a word with Lord Munslow.

The participants in the race made up a sizable group even though several men and a greater number of the ladies had declined to risk their necks dashing through the countryside. Gilbey could not help being impressed by the sheer quantity of magnificent horseflesh that awaited them in the paved stableyard. Gleaming animals for eleven men and nine ladies stood in the large courtyard with grooms at their heads, some standing patiently and others moving about with restless energy, eager to be off.

The riders were almost equally resplendent in their fine riding clothes; the men were garbed for the most part in sober reds and browns, while the ladies wore fashionable habits in practical colors, predominantly blues and shades of gray. Gilbey could not help noticing Venetia as soon as she arrived—the brilliant amethyst of her beautifully fitted habit stood out amongst the others. Her golden hair peeped out from beneath a beaver hat that could only be distinguished from those of the men by a matching band of color and a lace veil draped artfully around the brim. Vivian was not with her and apparently was not going to join them.

It took some time to sort out the riders and match them up with their assigned mounts. A handful of the guests had brought their own horses and grooms. While the rest were waiting, Nicholas joined Gilbey at one side of the fairly crowded courtyard. Voices and laughter bounced off the surrounding walls of stone and seemed to fill what space was left.

"I say, Nicholas, looks like your sister had to borrow one of your hats," Gilbey joked. "You haven't been letting her go down by the river again, have you?"

"No, but I am thinking I ought to encourage her to do so, after the way she treated you last night, old man. I imagine about now you are wishing that you hadn't fished her out for us the last time."

If you only knew, Gilbey thought. *Nothing has been the*

same since the moment I touched her then. But try as he might, he could not bring himself to wish that some other man had been there in his place.

"I am truly sorry for her abysmal behavior," Nicholas continued when Gilbey did not answer immediately. "I cannot conceive of what has suddenly got hold of her to treat a guest so badly."

"Don't let it concern you. I am not so fragile that her scorn can cause any damage."

"I suppose it is a good thing that she had not won your heart. People tell me those are more fragile than we think."

Ah, that. Well, Gilbey did not care about his, anyway. He considered it a liability. "I see that quite a few of the ladies are not joining us, including Lady Vivian," he said. "Is it such a rough course, or do you think they were just disinclined to race?"

Successfully diverted, Nicholas launched into an enthused discussion of the course the race was to follow, and explained in passing that Lady Vivian seldom rode. He did not say why. Then he was called away to claim his horse, and Gilbey was left to wait by himself.

He began to get a sinking feeling as each of the finest animals was assigned to a rider and he continued to stand by, waiting. The tamest horses were given to the ladies who requested them, of course, but he noticed that Venetia and Lady Caroline were both mounted on spirited animals who danced in place and were obviously eager. Gilbey was given the very last horse, an old chestnut mare who looked as if she achieved a fast gallop only in her dreams.

Gilbey took one look at the horse he'd been given and gave thanks that his own part in the race meant nothing. He'd been given the closest thing to a nag in the lot. Had Lady Venetia had a hand in this, or was it purely by chance?

Nicholas looked over and began to protest, but Venetia cut him off. "Someone has to ride Jonquil, Nicholas. I'm certain that Lord Cranford does not mind."

Of course, he did mind. Jonquil rolled her eyes at him as if she blamed him for the whole idea. But Venetia had placed him squarely in a position where any protest on his part would seem ungentlemanly. He shrugged in response to Nicholas's questioning look. He would arrange for a proper mount to ride on another day, that was all. Since he had no desire to compete in the race, he supposed he was a better candidate to take the mare than any of the other riders.

Instructions for the race were given while everyone was still gathered in the stableyard, and then the riders filed out one by one to reconvene on the sweeping carriage drive in front of the house. They would all set off at once when the signal was given.

Lady Vivian and the others who were not participating had gathered on the steps in front of Rivington to see them off. Gilbey noticed that Miss Whitgreave was the only other one of the younger ladies who was not riding. Colonel Hatherwick and Lord Amberton were the only two unmarried gentlemen staying behind.

At the crack of a pistol fired into the air, the twenty riders whipped up their horses and raced off, producing an earth-shaking thunder of hooves and a great cloud of dust. Soon the pack began to thin into a long line stretched along the road-way, and once they turned off the road onto the bridle path through the woods, they left both the dust and Gilbey behind them.

Jonquil was a follower, but as Gilbey had surmised, she was not fast. Despite his masterful efforts, the mare quickly fell into last place. He felt they were fortunate to be able to keep the rest of the group in sight. After a time, even that was no longer possible, as the twisting course wound up through the Cotswold hills and down into hidden valleys. Gilbey kept a sharp eye out for the red flags that had been set out to mark the way, for there were many places where they emerged from the woods to cut across open pastures, only to dive back into the forest again on a new path.

Gilbey began to enjoy himself, despite Jonquil's limitations, for the day was particularly fine, and the views from the hill-tops were sometimes breathtaking. Although she was slow, the mare had an easy, steady gait that allowed him to relax. He had a sense that they were not too far behind the stragglers of the main group, for every so often the sound of shouts or laughter or the occasional whinny of a horse carried back to him on the breeze.

He was surprised, however, to catch a fleeting glimpse of Venetia as he and Jonquil came down a steep decline toward a small bridge in the bottom of a ravine. She and her fine roan were just disappearing over the crest of the hill on the opposite side.

How has she come to be so far behind the others? was the first question that popped into his mind. He was distressed by the way his body reacted to the mere sight of her—his heart jumped and his pulse began to race as if they'd been struck with a whip. With a sudden urge to try to catch her, he attempted to inspire a similar reaction in Jonquil.

It was only because the road ran blessedly straight for a short ways beyond the top of the hill that he saw Venetia turn off the route into the woods. *Where in God's name did she think she was going?* He pressed Jonquil onward with an urgency the horse seemed to sense, for she cooperated with more spirit than she had shown at any earlier time.

The path Venetia had taken was much narrower and very obviously less traveled than any that had been used for the race. Ducking tree branches, Gilbey guessed that she had chosen a shortcut in an attempt to catch up to the main group. He did not think she knew he was following.

The path led generally downward and Gilbey was careful to keep his weight centered. He was not at all prepared to pull up quickly when he and Jonquil rounded a curve and nearly ran full tilt into Venetia's horse. The roan was standing riderless by a fallen tree across the path.

It was clear at once what had happened. The ground sloped downhill rather steeply on the other side of the tree trunk, and the horse had obviously refused the jump. Unprepared and riding a bit too fast, Venetia had sailed over it without him. She sat hatless in a muddy pool at the bottom of the decline with leaves sticking to her habit and her hair halfway unpinned. To Gilbey's relief she did not appear to be injured.

Gilbey dismounted. Pushing some branches out of the way, he climbed over the fallen tree and started down the leaf-shrewn slope toward her. He spied her hat and retrieved it from a bush, brushing more leaves from the lace veil. He noticed that there was a rip in it. In the meantime, he heard Venetia mutter a few rather unladylike phrases.

"Forget something?" he asked as he reached the bottom. "I noticed your horse decided not to join you."

"It would have to be you that came along," she said ungraciously.

"It was me or no one." He grinned. "Where on earth were you going? Besides down this hill, I mean."

She did not answer.

"I found your hat. Looks a little the worse for wear." He held it out to her and she jammed it onto her head.

She looks ready to spit, he thought, and reflected that he had never seen her angry before. The fact was, he thought she looked particularly charming, with her hair coming loose and a smudge of mud on her nose. This was the real Venetia, not the perfectly groomed beauty he was used to seeing, and he liked what he saw.

"This happens to be a shortcut," she said finally. "I lost my hat earlier and had to go back for it. I wanted to catch up."

He waved a hand at her sitting in the puddle. "Looks like an odd way to go about it, if you ask me. But then, you didn't ask, did you? I'm certain you know best."

He turned and started back up the slope.

"Where are you going?"

"To get Jonquil. I want to show her that there is a place to land on the other side of the tree."

"You aren't going to help me up?"

"Oh, I doubt if I have enough wit to do that."

Retribution might not be gentlemanly, but it tasted very sweet. Behind him he heard the sounds of her struggling to get up.

"Ooh, you are a wretched man! I hate you!"

Something struck him just below his shoulder blades. He put a hand back and brought away gloved fingers covered with mud. *The little vixen!* He turned and saw her standing there, her heavy skirts soiled, wet, and clinging to her. As she bent down to scoop up another handful of ammunition, he bounded back down the hill.

"Is it full-fledged war, then?" he asked, grabbing her arm. "Flinging insults is no longer enough?"

But something happened the moment he touched her. He did not feel at all warlike. "Rumor has it that you think I am witless and utterly boring." He stared down into her beautiful eyes, searching for the truth.

"Well, I—"

She did not finish. The very air around them seemed charged. In her eyes he thought he saw a message quite different from anything she had said.

"Tell me if you find this boring, then," he said softly, his voice husky. Quite ignoring the mud that covered her, he slipped his arms around her and brought her against him. He found her sweet lips and proceeded to kiss her as thoroughly as he knew how.

Chapter Eleven

Lost in the arousing pleasure of Cranford's kiss, Venetia felt an almost overwhelming urge to surrender. His mouth was gentle yet demanding; he tasted warm and slightly spicy. She was aware of every inch of her body that pressed against his, of his arms around her, of her clinging wet skirts.

Give in, called a seductive voice inside her. How easy to yield everything to him—her struggle, her secrets, her body, her heart! She did not hate this man. She was very much afraid that she loved him. At least for that moment while they stood kissing in a puddle of mud up to their ankles, she did love him.

No. It was impossible, of course. Like a dreamer slowly coming awake, she struggled to regain her reason. What of Vivian? What of her father? She had obligations. What of the group of riders somewhere ahead of them, racing further away at every moment? And not least of all, what of the blackmailer who was someone among them, someone who watched her each day, waiting, if he was not the man here with his arms around her? How could she have forgotten any of that for even an instant? That it had happened so easily frightened her.

Gilbey felt the change come through her like a sudden erratic current in a stream—the infinitely sweet, deep receptiveness he had found was swept aside and she started to push him away. Reluctant to give her up, he held her tighter for a fraction of a moment, but then he released her. She was right, of course, and this time he had made himself the fool.

"Oh dear," she said. "Oh dear."

He stepped back from her, straightening his spectacles. "Lady Venetia, I beg your forgiveness! I think I may have proved you to be half right, after all. I must indeed be witless, to have done such a thing."

She looked down at her muddied gloves and then plucked at her skirt. She did appear terribly distraught.

"No, no, I don't know what came over us," she murmured, shaking her head. At some point she had lost her hat again—he was surprised that neither of them had noticed.

He stopped to retrieve it and tried to brush off the mud that had splashed on it before he handed it back to her a second time.

"Oh dear," she said again. "You truly are dangerous." She lifted her gaze to meet his, and he saw not distress but something much more like a deep sadness in her eyes. She shook her head as if that would rid her of it. "I should never have thrown the mud at you. I'm sorry."

He wanted to reach out to her, to touch that fleeting sadness and soothe it away, whatever it was. But he sensed that she would not let him.

"I must admit that I would rather be thought dangerous than boring," he said, cocking his head to one side and smiling at her. "I am afraid I hardly look the part, however." He looked down at his own clothes and began to laugh.

"In the four days that I have been here, my clothes have been doused with wine, soaked in a river, and now coated with mud. If I had only known, I would have made sure to bring a second trunkful. Your brother should have warned me." *He should have warned me about a lot more than that,* he thought.

His tactic succeeded, coaxing a smile from her. "I think the trunk would only have been full of books, sir."

He staggered, pretending to be wounded. "Ah, *touché!* But what else would you expect from a witless fellow?" Tapping his head, he continued, "We can't keep anything up here, so we have to cart it around with us in trunks. But now you have learned my secret." *How much I would like to know yours.*

"I am sorry about the remark I made last night. I did not mean it, and I never intended that anyone else should overhear it. You may call me witless, if you like."

She looked so utterly sincere, he could not help grinning, fool that he was. Part of him knew they would both be better off if she did think him boring and witless. But part of him thought he had tasted the truth in their kiss.

* * *

They decided that there was only one possible way to explain the state of their appearances when they caught up to the rest of the group, and that was to tell the truth, minus a few major details, and to hope for the best. Gilbey would say that he slipped while helping Venetia, to explain the mud on his own clothes. If they were not believed, the consequences could be disastrous for both of them. It was a sobering thought.

Most fortunately, Venetia's shortcut brought them back to the main route just ahead of the last few slow ladies who had given up all hope of the race. Lady Colney was horrified at the sight of Venetia's muddy clothing, and Lady Sibbingham clucked sympathetically at the story of her fall. But no one questioned the truth of the tale, and indeed there was no way for anyone to guess how much time had elapsed while Venetia and Lord Cranford were alone. Because the errant pair returned home in company with the other ladies, the damaging questions from the rest of the group were minimized and the potential disaster avoided.

Gilbey was so relieved, he did not mind the sly comments and looks that the other men directed at him during dinner and the evening's activities. Besides, one other thing had gone right. Lord Chesdale had won the race.

Cranford's remarkable blue-green eyes haunted Venetia's dreams through the night, as did a craving to feel his arms around her. She awakened late the following morning, sore in several places from her fall the previous day. After her maid helped her to dress, she went stiffly down to breakfast.

Only a handful of guests were still at their meal in the Italian room, which featured paintings by Italian masters on its walls. Venetia was not surprised that there was no sign of Vivian, and if she was disappointed not to see Cranford, part of her knew that it was just as well. The Duke and Duchess of Brancaster sat at one table near the French windows overlooking the small courtyard known as the Roman court, so named because Venetia's grandfather had designed it to look like the atrium of a Roman villa. Venetia noticed Lady Norbridge and Lord Munslow out strolling in it. Colonel Hatherwick sat by himself at another table, feasting happily on a breakfast that looked quite sufficient to feed five people.

The duchess called her over. "My dear, how are you this morning? We were so sorry to hear that you took a fall yesterday. Oh, but the race was just splendid! His Grace and I cannot remember the last time we enjoyed ourselves so much."

"I am glad you enjoyed it, Your Grace. I am a bit sore this morning, but nothing to be concerned about."

"I confess to being a bit sore myself this morning," the duchess said. "Most of us continued racing just to keep up enough to see what would happen. Such a surprise that Lord Chesdale should win, although afterwards we wondered why we did not expect it." The lady chuckled. "Lord Newcroft certainly did give him a run for his money."

A man of few words compared to his wife, the duke made a rare comment. "Humph. Lord Newcroft thinks he must prove himself over and over again—always afraid someone will cast up to him the fact that his father was in trade."

Venetia had noticed that Lord Newcroft worked very hard at winning. Yet he had not seemed overly attentive to either her or Vivian. How badly did he want to win the hand of one of the twins? She had assumed the blackmailer's motivation must be financial, but now she wondered if that might not be the case. A connection by marriage to a powerful duke would certainly be an asset to a very ambitious and wealthy viscount.

She hurried through her breakfast and went in search of her sister to share this new insight. Vivian was not to be found in the gardens, so Venetia returned to the house. She enlisted several footmen to help her, for Vivian could be anywhere in the huge residence. She tried the ancient chapel, a fourteenth century relic that had been incorporated into the house, knowing that Vivian at times liked to go there. Failing that, she tried the library, half expecting that not only her sister but also Lord Cranford might be there.

The viscount was indeed in the library, so engrossed in a large book on Italian architecture that he did not notice her until she stood directly before him, coughing discreetly to catch his attention. Obviously startled, he leaped to his feet, still clutching the heavy leather volume.

"Lady Venetia! I did not see you there. Uh, good morning."

She smiled, amused to watch his face reflect surprise, pleasure, and then embarrassment in turn.

"I wondered whether you might have seen my sister Vivian this morning?" *You must not let on that you know they have met here before*, she reminded herself. "I came down late to breakfast, and I am looking for her."

"I did see her at breakfast, a good while ago. She was dressed to go riding. I noted it, actually, not only because she looked splendid, of course, but because I thought Nicholas told me yesterday that she seldom rides."

A frisson of alarm went through Venetia. "That is true," she said quietly, trying to cover her reaction. It would not do to show unusual concern over something that for most people was a normal activity. And the chances were that Vivian would be fine. Perhaps she had gone out with Nicholas, or one of their own grooms. But all of Venetia's instincts were suddenly screaming at her in warning. "I—I think I'll go to the stables to check," she said, hoping she sounded calmer than she felt.

"I'll go with you," Cranford volunteered.

Venetia was too upset to protest. Having Cranford with her forced her to act calmly. Otherwise she might have run all the way to the stableyard, causing a host of unwelcome questions. She walked, but quickly.

"Did she happen to mention if she was going with anyone?" She winced. To her own ears she sounded breathless, like her aunt.

"I don't believe she said."

"It is not like her to go off this way. She doesn't ride often, and when she does one of us is always with her. I don't understand." She was talking more to herself than to him.

By the time they reached the stables, she no longer cared if Cranford saw that she was worried. He might wonder why all he liked. Something more had pushed her closer to the edge of panic—the rumble of thunder in the distance.

Riding itself was no threat to Vivian; the danger was the possibility of a seizure while she was doing it. The twins and Nicholas had learned to recognize when seizures were most likely to strike: if Vivian became overtired, for instance, or if she was exposed to abrupt changes of light. They had learned to cope and to compensate, but occasionally a seizure would strike without warning, for no apparent reason at all.

The flashes of lightning that came with a thunderstorm guaranteed trouble. Venetia prayed that Nicholas was with her twin, or at least that Vivian would have returned by now. The safest place for her sister was in her own room until the storm was over.

One look at the uneasy stablehands confirmed Venetia's worst fear. "She has not returned, has she?" she blurted out without preamble. "Is my brother with her?"

The head groom approached her, hat in hand, his eyes on his boot toes. "No, my lady."

"Who is with her, then?"

"The Marquess of Ashurst. And I sent Tom Dixon with them. She was determined that she would go, miss. 'Twas not my place to argue."

He was right, of course. "I'm sorry, Griffiths, it's not your fault. Have you any idea where they went?"

"No, my lady. Wish to God I did."

Venetia paced a few steps in a circle. "I don't know what to do."

"Will they not be all right?" asked Cranford.

"I am sure they must be returning." What if they did not get back in time? Would Tom Dixon know what to do, or be able to explain to Lord Ashurst? As far as Venetia knew, the young groom had never seen Vivian actually suffer a seizure. And what of Ashurst? He would likely be horrified. Would he then feel obliged to tell everyone what he'd seen? The blackmailer would be thwarted, assuming it wasn't Ashurst, but the family would be ruined and God only knew what fate would befall Vivian then. Oh, why had Vivian insisted on doing this? She would have to go after her.

Hands on her shoulders abruptly stopped Venetia from moving. She looked up to see Cranford, his eyes full of concern. "You will make yourself dizzy."

She realized she had been pacing in a tight little circle with increasing speed that reflected her agitated state. She also realized with surprise that she was not used to having someone express concern over her own well-being. She was the strong one, the lioness, the one who had escaped from the accident with hardly a scratch. She was always fine—everyone expected it, including herself. It surprised her that she rather liked the concern, especially coming from Cranford. Even so, she could not allow him to come with her. If Vivian had a seizure before they got back, he would only be another witness.

"Thank you," she said, offering a shaky smile. Before she could go after Vivian, she would have to get him to go back to the house. "Since Lord Ashurst and one of our grooms are with her, I'm certain she will be fine. You may as well go back in."

"Without you?"

"I think I will wait here for them, but you do not need to. Thank you for your help."

Did the man not know a dismissal when he heard one? She was not dressed to go riding; there was no reason for him not to believe her. He looked dubious, and for a moment she feared he would not go. Then with a "very well, then," he took himself off. As soon as he was gone, she called for her horse Artemis. By the time the mare was saddled and she headed out of the stableyard, she assumed Cranford was safely back in the main house. She had an idea where Vivian might have chosen to go and set off for a trail that led up to the north pastures.

Gilbey was not surprised to see Venetia head out of the stableyard without him. He took note of her direction and ducked back into the stables, calling for a horse and letting Griffiths know by the look in his eyes that he would tolerate no questions or delay. "And don't try to foist old Jonquil on me, either," he added. "She and I are well acquainted after yesterday."

Gilbey guessed that the stablehands may have been relieved to see him go after Venetia, for although Griffiths said nothing, the horse they provided had to be one of the duke's finest. "Might 'ave won that race yesterday, with a different rider," was all the groomsman said as the animal was brought out.

"Well, this is a race, too," Gilbey answered as he mounted. A rumble of thunder dramatized his remark.

It did not take him long to catch Venetia. He was riding hell-bent as fast as he dared, while she had no idea he was coming behind her. He caught up with her in an open field. When he came into view she made a halfhearted attempt to sprint away from him but apparently she thought better of it after a moment, circling her horse around to face him.

"Why did you follow me?" she demanded, her words more accusation than question.

"Why did you pretend you were not going to go?"

"You spied on me!"

"You lied to me!"

"What if I did? What makes it your business? Why can't you leave me alone?"

That last was the real question, wasn't it? What could he say? *Fate hasn't allowed it. I meant to. I wanted to. I'm too much of a fool?*

His best answer was a question. "If you are so worried about your sister out here with two grown men with her, why shouldn't someone be concerned that you are out here alone?"

That stopped her for a moment. "I—I am going to meet them."

"What if the storm spooked your horse before you found them? What if you fell, as you did yesterday? Who would find you? What in God's name can you do for them that they cannot do for themselves?"

She tossed her head in the arrogant way that he had grown to like, but as she did he thought he caught the glitter of moisture in her eyes. He urged his horse closer.

She brushed her eyes with a quick, impatient gesture. "I can't tell you. It's none of your business. Please, please, just leave me alone."

Thunder rumbled again, much closer now.

"No, I won't," he said. "I can't."

Chapter Twelve

Venetia stared at Cranford. What was she going to do about him? She could not allow him to interfere with her life. She would have to go to Nicholas—he was the one who had brought Cranford here. But now, just right now, what was she going to do?

Her horse moved restlessly as another peal of thunder rolled through the sky, adding pressure to her indecision. The greenish black edge of the storm clouds could be clearly seen advancing from the west. *Where are you, Vivian? You need to be home.*

As if in answer to her thought, three riders suddenly burst out of the woods into the field, riding as if devils were after them. Vivian, Lord Ashurst, and the groom slowed their horses as they approached Venetia and Lord Cranford.

"We came looking for you!" Venetia shouted over a clap of thunder. Artemis was backing and turning and she slapped the mare sharply with her crop to get her attention.

"Are you all right, Vivi?" Venetia looked for any signs that would warn her of trouble. The storm had not yet reached them, and there had not yet been any bright bursts of lightning.

"I am so far. I'm sorry, Netia. Do let us hurry."

Venetia wanted to know what had possessed her twin to go riding with Lord Ashurst, but now was not the time. Things seemed to be happening so quickly, they had not had time to talk over any of what had happened in the past few days. *Or we just aren't discussing them,* she admitted more honestly. She turned Artemis around once more and urged the horse back the way they had come.

The first bright flashes of lightning lasted hardly more than the blink of an eye, and Vivian was still all right when they reached Rivington. The twins barely waited for their horses to stop before they dismounted, throwing their reins to Tom Dixon and one of the other grooms who ran out of the stable to meet them. Without a word to the gentlemen, the young women dashed out of the courtyard toward the house.

"We aren't going to make it to our rooms, Netia," Vivian said woefully. Large splattering drops of rain were beginning to fall around them as they ran. A large clap of thunder sounded overhead, and although there was still a delay before the lightning flashed, this time it was brighter and more sustained.

"Oh God. All I wanted was to go riding for once, like a normal person."

"Hush, not now, Vivi. Think, where else can we go that would be private, that's nearer?"

"The chapel. Up in the gallery. No one goes up there."

"That's perfect," Venetia answered, altering her course. The chapel even had its own entrance. "We'll try that door. Pray to God that it isn't locked."

The twins hid in the chapel gallery while the storm rumbled and pelted the house with hail and rain. Vivian suffered a seizure as soon as they got there, but when she recovered, Venetia went to her and encouraged her to curl up beside her.

"Put your head in my lap," she suggested. "I'll cover your eyes with our skirts and maybe that will block out enough light to prevent any more attacks."

Huddled on the floor, they talked quietly against the roar of the rain on the chapel roof.

"Why did I go?" Vivian said, her voice somewhat muffled by skirts. "Because Lord Ashurst invited me. I did not want to say no. Do you know how it feels to be left out so often? Can you imagine how I felt yesterday, watching everyone ride off for the race, knowing I could not go with you? I get so tired of being so careful—just for once I thought I could risk it. How was I to know the weather would break this morning? It has been so beautiful."

"Shh. I know, Vivi. I don't blame you. It's just that you took such a risk. Even without the storm, you know that it was a terrible risk to take—you could have been hurt, but perhaps worse was the risk of exposing your epilepsy to Lord Ashurst. Who knows what he would have done? It is not like you to take such a gamble."

We have both been acting out of character, Venetia reflected, thinking of Vivian's meeting with Cranford in the library, which she had yet to mention, and then considering rather guiltily that she herself had no plans to tell Vivian about Cranford's kiss.

After an hour the storm faded away, and by then Vivian was fine. They were just making their way to the narrow twisting corner stair that led down from the gallery when they were startled to hear Cousin Adela's voice below them.

"I see you both! I found you. Do I get double points?"

"Adela! Why, what do you mean, 'double points'?"

"For finding two people at once. I'm on the hunters' team."

"Heavens," said Venetia, thinking quickly. *The guests must be playing hide and seek because of the rain.* "How clever of you to find us. Is it a point per person? I should think you have earned two, even though we were in one hiding place." She descended the stairs with Vivian behind her.

Adela giggled. "Not many people would think to look in here. But the person I'd most like to find is Lord Wistowe. Do you not think he is terribly clever?"

"Clever?" The twins exchanged a glance. "Handsome, at least."

Adela sighed. "Anyway, I must take you back to headquarters to prove that I found you before I can go looking any further. Come along."

Venetia put a reassuring hand on her sister's shoulder. They would play along, for wherever "headquarters" might be, it was probably nearer to their own rooms. They desperately needed to change their clothes, for Vivian was still in her riding habit, and both of them were damp from the rain and now dusty from the chapel gallery. They both smelled of horses. As they walked through the rooms and corridors in the north wing with Adela, they heard the faint rumble of thunder again.

"Not another one," whispered Vivian.

"I had forgotten, you don't like storms, do you?" said Adela. "Well, it makes perfect weather to play games inside."

"Why don't we let Vivian go along to her room, Adela? I can vouch for the fact that you found both of us."

Adela hesitated. "I don't know if that is good enough, Netia. I should think I'd have to show you both."

Venetia felt her patience waning. "Heavens, it is only a stupid game! I'll give my solemn oath if I must. Do you go along, Vivi, and change into your white muslin—you know, the one with the French work and blue embroidery."

She did not care if her cousin thought the conversation peculiar—if there were to be more storms in the coming hours, she would have to play two roles, and it was essential that she and Vivian dress alike. She hoped the hide-and-seek game would continue for some time, for it would certainly make her job easier. All she had to do now was make certain she had a chance to slip off to her own room to change as well.

Vivian fled up the nearest staircase, for thunder sounded again in the distance. Venetia went on with Adela to finish their business. As soon as she was free to hide, she, too, fled to her room, but only for the time it took to change her dress and check on her sister. Then she contemplated a true hiding place, wishing she knew what rules had been established. It suited her purposes to be found rather easily, since she needed to hide and be found twice as often as anyone else.

Lamps or candles blazed in many of the ground floor rooms, lit by dutiful servants. The guests, however, undid this work in many cases. The storms lent drama to the game and advantage to those in hiding, illuminating dark rooms with sudden startling brilliance only to plunge them into darkness again in seconds. For those in a position to watch, it created the peculiar effect of highlighting the movements of the seekers by fragments, showing one first at the entrance to a room, then halfway through it, next looking into an alcove or under a table, then gone.

Venetia watched several unsuccessful hunters pass through the long gallery in this fragmented fashion. She began to feel frustrated, as she was scarcely concealed behind one of her father's prized Italian sculptures. It was finally Lord Wistowe who penetrated far enough into the room to find her there.

"Aha! I have found one of you," he said as a flash of lightning lit the room. "Dammed if I know which one, but it cannot matter, eh?"

Venetia started to come out and was startled when he took one of her hands in his and put his other hand on her arm, pushing her back.

"Not yet, my lovely. Where is my reward for finding you?"

"What reward?" She felt uneasy, for he had stepped very close to her.

"Shy? Then it must be that I have captured the gentle lamb, Lady Vivian. I will be gentle, too, my pet." He lowered his face toward hers and she realized that he meant to kiss her.

Who had set these rules? No one but him, she was certain. Did he think he would take advantage of her sister? She averted her face and pushed back with all her weight, catching him quite unprepared.

"Your mistake, Lord Wistowe. I am Lady Venetia, and you have captured no one." It was the perfect exit line, but he recovered his balance faster than she had expected. As she tried to slip past him, he seized her around the waist and pushed her roughly back into the corner by the statue.

"Minx! You'll not escape that easily." He laughed, but there was an edge to his laughter that she did not like. "Pay my reward, or pay a forfeit."

"Which is?"

"Double my reward!" He claimed her lips quickly, before she could say more, kissing her hard and long. "Mm, I'll take the forfeit, too," he added then, without removing his mouth from hers. He probed with his tongue, and she was tempted to bite it. How dare he take such liberties? But he was still a guest, invited by her father. She held very still, waiting for him to finish. What would her father do if he knew about this? *I wonder if he would really care. He never shows his face except at dinner.*

Lord Wistowe stepped back from her, looking pleased with himself and somehow expectant. What was she supposed to do? Swoon at his feet? Thank him? Handsome though he was, she had not enjoyed being kissed by him. When she compared the way Lord Cranford's kiss had affected her, she hardly knew what to say.

"Well?"

Obviously she had to say something, "I think Lady Adela would be very pleased if you happened to find her. I can turn myself in, if you like."

As the game continued against a stormy backdrop, Venetia became more adept at juggling the two roles she had to play. When it was her turn to be one of the hunters, she would hide quickly in an obvious place and make sure that another seeker found "Vivian." Once "Vivian" had been sent off to hunt, Venetia would hastily find someone who was hiding and return in triumph as herself, pretending she had looked at length.

In both roles she was grateful for the advantage of knowing the house so much better than the other players. She knew every servants' door and passageway, and could get from one place to another quickly and unseen. She knew the best hiding places and the worst ones, and used them all.

"Vivi's an expert at hiding," she informed some fellow hunters at a point when she could not get away to play her twin. "If she really puts her mind to it, you'll never find her."

At another point she enjoyed listening to Lord Amberton pour the butter boat over her while he thought she was Vivian. His complaints about Venetia's lack of decorum and odd sense of humor were especially interesting. She would have to test if he still held those opinions sometime later when she was herself.

She counted herself fortunate that she did not run into Lord Cranford directly. She narrowly escaped him several times, ducking through a servants' door or around a corner when she saw him coming. Nicholas would understand exactly what she was doing if he stopped long enough to consider, but she did not want to risk the chance that Cranford might realize, also. She also did not wish to face the questions he was liable to ask after this morning's ride.

Her hope of avoiding him at least until she could have a word with Nicholas about him was dashed just as the game came to an end. Vivian was supposedly hiding, and Venetia was a hunter—it was the perfect opportunity to slip away to check on the real Vivian and see if she was up to rejoining the group. The series of storms had finally passed through, and fine, steady sunlight was streaming in the windows. As Venetia hurried through one of the drawing rooms, intent on reaching the south servants' stairs, Cranford hailed her.

"Ha, Lady Vivian—caught in transit! I'm afraid you will have to come with me. You are one of the last ones still out—we are ending the game once we have collected everyone."

Did he really take her for Vivian? He could hardly have gotten a good look at her, so perhaps he did. Venetia was stymied. Should she point out his error, or go along with his assumption? As Vivian, she thought she might escape the difficult questions she knew he wished to ask. But if she returned with him now, how was she to retrieve Vivian from her room? She doubted that the game could end until both of the twins made their appearances. They might wait a very long time for a "Venetia" who had never been summoned.

"You know, you and I have some unfinished business," he said in a low voice. "You did say on Monday that we could talk later."

That was when she had been playing Vivian before. If only she had found out what was between him and her sister!

"Now is not the right time for a discussion, but perhaps we could meet later this afternoon?" he suggested.

Now she was in a coil. Would Vivian wish to make this appointment or not? He was waiting for an answer.

"All right," she said softly, attempting to raise the pitch of her voice just slightly, like her sister's. "Four o'clock, by the entrance to the walled garden."

Venetia would deal with that problem then. What she needed to do now was escape. Her salvation came moments later when Lady Norbridge walked in on them.

"Ah, what have we here? Has Lord Cranford caught the elusive Lady Vivian? Or has she caught him? Or have I caught you both, now that the game is up? Perhaps it is Lady Venetia, after all. Come, you must confess all." She laughed at her own cleverness.

"I have caught Lady Vivian fair and square," Cranford began, turning to the countess. Venetia began to back away. "She is one of the last still out—I believe the others are looking for Lord Lindell."

Lady Norbridge could not see her, for Venetia was careful to keep Cranford's tall form between them until the last moment. She guessed that little would have distracted the countess from gazing at the viscount anyway—Lady Norbridge's attraction to him was obvious. She only hoped that he was paying similar attention to the countess. Finally she was able to turn and make a run for the door.

"Damnation! There she goes," cried Cranford, quite forgetting himself.

"Forgot to warn you that I cheat," Venetia called back over her shoulder. If he chose to pursue her she would be in a worse coil than before. *Lady Norbridge, I am counting on you*, she prayed silently.

She needn't have worried. Lady Norbridge latched on to Cranford's arm as fast as a trout leaping for bait. "Let her go," she heard the countess purr just as the door was closing. "Let someone else catch her. Now *we* can have a moment alone, instead."

Later, after the game was over and Gilbey had managed to part from Lady Norbridge, he wandered out into the garden to think. He wondered which of the twins would appear at four o'clock, or if either of them would come at all. He had said nothing more about the meeting when both twins had appeared at the end of the game.

He had known that the Lady "Vivian" he'd caught was really Venetia as soon as he had gotten a good look at her. It had occurred to him then that he had not seen the twins together since they had fled the stableyard that morning, although he had caught separate glimpses of what he had assumed was both twins all through the hours of the game.

Had Venetia been playing both twins all that time? He did not know. Certainly she had tried to fool him at the end. She had also pretended to be her sister on Monday on Sandler's Hill. Had there been other times?

He tried looking at the questions from another angle. Did Vivian ever try to play Venetia? Had they switched places any time when both were present? He needed to consider that, but he did not think so. Why did they do it? He did not believe that it was purely mischief—the look in Venetia's eyes was enough to tell him that. Was it one of their tests? Did Nicholas know? Surely he must be aware of these masquerades.

Gilbey pulled out his pocket watch and checked the time. *Half an hour still to pass.* If either of the twins kept their appointment, how was he going to handle the meeting? With chagrin he admitted that everything depended upon who came.

Slowly he strolled through the gravel paths and paved terraces of the gardens, making his way toward the walkway that led to the walled garden. He had discovered this walk on an earlier exploration, and thought it somehow ironically fitting that his confrontation with the twins should take place here, in the one magical spot he most admired and enjoyed.

The spot Venetia had chosen held everything that he liked about Rivington—the history that engaged the scholar in him and the beauty that appealed to his artist's eye. The stone wall that served as the west wall of the garden was an ancient relic left from the abbey or priory that had once stood in Rivington's valley and its heavy stone arch and wooden door served as the garden entrance. The walkway ran parallel to this wall, under a pergola made from six pairs of stone columns. The entire frame of the pergola and much of the ancient wall beside it were covered with a profusion of the most delightfully exotic plant he had ever seen, with gracefully twisting, woody branches, feathery leaves, and long plumes of mauve and lavender blossoms.

It was the kind of spot that might inspire a man to love—if such a thing could be permitted. After this day, he might never feel the same about it again. He might not ever be here again. He walked slowly through the pergola, staring up into the canopy over his head, studying the interplay of blossom, leaf, and sunlight.

Absorbed in the patterns, he almost forgot why he was there and felt some surprise when he arrived at the end next to the arched doorway in the wall. He looked about, but saw no one as yet.

By the entrance of the walled garden, she had said. Well, he was here. Now it remained to be seen if anyone else would be. He settled himself against the stone arch, where he could continue to study the flowering vines while he kept a watch on the walkway.

At what must have been precisely four o'clock, one of the twins came down the walk. She looked beautiful and fragile, a golden-haired vision in white, framed by flowers as delicate as she was. Was it Venetia, Venetia pretending to be Vivian, or Vivian herself? He studied her as she approached.

"I have been admiring your flowers," he began cordially, removing his hat. "I have never seen anything like them."

She smiled, stopping a few feet from him. "They are a particular pet of my father's, sent by a friend in America. I was very small when the gardeners first put them in and were trying to coax them to grow. We were absolutely forbidden to touch them."

"They seem to grow in great profusion, now."

She sighed. "I wish my mother could see how they've begun to take over everything in these recent years. She loved them. We called them Chinese teahouse flowers, although I don't know where she got that name. Since last year they have been named wisteria, after the American who had been cultivating them. I believe he died. I do think they are pretty."

She reached up and broke off a single tendril of blossoms, holding it gently in her fingers.

"You are very knowledgeable, Lady Venetia. And I see you are not afraid to touch them now."

She looked startled. "Why do you call me Venetia? I thought you and I were the ones with a discussion to finish."

"Ah, refresh my memory. What was it we were discussing?"

"My sister."

Ah, he thought, *she has done her homework.* At some time she must have spoken with Vivian to find out what this was about.

"Almost correct," he said "Your sister and I were discussing you."

She looked chagrined. "No, you and I . . ."

"You and I have been playing games, and it is time to stop. You don't fool me, Venetia. I have kept your little secrets, but now you owe me an explanation."

"I am not Venetia—Lady Venetia, to you. I am Lady Vivian, and I don't have the slightest idea what you are talking about, Lord Cranford."

He had moved out from the doorway and now he circled around her. "I kept silent on Sandler's Hill when you were parading around pretending to be your sister. I said nothing today, either." *Let her wonder how much I have noticed,* he thought. "Are you planning to continue to do this all the rest of the time your guests are here? Do you enjoy making fools of everyone? Does it entertain you at our expense? A week and a half is a long time to expect me to continue to keep quiet about your masquerades."

He thought if he upset her she might give in. He was wrong.

"What makes you think any of what you are saying is true?"

"I told you the first day I arrived that I could tell you and your sister apart, Venetia. With every day that passes, I learn more ways to distinguish you. You two may look alike, but in truth you are every bit as different as my twin sister and I. You toss your head like a wild stallion. Your sister tends to keep her eyes on her toes. When your sister looks up, she has an innocent, wide-eyed look of surprise about her. You always look as if you were born knowing all the answers. You have a way of turning your head to the side and looking down your nose at the same time that speaks volumes for your arrogance." He did not add that the way this exposed her neck made the blood race in his veins.

"Stop! That all means nothing. Any actress can learn to imitate those things."

"At least you admit that you have been acting."

"No . . ."

This was not going at all the way he meant it to. He had meant to be gentle and offer his help. Instead they were arguing, the last thing he wanted.

"Venetia." He spoke her name softly and reached for her hand. "I can prove that you are not Vivian."

She might have been going to ask how, but he did not give her that much time. Slipping off his spectacles, he pulled her toward him, and taking advantage of her surprise, claimed her lips.

Dear God, she smelled of jasmine and tasted like honey. He could not get enough of her sweetness. He did not wish to frighten her, but he wanted—needed—more, and his kiss began to demand it. He could feel his heart pounding in his ears, his loins, everywhere. He could feel her responding, and he brought her closer against him, as if he could make her warm softness one with him. His lips left hers and trailed down across her small jaw to her neck, where he nuzzled her soft skin. She moaned and he felt as if she had set him on fire.

"Venetia." He whispered her name, resting his cheek against hers. "I could no more mistake you for someone else than I could my own self." He knew he had to stop, to let her go. With the greatest reluctance, he drew back.

She was looking up at him, her clear blue-violet eyes now brimming with moisture. Botheration! He had not meant to make her cry. He tried to keep his voice gentle. "Don't you know that you can trust me? Even Nicholas would tell you so. You are a fraud, Lady Venetia St. Aldwyn, and never more so than at this moment. I am asking you to be honest with me. Please, let me help you."

Would she turn and walk away? The words had come out all wrong. But she just shook her head.

"I cannot."

"Why?" He felt so close to reaching her. "Just tell me why."

Chapter Thirteen

"You truly do not know, do you?"

If Venetia had harbored any lingering, secret doubts about Cranford, in that instant they were gone. Perhaps they had disappeared long before, even before the first time he had kissed her, but now she could no longer fool herself. She had tasted caring in his kiss, and total honesty. She practiced honesty so little now, she wondered that she could even recognize it.

He was waiting for her to say something more, holding out his handkerchief to her for the tears that had spilled over. She took it and mopped her eyes.

She did trust him, and trusting him restored her faith in Nicholas, too, that he would have such a friend. But her response to Cranford's kisses had showed her that she felt more than trust—dangerously more. To have him help would be foolish, possibly disastrous. She could not trust herself.

No, she could not let him help. Above all, she could not tell him why. She needed to keep him at a safe distance—as far away as possible. Perhaps there was still a chance that she was not already in love with him. No matter what she felt, she had to put Vivian's needs first.

Vivian trusts him, came a wicked little voice. Vivian had liked and trusted him long before now. And they did need help. They were no closer now to finding out the blackmailer than when they had started—perhaps even less close. At least when they'd started she had been half sure the villain was him. Now she did not know what to think.

A man can investigate in ways Vivian and I cannot, simply because we are women, she told herself. They had not dared to go to Nicholas for help; they feared he might expose their secret in his rush to do something heroic. Lord Cranford might be far better-suited to help them, with his quiet, unassuming manner and studious ways.

She looked at him. He was still waiting, his sea-colored eyes roaming her face as if he would read her thoughts flowing across it. She could not deny the attraction she felt to him. Even if she closed her eyes, she would still see the handsome angles of his long face, the silver highlights in his pale hair, those remarkable eyes behind their spectacles.

Was she wrong to refuse his help? Was she putting her own needs ahead of Vivian's by doing so? In a week and a half he would be gone, she and Vivian would each be betrothed, and life would move on. Could she not barricade her heart for that little while? Was she not strong enough to resist him? If she confessed the reason for her deceptions to him, he would have less reason to watch her or approach her. He could investigate other people instead. If she confided Vivian's secret and the blackmail attempt, she need never divulge the rest of the truth, if she had not revealed it already in her kiss. Would he be horrified by what she told him? Was telling him what Vivian would want?

Someday you'll have to trust someone, Vivian had said—Vivian, who had suffered more and had even more to risk than Venetia did. She closed her eyes.

"My sister is an epileptic."

There! She had told him. She tossed her head and looked away. Then, fearfully, she looked back, for she had to know his reaction.

His eyes were on hers. He was not smiling, but slowly he reached out for her hand and took it. He brushed it with his lips and then enclosed it between his own hands as if it were something precious and infinitely fragile.

"By God," he said softly, exhaling as if he had been holding his breath, "that is a heavy burden indeed. It explains much."

"You are not appalled?"

"I am surprised. She seems so perfectly normal."

"She *is* perfectly normal," Venetia answered vehemently. "She just happens to have occasional seizures. There is no harm to her or to anyone else, no matter what you may think you know or have heard. The problem is having to hide it because people do not understand, and not being able to predict when or how often the seizures occur."

He tucked her hand into the crook of his elbow. "Come, let us walk a bit. You can tell me about it, and we can make certain we are not overheard."

They headed away from the walled garden entrance, following the walkway down to the end and turning onto a gravel path. Cranford steered them into open parts of the gardens where they could see that there was no one nearby. Venetia was grateful for this small sign of his understanding and sensitivity. She began to talk, unburdening herself more freely than she had ever done.

"Vivi was not born this way. Six years ago we were in a terrible accident. Vivian, my mother, and I were in our carriage, driving home from a visit to some friends. Father and Nicholas were riding behind us. We left much later than we had intended, and the road was very dark. Something happened—we hit a deep rut, or a wheel came off—I never knew, really. Our carriage overturned. It was terrifying! The horses were screaming, we were screaming, everything was falling around us, the cushions, the doors, big splinters of broken wood, but then suddenly I didn't hear my mother or Vivian anymore. That frightened me more than anything."

She closed her eyes, remembering. How many times that scene had been repeated in her nightmares! She felt Cranford's hand cover her own at his elbow, and realized suddenly that she was trembling. She swallowed, trying to clear the tightness in her throat.

"I crawled out of the wreckage and saw my father cradling my mother against him. She was dead. I thought then that Vivian was, too. I don't remember how we got home, or anything else at all about that night.

"All I remember of the next few days is the doctor coming and going, over and over again. Vivian was alive, but she had a head injury, and no one knew how it might affect her, or if she would die. A thousand times I wished I could trade places with her then—too late! Too late. I promised God I would take care of her if he would only let her live."

Cranford had stopped, and now he took her into his arms. Tears were streaming down her face, and she could not stop them. "When she recovered, we thought everything would be fine. But my father could not get over the loss of our mother. And then Vivian's seizures started. He would not—and still will not—accept them. He makes up any excuse—that she has delicate nerves, or that she is just overtired—anything to escape the truth. To have him react that way was bewildering, as if he had abandoned us when we needed him most. He refuses to accept that there is something besides death that he cannot control. Epilepsy is not allowed to exist in his world, in his family.

"Then there is Aunt Alice." Venetia laughed bitterly. "She knows very well that my sister has fits. She believes that Vivian can control them and simply refuses—oh, it is so illogical! Sometimes I just want to shake her. She thinks Vivian does it to get our sympathy and attention, a way of dealing with the loss of our mother. Aunt Alice lives in fear that someone will find out about it."

"And what of Nicholas?"

"He knows, of course. He tried to help, but as you must know, he is not here that much of the time. I think he often feels at a loss to know what to do—he is caught between Father and us."

"Yes, I can see that." His handkerchief was out again, but this time he kept it and very gently dried her tears himself. "You must feel very much alone at times."

The comment was so perceptive and so unexpected, she left off staring at his waistcoat and looked up at him.

"You have tried to shoulder the burden all yourself." His handsome face was full of sympathy and concern. *Who could not fall in love with such a man?*

She stepped back from him and turned away, shaking her head as much to clear the thought as to deny his words. "Vivian has the greatest burden, having to live her life so carefully, always in doubt, always wondering when the next attack will come, never knowing for certain. She has to tolerate Father's denial and Aunt Alice's insensitivity, and the looks of the servants. Some of them are afraid of her, I know. The seizures are frightening, and she is always mortified afterward, as if she were at fault! It should have been my burden. I must do everything I can to help her."

"Do most of your servants know?"

"Yes, most do. They are well paid, and there are not many positions like theirs in this area. A few would not stay when we first learned of the epilepsy, because they were afraid. But we have managed well enough in the years since then, until now."

"Now?"

"Yes, this party. This insistence that Vivian and I should both marry. Our father's decision that he will wait no longer."

She had moved away as she talked, and now in just two easy, long strides, he made up the distance. With a gentle hand on her shoulder, he turned her to face him again.

"The tests, the schemes, the capriciousness for which you have become infamous—they have all been because of your sister's affliction?"

She nodded, closing her eyes again. It was easier to talk if she did not face him. "They have all been because of my father, who will not see the danger in marriage for Vivian. It matters so much who she marries! She would be so much safer if she just stayed with me or with Nicholas."

She opened her eyes and looked out past him, at the tree-fringed hills and the sky beyond Rivington. "Her husband will have absolute power over her. The wrong man could destroy her, even if he did not abuse her or commit her to a house for the insane. Yet, if we could find the right man, if such a man exists, she could have a chance for a life of happiness, even with the epilepsy. I would sacrifice anything to make that happen."

"Even your own future?"

"Yes. Anything."

"And just what would this paragon have to be like? Just in case I should happen across one," he said.

She turned her gaze back to him and found him smiling. "He would have to be patient, and kind, and understanding . . ." *He would have to be like you,* she thought with dawning amazement. She felt as if a thunderbolt had struck her, but of course he did not notice.

"Willing to live with a secret?"

"Yes."

He rubbed his chin thoughtfully. "Are those qualities indeed so difficult to find?"

"They seem to be. We have been looking for two years."

She smiled. *But now we have found you!* Why had she not thought of him before now? *Because you were too busy falling in love with him yourself,* said the voice in her head. *Because he was only Nicholas's friend, or maybe the blackmailer, or witless and boring—whatever other image you tried to put in the way.* She had only tried to protect herself; she knew she would never have been allowed to marry him. But perhaps there was a chance for Vivian. There might just be a way.

"I had always hoped that we would be successful," she said, realizing that he expected some further comment. "But now my father forces us to choose from among the guests that he has gathered here. And there is also another who wishes to force our hands."

He looked surprised. "Your aunt?"

She sighed. "She will be well pleased to see us married off, but it is not she. Someone among the guests knows our secret, and has threatened to expose us."

She was astonished to see how quickly his expression changed. Color flooded into his cheeks and his brows drew down in anger. His eyes darkened. Suddenly he looked very much like a dangerous man.

"That is blackmail!"

She nodded and began to walk again. He fell into step beside her.

"To what end?"

"To force me into marriage with him." A small stone had trespassed on the gravel path and she gave it a vicious kick. Cranford was curiously silent. Finally she said, "I must confess that for some time I thought it might be you."

"Me?" He was clearly dumbfounded. She found that reassuring.

"I could not conceive that anyone else had a motive."

"What was mine supposed to be?"

She glanced sideways at him. "Oh dear. This *is* awkward. Why did I have to mention it?"

He grasped her elbow and brought her to a stop. "Half a confession will not serve. Finish it."

Her elbow was burning from his gentle touch. This would never do—she must go through with the rest of this, so there would be no more glances, no more touches between them.

"All right. I learned from Nicholas that you were in need of funds, to build back your estates. He—he said that your uncle had swindled you a few years ago."

"That's true," he said, and then he laughed. Laughed! She thought most men would have been angry. "And when did you decide that I might not be the blackmailer?"

"When I realized that money might not be the only motive, and I could see that you were genuinely puzzled by what was happening here." She could not admit that it had only been this morning.

"So, have you other suspects now?"

"Well, perhaps one."

"What does Nicholas say about all this? Did he know you suspected me? What is he doing to help?"

"He does not know."

To that point the conversation had made Gilbey feel as if all his emotions had been set off inside him like rockets in a box, bouncing and ricocheting in a dozen directions. But at that particular moment, the uppermost one was definitely anger.

"He-does-not-know? Anything? Do you mean to tell me that neither you nor Vivian has told him about this blackmail attempt?" He snatched his hand away from Venetia's arm, for he realized that he had an overwhelming urge to shake her.

Making an effort to calm his voice, he said, "Please tell me if I understand this correctly. You have been trying to protect your sister's secret, find her a husband, find yourself a husband, please your father, entertain these guests, and secretly thwart a blackmailer, all without any help?"

In the meekest of voices she said, "And unmask a bad poet."

Gilbey threw up his arms to dispel the explosion inside him. "Who do you think you are, Boadicea?" he roared. In the heat of the moment he could not think of a better example. "Even she had the help of her troops!"

Truly, he had not meant to yell. Venetia stirred all kinds of passions in him that were best left alone. It only proved to him what he had already known—that a marriage based on love would be a disaster for the likes of him. Parting from her at the end of this visit was inevitable, and he knew it was for the best. He thought he could survive the pain if he knew she was betrothed to a decent man. The blackmailer had to be stopped.

He took a deep breath. "Need I remind you that, despite her victories, Boadicea lost to the Romans in the end?"

Venetia raised her head defiantly. "She took poison." Her eyes told him that she would have done the same.

"Venetia." He tried to speak gently. "I'm sorry, I know I must still say Lady Venetia. If you would let me help you, and let Nicholas, you might not have to lose this war. You might find us useful allies."

"Nicholas is so impulsive. You see how angry you just became? What do you suppose his reaction will be like when he learns of this? He is our brother. What is to stop him from roaring off like a charging bull, exposing the secret to everyone anyway by the time he gets done?"

"I know how to handle Nicholas. I'll stop him from roaring off. Will you trust me?"

Opening her hand, she held out to him the small fragment of wisteria blossom she must have kept in it the whole time. Slowly she nodded. "It seems I have already begun."

At dinner the guests were divided and seated at three different tables, as they had been on one of the previous evenings. This time all the younger guests were seated together, and the conversation was lively. Gilbey had no chance to speak to Nicholas until the ladies withdrew after the meal, and even then he could only say he wished a few private moments with him. As the guests reassembled for cards in the blue drawing room, the two friends ducked into an anteroom and Gilbey quickly sketched out what had happened.

"It is more than essential that you stay cool about this, Nicholas," he counseled. "The situation is delicate and calls for subtle handling. We do not want to alert the blackmailer to our efforts any more than we wish to see your sisters' secret exposed."

Nicholas was understandably upset. He paced restlessly and repeatedly struck his palm with his fist. "Who could it be? My aunt and my father handpicked these guests. I'll kill the blackguard, whoever he is! How dare he come under our roof with such intentions?"

"Get a grip on yourself, man. Do you want someone to overhear? Look, what we need to do is have a war council, the four of us." Gilbey knew that if he could get Nicholas focused upon some specific steps to take, he would calm down.

"All right, all right." Nicholas stopped and pushed the hair back from his forehead. After a moment's thought he said, "We will take my sisters for a drive tomorrow morning. It is the only way I can think of to ensure utter privacy."

Venetia lay awake part of the night thinking out her plan to put Vivian and Cranford together. She had had no opportunity to speak privately with her sister until they had retired to their rooms for the night. In their dressing room she had finally recounted her conversation with the viscount in the garden. But her thoughts she could not share. Now she stared up at the blue velvet hangings of her carved four-poster bed, their tasseled shapes comfortingly familiar in the darkness.

Five things were necessary for her plan's success, as far as she could see. First, Vivian must want Cranford for her husband. That seemed to Venetia to be the easiest part. Vivian liked the viscount and had noticed how handsome he was from the first moment she had seen him. If Venetia had come to care for him so deeply, certainly it should not be difficult for her twin to arrive at similar feelings if she were given enough opportunities to be with him.

Second, Cranford must be willing to marry Vivian. *That should not be too difficult, either.* Unless she had completely misjudged him, he was not exactly indifferent to her, and Vivian was her twin, after all. He had not been disgusted or horrified at the revelation of Vivian's epilepsy, and he certainly had the patience, kindness, and understanding that they had hoped for so long to find. Surely a quiet, scholarly man such as he would not mind the limited social participation that Vivian would need to observe. What man in his position would turn down the chance to marry into a family as powerful and wealthy as the St. Aldwyns? A fraction of Vivian's dowry would undoubtedly restore all of his estates and triple them.

Plus, Nicholas was his best friend; surely their brother would lend his support to the match.

A bigger obstacle would be obtaining their father's approval. Determined to present two perfect daughters to the world, the duke fully expected both of the twins to make excellent matches. How could she get him to see the truth? Cranford was indeed an excellent match for Vivian—they were perfect for each other. His lack of funds should not matter, and what other objections could there be? Lord Newcroft was only a viscount, and her father had deemed him eligible enough. Undoubtedly it was because Lord Newcroft was rich enough to loan money to Prinny himself.

The solution was twofold: her father would have to be convinced that the family would not be diminished by a connection to Lord Cranford, and Venetia would have to make the most brilliant match possible to compensate. That meant, of course, the Duke of Thornborough for her, or at the very least one of the three available marquesses. Old as he was, the Duke of Thornborough obviously still thought he could father an heir, and Venetia hoped so. A child would give her life meaning after the old duke passed on.

She nearly choked on a sudden thought: could the duke be the blackmailer? How ironic that would be. With his high opinion of himself, might he still fear that his matrimonial chances were poor because of his age? Now that she had realized money need not be the only motive behind such desperation, the other possible motives seemed limitless. It was more essential now than ever that the blackmailer be discovered, for her choice of mate mattered now much more than before. She had believed that if they failed to stop him, she would go through with marrying the villain to protect her sister. But if he was not among the prime candidates that possibility now became unthinkable.

As difficult as unmasking the blackmailer might be, she thought the last part of her plan might prove to be the hardest. She would have to overcome her feelings for Cranford. If he was to marry Vivian, he would never be gone from her life, and the pain of loss in her heart would be renewed every time she saw him if she did not succeed in exorcising it. But at least failure here would not jeopardize all. It would only condemn her to years of self-torture for her sister's sake.

Not surprisingly, Venetia's rest was troubled when sleep did finally overtake her.

Chapter Fourteen

"There are two things that any blackmailer most specifically must have," Gilbey commented to his companions the following morning as the St. Aldwyns' landau crested a hill overlooking Rivington. Venetia, Vivian, and Nicholas sat with him in the carriage, en route to the nearby estate village of Colby Compton. On the floor at their feet were several packets of food, medicine, and clothing to be delivered to poor families in the village.

"I think you had both of these very much in mind when you suspected me, Lady Venetia. After considering the situation, I have come to understand why you thought as you did."

"You suspected Lord Cranford?" Nicholas cast an angry glare at his sister. "He is my best friend!" Turning to Gilbey, he added in accusatory tones, "You did not tell me about that part."

"I could not tell you about every detail," Gilbey said with a smile, remembering Venetia's warm response to his kiss. "Let us not digress. The two things are: motive and knowledge of a secret."

"Netia! What possible motive did you think Cranford could have had for blackmailing you into marriage?"

"You force me to be rude, Nicholas. You told me yourself that his uncle had swindled him and that he had been struggling to restore his estates. I am perfectly aware that Vivian's and my dowries are sweet enough by themselves to attract suitors like bees. Or maybe wolves. It seemed rather clear that Lord Cranford was not numbered among the eligible, so I thought that gave him motive enough."

"And you thought because of his friendship with me, I

might have betrayed the family secret?" Nicholas was rigid with indignation. "I am truly insulted!"

"Will you two stop? We must cooperate if we are to have success." Vivian's attempt to intercede was ignored.

"Lord Cranford's behavior seemed to support my suspicions, Nicholas. No one was less interested in courting us than he, and he seemed to be going to great extremes to avoid attracting any attention. For instance, his deliberate attempt to lose the archery competition." Venetia's chin was up and one eyebrow was arched quite impossibly high, even for a St. Aldwyn. Her tone was a mixture of defensiveness and challenge.

"How did you know about that? I am surprised you have not uncovered the blackmailer yourself if that is an example of your investigative skills."

Venetia sighed. "It took no skill at all—I overheard you saying that he was a Cambridge champion."

She must have heard me ask Nicholas to change the prize, too, thought Gilbey uncomfortably. Suddenly he felt rather loath to explain himself. "Could we please apply ourselves to the problem at hand?" he asked, only partly as a diversion. "We should determine who among the other guests are likely suspects."

"Yes, indeed," agreed Nicholas, recovering quickly from his agitation. "Enough time has already been wasted suspecting poor Gilbey, who is the most unlikely candidate of all. He has no interest in marriage at all just now, have you, old man? Planning to bury himself in his studies, travel the world, improve his estates, and enjoy the beautiful simplicity of his Cambridge fellowship stipend for a few years. Plenty of time for marriage later, eh?"

No doubt Nicholas was only trying to help, Gilbey reasoned, quelling a mighty urge to punch his friend. Every word was true, but at the moment it sounded like a very poor plan indeed, and this seemed a most unfortunate place and time to advertise it. He glanced at Venetia, but found her expression unreadable. Was she thinking of the secret kisses they had shared? She had every right to think him the worst sort of cad.

"A-ahem. I think we may assume the other guests are here with a definite interest in matrimony," he said awkwardly. "After all, they have chosen to be here instead of in London just as the Season swings into full stride. We know all of them appear to be respectable and highly eligible, 'else they would never have been invited. But we also know that one among them is not as he appears."

Nicholas took up the thread of questioning. "Who among them has a motive, then?"

"Or, who does not?"

"Lord Lindell," said Vivian with conviction. "His parents and sister are here with him, so I think it highly unlikely that he would attempt something of this sort, even if he lacked scruples, even if he had a motive. But he is almost too young to marry. Indeed, I think it is Lady Marchthorpe's ambitions which push both him and Lady Elizabeth to pay court to us. The worst we suspect of him is that he writes undistinguished poetry."

It was quite a long speech for the quiet twin. For a moment everyone looked at her.

"What? Do you mean to say it is not my personal charm that has attached the Lady Elizabeth's interest?" Nicholas feigned horror at the very idea.

"Silly. It would hardly be the first time that happened." Venetia had no mercy.

"How ambitious is Lady Marchthorpe?" Gilbey asked quite seriously.

"Oh ho. He sees a villain behind every tree," Nicholas teased. "Not ambitious enough for desperate tactics, my friend. Consider how highly placed they already are! And they have plenty of feathers to fly with. No, I am inclined to agree with Vivi. It is not Lord Lindell."

"By that reasoning, then, may we eliminate the Duke of Thornborough, the Marquess of Ashurst, the Marquess of Wistowe, and the Marquess of Amberton? They are all top of the trees, are they not?"

"No."

Now everyone looked at Venetia.

"I don't mean that they are not top of the trees, but that we may not eliminate them." She sighed. "Although it seems the most probable, money is not the only possible motive. Consider. His Grace the Duke of Thornborough might believe he is too old to win one of us by the usual methods. He is so proud, perhaps he will not settle for someone of a lower rank. Certainly he is running out of time to produce an heir—he might be desperate."

"Or simply ruthless."

"Lord Wistowe might believe his reputation is too sullied. Lord Ashurst might fear that we are put off by his reclusive ways and his reputation as a cynic. The only one of them I would excuse from suspicion is Lord Amberton—I don't believe he has the wit to put together such a scheme!"

"Ah, another witless wonder." Gilbey could not resist the comment. When Venetia looked at him sharply, he grinned.

"The point is," she said impatiently, "the motive depends upon their own perception of their status. How are we to know that?"

"Well, I shouldn't think that either Lord Wistowe or Lord Ashurst would feel desperate, even if they harbored doubts about their chances for success. They have a good deal more time left than the duke." Honor forbade Gilbey from revealing that he had an idea of Lord Ashurst's state of mind.

"All right, that is true," Venetia admitted. "If we are looking for desperation, however, something that the Duke of Brancaster said the other morning made me wonder about Lord Newcroft. His Grace said the viscount is extremely ambitious, always trying to prove himself. We have noticed how competitive he is. He has such tremendous wealth, it seems natural that he would seek higher rank to go with it, and marriages always do have political ramifications as well as economic and social ones. Perhaps he is not willing to take his chances along with everyone else."

"Then we have two suspects, so far, the Duke of Thornborough and Lord Newcroft."

At that point the carriage swayed and rumbled to a halt, surprising them. They had arrived at Colby Compton and the discussion had to be interrupted.

"Oh dear, we did not make very much progress, did we?" lamented Venetia. "Nicholas, I promise I will not argue on the way back if you will promise, also."

"Done."

"Lord Cranford, you go with Vivian to deliver these packets, while I go with Nicholas. That way we will not overwhelm anyone's hospitality."

It was a logical, thoughtful thing to do, but Gilbey was surprised by Venetia's instructions—surprised and disappointed. Had Nicholas's unwitting comment destroyed so easily the fragile friendship he thought had begun to blossom between him and Venetia? Perhaps he was reading too much into Venetia's choice. Perhaps he should not be concerned over it, anyway, since their friendship could lead nowhere.

They descended from the carriage into a crowd of small children quite naturally attracted by the elegant equipage. Venetia and Vivian seemed to know all of the urchins by name and greeted them cheerfully.

"Many of the families in the village are supported by members working at Rivington," Vivian explained as she patted a last few heads and then began to walk along the row of neat stone cottages facing the street. Gilbey noticed that she never looked at him directly the way her sister did, but kept her eyes on where she was going. "Some of the others are sheep farmers or simple shepherds." She nodded at the bundles he carried. "We try to give extra help to any who need it."

They stopped in at three houses, and were offered refreshment at each one despite the obvious poverty. Vivian handled her duties with tact and diplomacy, leaving the gifts without injuring the pride of those receiving them. He was impressed. His sister Gillian had always performed this duty at home, and since her marriage, he had asked his managers to take care of it. One day he would have a wife to do it. He stopped himself, appalled, when he realized he was picturing Venetia in that role.

Instead he tried to focus on Vivian. Did the villagers know she was epileptic? Would not the servants from Rivington share the secret with their families? From there it was easily spread to neighbors. He could not decide if the deference they showed her was more than the usual to be expected for one of her rank. Did he notice a few odd looks? Did she? He was not certain, and he realized suddenly that she must be accustomed to living in that state of uncertainty. Was that part of the reason she was so quiet and self-effacing, or had she always been like that? He was slowly coming to understand how thoroughly her condition must have changed her life and Venetia's.

They met Nicholas and Venetia walking back to the carriage. The whole visit had taken less than an hour. Once the four were comfortably settled on the leather squabs of the landau and the vehicle started off, they resumed their discussion.

"We have eliminated Lord Lindell from among the earls, but what of Lord Chesdale and Lord Munslow?" Gilbey asked. "What do you feel about either of them?"

"Neither have pressed their suit with much energy," Venetia said thoughtfully. "Perhaps they feel their chances are not good. Lord Chesdale is more interested in horses and gaming than anything, and Lord Munslow seems to be interested in Lady Norbridge."

"On the other hand, one of the reasons you suspected me was that I did not show interest in courting you," Gilbey pointed out. *In the beginning, before I became a total fool.* "Could either of them have a motive?"

"How can we know?" Venetia said crossly. "I don't believe we are getting anywhere with this. Colonel Hatherwick is the only suitor left whom we haven't discussed, and if he is the blackmailer then pigs fly and fish dance."

Gilbey smiled. "The colonel is a close friend of the family. Is it not possible that he might have learned Vivian's secret? If he felt certain of achieving his goal, he could afford to relax and spend his time fishing, could he not?"

"You are no help whatsoever!" Venetia folded her arms across her middle and with a toss of her head fixed her gaze on the scenery outside the carriage window.

"On the contrary, Netia," Nicholas protested. "We have managed to reduce the list of suspects by four."

"What is the colonel's motive, then?"

"He is only a baron. Perhaps he wishes to advance his close ties to the family through marriage, but despairs of the chance that either of you would choose him."

"Fiddlesticks!"

"We must consider who among the remaining five might have had some opportunity to learn of Vivian's trouble," Gilbey persisted. "It strikes me that it probably happened quite accidentally—few people would have suspected that there was anything wrong to spur an investigation."

"You did." Venetia's tone was accusing.

"Lord Cranford is extraordinarily observant. That is one of the reasons I invited him to come," Nicholas said. "It is also why he will be able to help us now."

Damn Lord Cranford, anyway, Venetia thought, still staring out at the familiar landscape beyond the carriage window. Just what *were* Nicholas's reasons for inviting him? The viscount might indeed now be trying to help, but at the moment she felt unaccountably vexed with him. Well, perhaps not so unaccountably.

Not interested in marriage! How had she so misjudged him? How had she allowed him to take liberties—not once, but twice! She should have slapped his face, but instead she . . . well, never mind that now. This was an unanticipated obstacle to her plans. Perhaps, just perhaps, he was not quite so set on those plans as he had once been. Perhaps if he developed a *tendre* for Vivian, he would change his mind. Perhaps, if he did not, there was still another way. . . .

Venetia stopped herself, shocked that she would ever consider trapping a man into marriage. How desperate she was becoming! But time was growing shorter with each day that passed. Tomorrow was Friday, one day short of the halfway mark. Could so much be accomplished in the week that remained?

"Yes," Cranford was saying in the carriage. Startled, Venetia forced her mind back to the present moment. "It would indeed be helpful to consider anything we know about the delivery of the note."

They were not far from Rivington now. Venetia answered quickly to cover her lapse in attention. "It was slipped under our door after we retired from playing cards Sunday night. The note was written in block letters, on Rivington paper that is available to any of the guests. No one but Lady Duncross retired before we did. We asked among the servants, but found none who knew anything about a note being delivered."

"I retired just after you did," Cranford observed.

"So you said," Venetia replied. "It was another thing that made me suspicious of you."

"Nicholas, you are our only hope there, then," said Vivian. "Can you recall if anyone else left at about that time?"

"I will think on it. Blamed if I can recall at this moment, however. Lady Elizabeth was quite intent on occupying my attention that evening, as I recollect."

The entrance facade of the house loomed closer by the minute, cutting short the time for discussion.

"We need more information about our suspects than can be learned here at Rivington," Cranford said. "My brother-in-law is in London at present—I will write to him. He is extremely resourceful, and he will not question my need for the information."

"Your brother-in-law?" Venetia did not know why she was surprised. Cranford had mentioned a twin sister in the garden, but she had not been able to ask him about her with all that had happened after that. She had not thought about the fact that he had family, or how that might affect Vivian once they were married.

"The Marquess of Radclyffe. Your Duchess of Brancaster told me that she knows him. He was recently elevated by the Prince Regent after becoming Earl of Grassington. He is better known as the Earl of Brinton."

"Splendid idea, old man," Nicholas said, reaching over to shake his friend's hand. "I'll have the letter taken into Northleach first thing. That way it will go straight into the Gloucester post for London. In the meantime, we will poke about with ears open and see what we can turn up for ourselves."

Chapter Fifteen

Venetia had little opportunity to advance her plan that afternoon. The beautiful morning the foursome had enjoyed for their drive to Colby Compton clouded over by midday and rain soon followed, postponing the scheduled driving race in favor of a fencing match to be held indoors. To everyone's surprise, the Duke of Roxley actually emerged from his study to take charge of the exercise. He banished the ladies to the gallery of Rivington's entrance hall, where they could watch in separate safety while the gentlemen fenced below.

Nicholas and Gilbey, however, welcomed the opportunity to begin implementing their plan. Clad in shirts and pantaloons, all sixteen of the gentlemen at Rivington were to take part in the double elimination match. The two friends planned to watch their five suspects carefully.

"I am paired with Colonel Hatherwick in the first round," Gilbey said to Nicholas as they waited for their turns. The hall was so large that as many as three pairs of opponents were able to fence at once. "I will try him a little, to see what surprises may be revealed in his response."

"I am paired with Lord Amberton," Nicholas replied. His father was already engaged against the Duke of Brancaster, and his eyes never left the dueling opponents. "I anticipate no surprises there—by Jove! Did you see that nice riposte by the Duke of Brancaster?"

"You sound as if you hope your father will lose."

"Not at all. I fully expect him to win—fencing is his sport. But His Grace is giving him a good run for his money."

"The Duke of Thornborough appears to be trouncing Lord Marchthorpe. I find that a surprise."

"Because of his age? But you see, he is reasonably fit, and

even though he is a bit stiff in the knees, Marchthorpe hasn't the heart for fencing. You can see he hesitates and holds back."

"Perhaps they should have let his wife take his place," Gilbey said with a chuckle that Nicholas echoed.

"You've been spending too much time with Ashurst. His humor is rubbing off on you," the duke's son chortled.

When it was their turn, both young men donned the protective coverings handed over by their predecessors and proceeded to win their respective bouts handily. Gilbey met nothing but affable good nature and poor skill in the colonel.

"He is almost too easy and amiable to be believed," Gilbey complained afterward as he removed his chest protector and wire mesh mask. "I feel as if I learned nothing."

"I doubt either of us will have the same complaint after this next round," Nicholas commented. "I am pitted against Lord Wistowe, and it appears that you have the honor of contesting Lord Newcroft. Yours is an interesting casting of opposites, eh?"

Lord Newcroft clearly had no intention of joining the losers' list so soon as the second round, and he let Gilbey know it immediately once they had made their salutes. His style was not elegant, but as Gilbey expected, it was aggressive and effective, rather like a bulldog's. Gilbey mustered his powers of concentration and focused them all on his opponent. He did not particularly care if he won or not, but as the contest became more heated, he lost sight of that. His shirt, barely moist after the first round, was soon soaked, and perspiration dripped off his forehead.

Newcroft darted in and out, parrying constantly and matching Gilbey thrust for thrust, executing a number of impressively complex attacks and moving with challenging speed. But the smaller viscount's thirst for victory ultimately cost him that reward. He redoubled, extending in a lunge and then as Gilbey retreated, lunging again. Newcroft could not pull back quickly enough to escape Gilbey's long arm. With a supreme sense of satisfaction, Gilbey reached over his opponent's foil and delivered the decisive coup.

His next round was against Lord Chesdale. The ex-cavalry officer fenced with a style totally different from Lord Newcroft's, strong and decisive, yet very trained and disciplined, with none of the affected flamboyance Gilbey half expected. It was easier to compete against a style that was a bit more like his own, but Gilbey found Chesdale's defense almost impenetrable. As their bout wore on, he began to wonder if they would still be at sword points when night fell. However, he respected the earl's absolutely forthright manner. *Unless I am no judge of human nature*, Gilbey thought, *this is no blackmailer*.

The bout ended when the earl slipped. Gilbey generously waited while the man regained his balance, but apparently he had lost his concentration, for he left himself open and Gilbey scored. Victorious in the third round, Gilbey discovered he would next face the Duke of Roxley himself. Fortunately, a halt was called to allow the opponents to catch their breath.

Nicholas sauntered over. "I lost to Wistowe, then he lost to my father. I swear he cheated."

"Your father?"

"Wistowe. He slapped his blade against me every time he passed. Probably how he defeated Ashurst in the first round, too, by distraction. Maybe we should put him back on the suspect list."

"We can take Chesdale off. I am certain of it."

"Based only on his fencing?"

"Utterly honest, thoroughly straightforward. Thought he'd be more of a saber man, but he's very good with a foil."

"I won against Thornborough, but I can't say I was able to read him so clearly. He could be utterly ruthless and wise enough not to let it show."

"So you are alive in the losers' list. Who is your next?"

"Newcroft."

"Ah. He is his own worst enemy. If you are lucky as I was, his own aggressiveness will trip him."

The break was over. Gilbey determined that it was both tactful and politically astute to make certain that the Duke of Roxley won their bout, but in the end he needed no special effort. The duke was obviously an expert in his element and enjoying it. Gilbey put up a defense that convinced even himself.

When it was over, the two shook hands and the duke fell into step beside Gilbey as they left the center of the room.

"You have been seeing a good deal of my daughter," the older man stated flatly.

Botheration. Somehow Gilbey had sensed this was coming. The duke knew much of what went on in his domain, despite an appearance of disinterest. "Not intentionally, Your Grace. Circumstances seem to keep throwing us together."

"Interesting choice of words. Should I be concerned that this trend will continue?"

How the devil should I know? "I trust not, Your Grace, but as I said, these events were not exactly planned."

The duke nodded. "See that they remain so." Just before he walked away he added, "Your technique is good, by the way. Your feint to the left shoulder tends to droop a little, however."

Venetia watched her father while he walked with Lord Cranford. *Perhaps he is complimenting Cranford on how well he fences,* she thought optimistically. Fencing was her father's favorite sport—surely it would help her cause that Cranford had proven himself so skilled. Certainly she was impressed. The expression on the tall viscount's face was not that of a man who was receiving compliments, however, and the exchange between the men lasted only a moment.

Vivian turned to her. "Did you see how well Lord Ashurst fenced, Netia? Lord Upcott was no match for him at all."

"I was too busy watching both Father and Nicholas." Her reply was not untrue, just incomplete. "Did you notice Lord Cranford, Vivi? He has also been doing very well, although he could not defeat Father."

"Not surprising. I did notice that he won against Lord Newcroft earlier. Nicholas lost."

"Lord Cranford could have to fence with Lord Newcroft again. The four finalists will go against each other to see who will face Father."

"Two more rounds and then the final? They have been at it all afternoon." Vivian's dismay was echoed by many of the other ladies.

"Father will win no matter which one of them it is. He always wins."

* * *

The talk at dinner was all of the afternoon's fencing, despite the efforts of the ladies to discuss anything else. The final round had been between Ashurst and the duke.

"I have used up all the compliments I know," Venetia told her sister wearily when the ladies finally escaped to the drawing room. "Would you not think well-bred gentlemen had been taught better manners than to be so boorish at table? I am ready to wash my hands of the lot of them."

Vivian giggled. "Those were not gentlemen at the table, Netia, there's your mistake. That was a great lot of crowing schoolboys after an exciting afternoon."

Mellowed by after-dinner port, the gentlemen in question behaved with more consideration as they played cards for the rest of the evening, limiting the number of comments related to the fencing match to what they deemed a reasonable number. Cranford and Nicholas even remembered their mission as sleuths and asked questions under the guise of polite conversation.

"Ever spent any time in this area before? It is very scenic, is it not? Beautiful hills and valleys, lovely little villages," Nicholas would say.

"How long have you been acquainted with His Grace and the family?" Cranford would ask.

Venetia appreciated what they were doing, but she concentrated most of her attention on her cards and the Duke of Thornborough. She had arranged to be his partner with a bit of assistance from her aunt. Every now and again Aunt Alice would look over with an approving smile. The duke seemed to accept Venetia's sudden interest as his due, prompted by his show of skill in the fencing match.

"Bad luck of the draw, I'd say, to have faced your father and then your brother in the second and third rounds," he said. "No dishonor to be bested by them, I must say, my dear, but I could have made mincemeat of some of the others."

Venetia looked down at the cards in her hand while she adjusted her expression to reflect something that could pass for admiration. She had been dealt a poor assortment herself, but she still felt little sympathy for the duke.

You looked thoroughly winded by the end of the third round, she thought, yet she could hardly say so. She hated the flattery that came out of her mouth in response to most of his remarks, but it was clearly what he expected. She forced herself not to move her hand away every time he reached across to pat it. Could she spend the rest of her days living out a lie? Could she keep her sister from knowing the price she was ready to pay for her happiness?

"You were splendid, Your Grace. Just bad luck indeed. Of course no one was able to defeat my father." *Most probably no one had dared try.*

As Thornborough seldom appeared before noontime, Venetia was spared having to suffer him at breakfast the next morning. Nicholas and Cranford were still finishing at one table, and when she and Vivian joined them, she was careful to sit beside her brother, leaving an empty seat next to the viscount for her sister.

Cranford greeted them politely and went back to polishing off the last of some kippers and freshly prepared trout on his plate.

Nicholas arched an eyebrow in his direction. "Wise decision of yours to go fishing this morning, old man. At the rate you have been consuming fish every morning, we undoubtedly need to replenish our supply."

The viscount ignored his teasing. "A fine morning and a good trout stream are all the excuse I need, thank you."

"You are going fishing this morning?" Venetia tried to conceal the disappointment in her voice. She had envisioned a number of possible activities which she had planned to suggest he and Vivian could pursue.

He nodded. "Getting a very late start, too." Venetia thought she caught a twinkle in his eye as he added, "Did you know that the Countess of Duncross likes to fish? She is really quite a remarkable woman."

"Must be all that hardy old Scottish blood in her veins."

"Netia!"

"Why, Lady Venetia, you'll make me think you are jealous, and we know *that* can't be true." He took a moment to grin at her and then, finished with his meal, he wished them a good morning and took his leave.

Venetia was not sure why the rude remark had popped

out—she seemed to lose control of her tongue when she was around Lord Cranford. Maybe she *was* jealous. "Whatever possessed you to invite Cranford here, anyway, Nicholas?" she said in annoyance.

"'Cranford' is it now, Netia? You have become familiar quite quickly, I see."

She felt the heat rush into her face and blushed all the more to think that she was blushing, a thing she rarely did. She should be more careful.

"I meant to say Lord Cranford." *I just have not been thinking of him in quite such a formal way.*

Nicholas leaned close to her. "He is after more than one kind of fish, Netia. He hopes to have some enlightening conversation with Colonel Hatherwick while he is at it." He sat back smiling as his meaning dawned on her.

"Have you made some progress?" she asked in a low voice.

"Cranford wrote to his brother in London last night, and the letter went off very early this morning. Hope we'll have something of our own to report to you this evening, if we can find an opportunity."

Venetia decided that Cranford's plans to go fishing did not necessarily void all of her own plans. As she sipped her second cup of chocolate, she conceived a new scheme to put him together with Vivian after enough time had passed for his talk with the colonel. She pushed any vague misgivings about the idea to the back of her mind.

"Lord Cranford has the right of it about the morning, Vivi—it is a fine one," she began casually. "A perfect morning to go sketching down by the lake. Shall we? We have hardly had any chance to indulge ourselves since all these guests arrived. Let us just go off by ourselves—it will only be for a few hours."

If Vivian suspected any ulterior motive, she gave no sign but simply agreed with a nod of her head. Thus it happened that a short while later, Lady Venetia and Lady Vivian set off across the south lawn armed with parasols, sketch pads, and paint boxes, followed by a diligent footman lugging an easel.

They arrived at the edge of Rivington's scenic lake a few minutes later. The lake was manmade; in the previous century a branch of the river had been diverted into a hollow at the foot of the vast, sloping lawns and dammed up. It was quite large enough for boating and other pleasures—it even boasted a pair of small islands. After so many years, it appeared quite natural and was fringed with reeds, yellow flag, and other moisture-loving wildflowers. Venetia studied the scene and frowned.

"No, not here," she decided. "We have painted and sketched this far too many times."

So saying, she marched off again, with Vivian and the footman following in her wake.

"Truly, Netia, what is the matter with any of these places?" Vivian finally said some while later. They had been trudging along the riverbank for quite a distance. "By the time you settle on a spot, we will have no time left for sketching. Have you forgotten the driving race is supposed to begin at one o'clock? We do have to be there to watch the start and finish."

"I have not forgotten." None of these places had yet yielded a certain fisherman. Almost as if she had conjured him, however, Venetia just then caught sight of Lord Cranford peacefully fishing on the riverbank ahead. He appeared to be alone. The simple sight of him caused a small thrill of anticipation to lift her spirits. How was she ever going to rid herself of such reactions?

"Why, look, there is Lord Cranford! Do let us go and see if he has met with any success." She ignored the audible sigh that came from their footman as she set off once again.

More difficult to ignore was the unmistakable expression of dismay on the viscount's face when she hailed him. *Oh dear*. The niggling suspicion that she was making an error suddenly swelled into a full-blown conviction. *Too late now. Nothing for it but to charge ahead*. She armed herself with a devastating smile.

"Why, Lord Cranford, you do not appear pleased to see us. What sort of greeting is that?"

"You truly do not care a fig about fishing, do you, Lady Venetia? Would it matter to you to know that you have in this past minute destroyed anyone's chances of fishing along this stretch of river for the next several hours?"

She knew her smile wobbled. "Why, I don't know how we

could have done that. Certainly that was never our intention."
Dear God, she sounded just like Aunt Alice again. Turning to
the footman, she said, "Here, Robert. This will do nicely. You
may set it up and leave us, thank you."

Cranford sighed. "Trout, my dear woman, are very wary
creatures. Particularly in slower, deep water like this stretch
along here. They hide in under the bank, and any unusual vi-
brations, such as those made by marauding lady artists and
their servants marching along the riverbank, will put them off
feeding for hours until they believe it to be safe again."

"Oh dear. I am truly sorry. We had no idea. Perhaps you
should teach us more about fishing. What do you think, Vivi?"

Vivian had already laid out her sketching materials and had
seated herself on the mossy bank. "I think it is a shame that we
have come all this way to disturb both the fish and Lord Cranford. The least we can do is make an attempt at sketching,
which was supposedly our purpose in coming."

Dear, practical Vivian. There was definitely a hint of irrita-
tion in her voice.

"Perhaps the trout won't stay in hiding as long as you think,
Lord Cranford," Venetia said. They were still talking about
fish, were they not? "If we are quiet, may we stay?"

"It is your riverbank," he replied. He eyed his line and the
perfectly cast fly playing along the surface of the water. "They
say every true fisherman is an optimist. I suppose it is true."

And we are all fishermen of some kind, Venetia thought.

She was not at all comfortable standing near him. The fact
that he was displeased with her did not seem to have any
dampening effect on her feelings. The sunlight made his hair
gleam almost white and her fingers itched to touch it. The
black silk kerchief casually knotted around his neck looked
invitingly soft. His lips . . . Really, she could not just go on
staring at him. Where were her wits?

"Did you have any success with the rest of your morning's
plan? Nicholas mentioned Colonel Hatherwick."

He never took his eyes off the river, which she thought was
just as well. "I had quite a frank conversation with him. He
would be very well pleased to marry either one of you—loves
you both like daughters. He doesn't harbor much hope in
changing that, but assumes he had nothing to lose by putting

his hat in the ring. If he is our blackmailer, he is supremely crafty and a better actor than Kean."

Venetia shook her head. "We have known the colonel for too many years. I cannot imagine that he is anything other than just what he seems."

"After fencing with Lord Chesdale yesterday, I have come to doubt that he is our culprit, either. So you see, we are making some progress."

"What was it about Lord Chesdale?"

"Just an instinct, I suppose. A man's fencing style reveals a good deal about him. His was very honest and straightforward."

She was not quite sure what she thought about that. She settled herself beside her sister and opened the paint box. "That leaves the duke, Lord Munslow, and Lord Newcroft."

Gilbey decided not to tell her that Lord Wistowe was back on the list of suspects. The man's fencing technique had offended Nicholas, and Gilbey had reacted the same way when he had finally faced the man himself in the fifth round. But by all reports, the marquess had treated every one of his opponents the same way, and Gilbey wondered if emotions were coloring his judgment simply because he did not like the man. Would not a blackmailer go to greater lengths to conceal his character?

At any rate, there was no need to alarm the twins any more than they were already. Venetia was acting strangely, and he thought it must be due to growing anxiety over their difficult situation. He must try to keep his mind off her. *It will prove difficult indeed if she keeps showing up wherever I go.*

Quiet descended on the trio for a few minutes until Venetia exclaimed, "Why, Vivian! That is quite lovely. Oh, do come and look, Lord Cranford. She has made a sketch of you fishing."

He sighed in exasperation. "That tears it." He brought in his line and flung down his pole. If the fish had even begun to feel safe again, her noise would have frightened them anew.

"Oh, I'm sorry!" she said, covering her mouth with her hand. He wished she would not do that, for her instinctive action directed his attention where it had no business. He moved toward her and forced himself to look away, down at Vivian's paper.

Her sketch was quite good, and he realized that the twins were endowed with some genuine artistic talent. The riverbank, the water, the willow tree behind him, and his own figure wielding his fishing pole were all there. "You have quite captured me, Lady Vivian," he said warmly, "although I think you have been kind. I see no hint of my slouching posture or the crazed look of hope in my eye."

Vivian laughed. "You do yourself injustice, sir. Had I seen those things, I would most certainly have included them."

He turned to Venetia. "And what have you created in these few minutes?"

She placed her hand over her work for a moment, laughing. "It is not finished!"

He squatted beside her and moved her hand. He compounded that mistake by looking into her eyes. He saw the laughter die out of them.

"Here. It is only this," she said stiffly.

On her pad was a small but perfect copy of a single yellow flag blossom, captured with all its exquisite, intricate detail.

It is lovely, like you, he wanted to say, but he knew he must not. He did not understand her at all. Was she angry that he had touched her? He was well aware of the attentions she had paid to the Duke of Thornborough the previous evening even though the duke was one of the suspects. What was she up to?

"It is lovely," he said. "It almost looks alive, as if one could touch it." He tried to steal another glance into her eyes, but she had turned her face away.

Quite abruptly, she rose, nearly knocking him over in the process. She tore the sheet from the pad and thrust it at him. "Here, you may keep it. I suddenly remember that I am needed at the house before the time for the race."

She gathered her things hastily and turned back to him. "I am certain I can rely on you to help my sister with the easel when she is finished. I will not have time to send out one of the footmen to chase it down." A moment later she was gone.

Gilbey looked at Vivian to see if she was as astonished as he was. She, however, appeared only slightly perturbed, staring down at her drawing.

"You do realize that she has done this on purpose," she said quietly. "It is really very bad of her to leave us alone together like this."

A prickle of sweat started on the back of Gilbey's neck. Venetia had indeed placed him in a deucedly awkward position. If anyone should happen along now and find him with Vivian, their situation would be open to all kinds of misinterpretation. Unchaperoned, in a remote and private spot . . . even his fishing pole offered no excuse, for it was quite obviously cast aside. On the other hand, he could hardly go off and leave her here.

"On purpose, you say?" His mouth was a bit dry. "Uh, to what purpose, might I ask?"

To his intense relief, Vivian was collecting her charcoals and packing them away. "I am beginning to gather that, well, she has an idea that you and I might suit each other, and she is trying to help. She feels compelled to manage my life."

"But, you . . . that is, I . . ." *Botheration*. The dryness in his mouth had developed into true incoherence.

Vivian giggled, which did not exactly make him feel better. Fortunately her words were more comforting.

"I do not think she will send anyone looking for us, if that is what worries you, Lord Cranford. If we start back now, we will be close to the house before anyone is likely to see us. If they do, I shall explain that you met up with me on the way and offered to help with the easel." She glanced up at him with a look of true sympathy. "I—I would never try to trap someone into marrying me. As for my sister and her schemes, you must trust me to take care of that. I hope you will be relieved rather than offended to know that, as much as I like you, I have something—or should I say some*one*?—entirely different in mind."

Chapter Sixteen

"I have learned something interesting," Nicholas told Gilbey in a low voice while they waited for the driving race to begin that afternoon. "We will have to find a moment to speak privately when this is over."

Gilbey nodded, wondering what his friend had accomplished during the morning. They could not speak here, in the midst of a crowd of excited onlookers. "What number did you draw?" he asked, in case anyone took note of their conversation.

"Five. Thornborough will go first. He is using his own equipage."

Nicholas was one of eight contenders in the race. They would each drive the course separately and had drawn lots to determine the order. Rivington servants had been posted at checkpoints along the route to give directions and monitor progress. Whoever had the fastest run would be declared the winner.

"Did you lay any wagers?"

Nicholas chuckled. "What sort of host would I be if I did not? You did so well putting money on Chesdale last time, I have bet on him this time. After all, he obviously has a special talent with horses."

"Ah, but driving is a different skill altogether from riding," Gilbey responded. "I have put a modest sum on Lord Newcroft this time. If anyone is to prove a true whip, I believe it will be he."

Nicholas arched an eyebrow, but before he could reply, his sisters descended upon them. Gilbey felt a familiar jump in his pulse at the sight of Venetia.

"Look, Vivi, here is Nicholas, and Lord Cranford. I am sure

you want to wish them luck," Venetia said, almost literally
steering her twin toward them. "I believe I must have a word
with the Duke of Thornborough before he sets off."

Neatly done, Gilbey thought, suppressing his anger and puzzlement. She had managed that more skillfully than the morning's scheme. He exchanged a glance with Vivian. Venetia
had left her no choice but to speak with them—any other action would have appeared to be a cut direct.

"But I am not racing, Lady Venetia," he said to her retreating back. *Fine, walk away. Just as well,* he told himself. He
did not understand her. Her actions were at odds with everything he sensed about her feelings. But he knew he had no
business being with her anyway.

"What is all abuzz with her?" Nicholas asked, staring after
Venetia with a puzzled expression.

Lady Vivian's words had not stopped echoing in Gilbey's
ears since he had heard them. *She has an idea that you and I
might suit each other, and she is trying to help.* Yet, he was
hardly the model husband they were seeking. He, too, would
have something to tell Nicholas later. He did not appreciate
being made the target of a scheme.

"Never mind," said Vivian. She smiled at Gilbey and then
addressed her brother in soothing tones. "I will wish you luck
at any rate, Nicholas."

"Thank you. I do have an advantage in knowing the roads."

"Do you know what the prize will be? Perhaps you don't
want to win," Gilbey said to cover his turmoil. "I hope your
father is not planning any more surprises."

All three of them laughed, but Gilbey's amusement did not
reach his heart.

A few moments later the crowd around them parted and the
twins' and Nicholas's father strode through. He would give the
signal to start the race. His pocket chronometer would be used
to time each contender's run down to the second. Whip in
hand, the Duke of Thornborough mounted the driver's box of
his glossy, dark green carriage and Gilbey noticed Venetia
giving the duke a sample of her magnificent smile. He turned
away as a stab of jealousy shot through him. Had she allowed
the duke a sample of her kisses? *Devil and damnation!* He had
no business thinking such thoughts. His only comfort was that

Venetia's father could plainly see that he was nowhere near her.

Venetia and Vivian excused themselves from their collected guests once the first two drivers had started off. Lady Caroline's father, Lord Upcott, was using his own equipage also and did not need to wait for the Duke of Thornborough's return. The race would take up a good part of the afternoon, and the twins had some other duties to attend. They would be called when it was time for the winner to be announced.

"It is a blessing that Aunt Alice did not insist on helping us, is it not?" Vivian said as they settled themselves with pen and paper in their private sitting room. "We can plan the treasure hunt better by ourselves."

Venetia shrugged. "Perhaps she or Adela should help. I feel more inclined to curl up for a long sleep than to set my mind on any project. Mayhap when I awake this nightmare will be over."

"Netia! You must not say so." Vivian was all concern upon the instant. " Nicholas and Lord Cranford will help us solve this coil. You must have faith in them!"

Venetia tried to smile. Vivian only knew a fraction of her nightmare. Her twin could not see the anger she was hiding—anger at herself for feeling as she did about Cranford, and anger at how difficult she was finding it to cast aside those feelings and push him and Vivian toward each other. She had made a botch of things this morning. He had not made it any easier by touching her hand and showing interest in her work. At the start of the race she had done a better job, but emotionally it had been no easier. And the prospect of pursuing the Duke of Thornborough depressed her thoroughly.

"We still have a week left, and we shall unmask the black-mailer," Vivian continued. "I had an idea of something we could try that might help."

"Oh?" Venetia simply could not summon the energy to sound enthusiastic.

"If we can get everyone involved in a game of twenty questions and make them write out the questions and answers, we could get a sampling of their handwriting. Maybe we would be able to tell who wrote the blackmail note."

"And who wrote our poems? I doubt it, Vivi. First of all, we'd have to insist that they print."

"We could do that."

"What would prevent the blackmailer, or for that matter our poet, from disguising his writing? I just don't see how it would help."

"Well, perhaps it would stir someone up, make him afraid that we were getting too close to him. Perhaps it would move him to do something more, something that would then give him away. What can we lose by trying?" Vivian was impervious to Venetia's doldrums.

"All right."

"We cannot do it tonight, for Aunt Alice has planned the musicale. But perhaps tomorrow night, after the treasure hunt."

"All right."

"Really, Netia! You are blue-deviled." Vivian looked at her closely, as if somehow she might determine visually the true cause of Venetia's state. "Have you the headache? You have not taken a chill, have you?"

Venetia shook her head. "I am sorry, Vivi. I am fine. Perhaps a bit tired. About the treasure hunt?" She dipped the pen in the ink pot and held it poised above the paper.

"The treasure hunt. First, we must think of all the things that might be found in a garden . . ."

Venetia closed her eyes. What might be found in a garden was a beautiful man with hair like pale silver staring up at a canopy of flowers . . . or making her feel loved and desired with his gentle kisses. . . .

"Netia, you are not listening. I asked if you thought it would place the peacocks in jeopardy to put one of their feathers on the list."

"I'm sorry. Yes, I do. We don't want the guests to terrorize them, and from what I have seen, some of our dear guests would not shrink from chasing the poor creatures and plucking the feathers out themselves."

Vivian giggled. "Oh, but think of the terrible noise the birds would make. They have really been quite good this week. I have not heard of anyone being frightened out of their wits by awful shrieking sounds."

Venetia actually found a small smile in answer. "That is true. Perhaps instead we could put the topiary peacock on the list. We could put a dish full of pebbles at the base, and they would have to bring back a pebble to prove that they'd found it."

"That is excellent. You see? We shall just keep working on the list until we have enough ideas. You will fight off this megrim."

Venetia sighed deeply. "I suppose I will." Perhaps she would at least reach a point where she would have enough energy to hide it. She really did not know what else she could do.

The final results of the race were very close to call. Lord Newcroft, Lord Lindell, and Lord Munslow led the rest with times that were less than minutes apart. Thanks to the accuracy of the Duke of Roxley's chronometer, however, it was clear that Lord Newcroft had won. Amid the general clamor and congratulations, Gilbey felt quite pleased.

"You devil," Nicholas teased, finding him at the edge of the crowd. "How did you know that he would win?"

"Simple logic, dear friend. I reasoned that if he was really as ambitious in character as we have said, he would have made certain to develop all the skills of a notable whip—you know, absolute proficiency in anything at all valued by the *haut monde*. What I wagered on was actually our assessment of him as much as his skill."

"So, you believe he is our man? Well, walk with me and we'll pop inside. What I tell you may make you less certain."

"I want to know, but I must collect my winnings first. Have you paid Lord Munslow yet for your loss?"

"Botheration!" Nicholas laughed at his own reaction. "Now I begin to sound like you!"

A number of gentlemen were gathered around Lord Munslow, paying or collecting their bets. The earl shrugged off their teasing with apparent ease.

"By Jove, didn't know you were so handy with the ribbons, Munslow," someone said. "Thought wagering was your only sport!"

"Surprised you, eh? I'm full of surprises."

"You and young Lindell both gave the little viscount a run

for his money. Expect he wasn't counting on either of you to show so well."

"Well, His Grace the old duke ain't well pleased with how he did. Nose a bit out of joint that his splendid animals didn't take the day."

"Takes more than the animals to do that," someone snickered.

"Where's Lord Wistowe? Here, I'm surprised you weren't racing, sir."

Wistowe answered in a lazy drawl. "Never claimed to be any good on the box. The way I see it, why waste time whipping up some cattle when you could be spending time with the ladies?"

Amid the laughter that followed this, Gilbey and Nicholas took care of their transactions and slipped out of the circle.

"I spent some time talking with our servants this morning while you were out fishing," Nicholas said as they walked toward the house. If he had any inkling that Gilbey had been with his sisters, he gave no clue of it. "What I learned is actually something about Lord Munslow."

Gilbey did not express his surprise until after they had entered the huge hall and gone through into a small anteroom that opened off one side. Nicholas closed the door behind them.

"I thought it might be helpful just to ask the staff in general about our guests—whether any of them showed any particular eccentricities that our family should know about. Our servants are trained to be discreet, and it took a little convincing to get them to open up to me. I had to remind them that two of these guests will end up as husbands to my sisters if my father gets his way. That loosened a few tongues."

Nicholas's plain statement of the facts made Gilbey shift uncomfortably. He glanced about him, taking in the gilt work that seemed to be the chief feature of the room. Every stick of furniture was gilded, as was every inch of plaster ornamentation on walls, ceiling, mantel, doorcases. "And?"

"Lord Munslow has made himself rather unpopular, it seems, by his regular failure to pay tips for any of the special services our servants have provided for him."

"Perhaps he is simply going to pay them all a handsome vail at the end of his stay."

"Perhaps. But I rather thought it smacked of a man who is either a pinchpenny or nearly rolled up. No one else has so distinguished himself."

"Going back to lack of funds as a motive?"

"Precisely."

"Well! We don't seem to lack for motives, do we? Thornborough has his age and his pride, Newcroft has his competitive ambitions, and Munslow may be dished up unbeknownst to us all. I don't take Wistowe seriously as a suspect, Nicholas. I think we just don't like the man. He's a bounder, but not a blackmailer."

"I suppose I agree, but you know that I don't like to take too much simply on faith. We are dealing with my sisters' futures here."

"Oh, I know." *Trust me, how well I know.* Gilbey hoped the pain he felt did not show on his face.

"We will have to find a moment to tell them this latest tidbit," Nicholas said.

"Ah. I had best leave that to you, my friend. Your father has made it abundantly clear that he does not want me near your sister Venetia." Gilbey opened his mouth to say more, then closed it. Somehow it felt wrong just now to betray what Vivian had told him about Venetia's scheme. *Trust me,* she had said. Apparently she had some kind of plan. Very well, then. He would give her some time.

"Talking to servants is something we might want to do a bit more of," he said instead, steering the conversation back to the blackmail investigation. "Ever since we visited Colby Compton I have been thinking about ways the knowledge of your sister's condition could have become known. We have not found any direct and obvious links between our suspects and Vivian, but perhaps the link we seek is more subtle. I thought some conversations with the servants who came with our guests might be helpful."

"Good idea. Thornborough brought at least four with him. Most have brought maids or valets, and a few brought their own grooms. The stables would be a good place to start."

Nicholas rubbed his chin thoughtfully. "You say my father

put in a word with you, did he? I didn't think he was paying enough attention to know you have been near Venetia."

"Ha. I believe your father knows twice as much as you, Nicholas. Do not underestimate him."

"He does not know about the blackmail attempt."

"Hm. As far as we know, but even now I begin to wonder," Gilbey replied. "I doubt I have ever met such a confounded family full of schemers. How did I ever let you talk me into coming here?"

Gilbey managed to avoid both of the twins for the remainder of the day. He felt as though he and Venetia were engaged in a silent game, each trying to attain opposite goals. Each time she made some move designed to put him in company with her sister, he had to make a counter move. At dinner he had to convince Lord Lindell to trade seats with him; during the musicale that evening he had to ask Lord Ashurst to take his place to turn pages for Lady Vivian at the pianoforte. When the company was invited to sing, he had to maneuver a different place to stand from the one Venetia tried to assign to him.

Was she testing him again? Was it really all a game? He did not think so. He sensed something was wrong—there was no light in Venetia's eyes, and although he heard other people's laughter from time to time, he never once heard hers. He would have defied her father to demand an explanation except for one thing—he happened to think that her father was right. If he did not want a wife, what business had he with her? If he *did* want a wife, still what business had he with her? He could not provide a proper life for the daughter of a duke. He needed to stay away from her, for both their sakes.

On Saturday he thought his job of staying away from the twins would be easier. The list for the treasure hunt was long and quite clever, and the participants in the hunt were encouraged to go about in pairs—ladies paired with ladies, of course. Most of the men preferred to work alone, Gilbey included, and he thought in the vast Rivington gardens it would not be difficult to avoid company altogether.

Indeed, once the group scattered into the various pathways and terraces, he began to find the event entertaining. He took himself off to one of the higher terraces, where he could command a view of the gardens spread below him. There he watched the ladies in their colorful muslins traipse to and fro, looking like flowers themselves with their matching parasols, frowning at their lists or laughing in delight when they achieved some success. Snatches of their conversations floated up to him: "A pink rose, a cream rose, a rose the color of blood . . ." "Stone stairs six in number . . . drat, these are only four! Now where . . . ?"

The men wandered about like independent shadows in their darker colors, occasionally meeting up and comparing notes. "How many fish did you count in the lily pool? Felt like a damn fool sitting there counting 'em . . ."

Gilbey felt relieved to put his mind to something besides the crop of troubles he had found at Rivington. He had already observed a number of the items on the list during previous walks in the garden. He knew that what was missing from the statue of Venus was her hand, and he knew the inscription on the sundial in the sundial court. "Love always" was part of it. He did not agree.

He filled in all the information that he could without having to circulate through the gardens, and then plotted a route that would move him through efficiently. He could count most of the fountains from his present vantage point, but he had never gone into the walled garden, and he did not know how many fountains, if any, might be there. That was also the location of the topiary peacock that had been endangered during the archery contest. A pass through there would bring him out by the pergola covered with Venetia's prized wisteria. She had said the set of vines were her father's pet and had been loved by her mother, but in his mind he would always connect them with her. Surely it was the only answer to "a tender climbing Chinese flower." He doubted many of the others would solve that one.

He found that the walled garden had no fountain at all, for it was designed like an Elizabethan knot garden in a geometric pattern, with neat gravel paths all bordered with boxwood. He retrieved a pebble from the topiary peacock, and let himself out by the old wooden arched door in the crumbling side wall. The door swung outward and almost knocked Venetia off her feet. He was so stunned to find her there that for a moment he just stood.

"My God, Venetia! Are you all right?" he blurted out when he found his tongue. "I did not expect anyone to be there."

She gave him a smile that was definitely sad. He felt his heart turn over. Should he shake her with anger or comfort her in his arms?

"I expected to find you here," she said.

"Did you, by George! What were you doing here, waiting for me?" Another scheme. Anger was edging out comfort.

"Yes." She had the nerve to speak plainly, but at least it was the truth.

"I am surprised you did not try to substitute your sister."

"I am constantly surprised by the way you know which one of us is which."

"How did you know I would come here?"

"You are the only one who knows about the flowers. No one else has noticed them or cared to ask. I put the clue on the list quite purposely."

He was strongly tempted to walk away. He knew he ought to walk away. But his feet seemed to be rooted to the ground as firmly as the vines around him. "All right, I am here."

She looked down and took a few steps along the pathway before turning back to him, almost as if she were embarrassed. "It seemed the only way. About my sister . . ."

"Yes, what about your sister? She has a mind of her own, and so do I, yet you seem intent on pushing us together. Why do you insist on meddling?"

She seemed taken aback by his aggressive response. *Good. Make her think.*

"I thought I explained before. I must make sure she finds a good husband. Her need is greater than mine . . ."

"And you decided since I was not a blackmailer I would make her a good husband? Did it ever occur to you that I might have some feelings about that?"

"Yes! Yes, of course. That is why we are here talking . . . You have been doing all you can to avoid both of us. I just thought, if you got to know her, if you would spend a little time with her, perhaps you might discover that you cared for her! Perhaps you would find the idea of marriage less displeasing . . . Oh, why will you not consider it?"

She looked straight up at him in her desperate appeal, and he found that he could not stay angry. She looked so beautiful standing under the flowery canopy. The leaves and blossoms threw a lacy pattern of sunlight over her. "Light and shade by turns, but love always," said the words on the sundial.

He did not realize he had said them aloud until he saw the look of utter surprise and then wariness on her face.

"Love is the thing," he explained quickly. "Your sister needs someone who can and will love her. I cannot be that man."

"But why? I mean, how do you know? How can you say that, when you haven't even tried?"

Because, he suspected, it was already too late—he had already given his heart to her. But he would not say that. "I am not a suitable match for either of you, as your father would be the first to tell you," he said instead. "In fact he has warned me to keep away from you. There are other reasons . . ."

"Will you not tell me what they are?" she asked very quietly.

He sighed. Maybe he should. "My own father . . ." he began, but at that moment they heard laughter. Lord Munslow and Lady Norbridge came around the corner at the far end of the pathway that led under the pergola.

"Why, I do believe it is Lord Cranford with one of our hostesses," Lady Norbridge proclaimed cheerfully. "I won't even try to guess which twin you are from this distance. I suppose you're going to say you are comparing your lists."

Chapter Seventeen

"Not at all, Lady Norbridge," Venetia said quickly. "I am not playing the game—how should I, when I made up the list? But Lord Cranford chanced to stop me in passing to ask a question . . ."

Lady Norbridge narrowed her eyes. "Of course. Lady Venetia, is it not? You are always so smooth. Well, never fear, we shall say nothing. How should we? After all, we are out here unchaperoned as well!" She laughed as if that were a supremely humorous jest.

As if you needed a chaperon, Venetia thought. She could easily have shot the older woman at that moment. Whatever Cranford had been about to reveal might be exceedingly important to her future and Vivian's, if it helped her to understand him. At least Lord Munslow looked a bit embarrassed and uncomfortable, which Venetia counted in his favor. But the moment between her and Cranford was lost. She only hoped she could find another such opportunity to speak with him in the days ahead.

The opportunity presented itself with surprising ease the following afternoon. Most of the party had gone with the St. Aldwyns into Withington to attend the parish church there, and had spent the early afternoon walking, writing letters, or pursuing other quiet Sunday pastimes. In the late afternoon, plans were made to go punting on Rivington's small lake.

Venetia thought she could go with Lord Cranford—if she could convince him to accompany her—and still go out a second time with the Duke of Thornborough, as there were not enough punts to accommodate all of the guests at once. The trick was getting a chance to speak to Cranford before he invited one of the other ladies.

"Please, Vivian, you must help," she begged as the twins walked across the lawn down to the water. "I know he will try to avoid me. He and I were interrupted in the middle of a very important conversation yesterday—we must finish it!"

"This is a switch," Vivian said wryly. "I thought you would be asking me to go in the boat with him." She was reluctant to be part of a new scheme, but after a little more begging, she agreed.

As it happened, Gilbey was in the process of asking Lady Caroline when Vivian stopped him. "I was under the impression that you had promised my sister," she said with a perfect mix of puzzlement and reproval in her voice. Behind her, Lord Chesdale expressed an interest in asking Lady Caroline.

Gilbey had no recourse without being rude; he could no more contradict Lady Vivian than he could insist upon taking Lady Caroline after Lord Chesdale spoke. The twins and Fate had outmaneuvered him.

"Am I to be delivered on a plate?" he asked Vivian as they walked toward her twin.

Color flooded into her face, the first time he had seen either of the twins blush. It was very becoming.

"I am sorry," she said. "She only wants to talk with you— she said something about an interrupted conversation."

He groaned. "Your father will be very displeased when he learns about this."

They were close enough so that Venetia heard his remark. "Everyone can see that this was not your idea." She glanced about, looking a bit embarrassed. "You look like a prisoner being marched to his execution. Truly, I did not know I was such an antidote."

Hardly an antidote, Gilbey thought. *More like a beautiful thief who has stolen my heart.* She looked resplendent in a dress of sky blue muslin with a spencer in a darker shade of the same hue worn over it. A modestly proportioned straw cottage hat with a brim that dipped artfully in front emphasized her eyes. Admiring her, he revised his thought. Maybe he was a prisoner, after all—captivated by her charms. But God help him, he could not say that to her.

"Well, never mind," she said, clearly piqued when he did not answer her comment. "This may not require much of your time."

Gilbey assisted her into the punt, marveling at how such casual contact between them could affect him so much. Fire spread from his fingertips through all his veins. Just looking at her seated in the little boat set off a craving that nothing could fulfill.

She said nothing as he poled them out from the shore. Other punts were still near them and the occupants could be heard laughing and talking. A few of the gentlemen were not used to punting and had trouble controlling their boats, spinning round in circles to the amusement of the others. No stranger to punting on the river in Cambridge, Gilbey soon had their boat out and away from the crowd.

"This is a peaceful spot," he said, smiling and giving an extra push to their pole. "Where to, milady?"

"Let us stay within sight of the others, but out of earshot—can you do that?" she asked. When he nodded she appeared to relax somewhat.

"I know what you must think of me," she began. "Meddling, managing, manipulative—all most unflattering to a female. I hope you can understand me a little—at least you know the reason for the things I do. I had hoped to understand you a little, also. You were talking about the reasons why you wish to postpone marriage when we were interrupted yesterday. You mentioned your father."

Perhaps if he explained, she would leave him alone. The thought of her turning her attention to the other gentlemen depressed him, but that was the way things must be. Looking out across the tranquil surface of the lake, he let the punt drift.

"My father must have been very passionate and romantic as a young man," he said. "He fell in love with a Scottish woman whom he desired above all else, and when neither of their families approved of their match, they eloped." He felt oddly detached, telling the story as if it were about someone he hardly knew. "He brought his wife to his home in England, and they had two children, a pair of twins. The mother pined for her homeland and taught her children Scottish songs. When this boy and girl were eight, she died in childbirth."

He took a deep breath. "Their father was so grief-stricken, they might as well have been orphaned. He all but turned his back on them. It was if the father's spirit had gone with the mother. Because the relatives were estranged, the children hardly knew anyone. They grew up without any parent's loving guidance."

Her eyes were dark with sympathy. "What happened to them?"

God help him, if only she would not look at him like that! He tore his gaze away from hers, back out across the water. They were very slowly making their way around one of the small islands in the lake.

"The girl grew up full of romantical notions, and when her time came to marry, she ran away to Scotland, to an aunt she had never met. Luckily for her, she met a man along the way who fell in love with her. They are married and have two children, and she is just as full of romantical notions as she ever was."

"What about the boy?"

"He sees all the pain and suffering the parents' love created. He will not make the same mistake."

"Mistake?"

"To marry for love. Now do you understand?"

He risked another look down at her. She nodded silently, staring down at her hands in her lap. She looked so dejected, he wanted nothing more than to take her in his arms. He gave the pole a mighty heave and sent the punt skimming out beyond the shadow of the willow trees on the island.

Past the trees, the lake seemed enchanted. The late-afternoon sun shone brightly on the water, shimmering and sparkling, dancing on the surface. The ripples from the small flotilla of punts plying the water multiplied the magical effect.

"Look," he said, hoping the beauty would offer her some of the comfort he could not.

She raised her head, but her reaction was not what he expected. "Oh my God," she said, her eyes widening with what could only be alarm. "Vivian. Where is Vivian?" With one hand shielding her eyes, she began to scan the other boats.

"What is it?" he asked, thoroughly puzzled. "She is with Ashurst."

She gestured impatiently with her hand. "The light. The bright sunlight. It could trigger a seizure. Abrupt changes in light often affect her that way." She was agitated now, twisting about in the boat.

"All right," he said decisively. "Sit still. We'll find them." He was beginning to understand a little himself. The light, the thunderstorms that one day. Venetia was reacting now with the same urgent restlessness as she had that morning when she learned Vivian had gone riding. He pushed the pole repeatedly, moving the punt much faster.

"I don't see them," Venetia moaned. "They must still be behind one of the islands."

"If they are, then she will still be all right, will she not?"

He had brought the punt around in a wide circle, and now started back toward the islands again. He saw Ashurst just as the other punt emerged from the shadows.

"There they are."

"Please, hurry."

"Can you tell if she is starting a seizure?"

"It is not always obvious, but there are signs. She will know. We will have to land on the island. I'll need to get her out of sight under the trees. I don't know what we can say to explain."

"We'll think of that later. You just do whatever you need to."

Vivian was trembling all over by the time they reached her. Ashurst was headed for the island but he looked relieved to see help arriving.

"We're having a bit of a problem here," he said. The grayness of his face and the white knuckles of his hands gripping the pole betrayed his worry.

"Just land us on the island," Venetia commanded. "I will take care of her. She'll be all right."

They landed the boats and Venetia hustled her sister into the center of the island, where the brush and willows offered protective shelter.

Ashurst looked at Gilbey. "What is it? Some kind of fit?"

Gilbey hesitated. It was not his right to tell, but the man deserved some word of explanation. How would Ashurst react? He nodded. "Lady Vivian has epilepsy."

Ashurst looked away, obviously shaken. "Epilepsy. Dear God."

Gilbey gave him a minute and then stepped over to him. The island was too overgrown to allow them to walk about. "I'm certain you understand how much they will appreciate your discretion about this. They need our help."

"Our help," the marquess echoed woodenly. "Yes, of course."

"Here, look about you. Pick some of these flowers, as many as you can. I think that will have to be our excuse for stopping—that the ladies wanted to pick these. We'll need enough of them to justify the time."

Ashurst still stood there like a man whose whole future has been wrested from him without warning. Gilbey supposed that if Ashurst had been entertaining visions of marriage to Vivian, this revelation might indeed feel like that. How unfair life could be!

He turned and snapped a few flower stems with unnecessary violence. "Here," he said, thrusting the stalks at Ashurst.

The movement required to accept the flowers seemed to bring the marquess back to life. "Yes, all right," he said. Glancing toward the willows, he began to pick the flowers around him. Then he stopped again. "How long?" he asked Gilbey. There was no mistaking the agony in his eyes.

Gilbey had no answer to give him. Spreading his hands apart in a helpless gesture, all he could say was, "I don't know, my friend. I don't know."

Venetia prayed that Vivian's seizure would prove to be a short one. Over and over she chastised herself for failing to realize that going on the lake would be a risk for her sister. Never before in the past six years had they come so close to disaster. More than a dozen people had almost witnessed the attack. But even more frightening was that if she and Cranford had not come in time, if no island had been close at hand, Vivian could easily have fallen from the boat and drowned during her seizure.

She glanced at her twin still trembling in the throes of the paroxysm, curled in a frightened ball, muttering unintelligible sounds. In a few moments more it should be over, but how

many minutes would the recovery require? She could not bring
Vivian out while she was still staring into space and disoriented. Even without that, Venetia hardly knew what she could
say to Lord Ashurst.

Tell the truth, came that voice inside her head. She supposed there was no other choice this time. Would he agree not
to tell others? Would he take the entire family in disgust and
leave? Almost as difficult, what would she tell Vivian? Her
sister would know that she'd had a seizure, even though she
would not remember what had happened. If Vivian thought
Cranford and Ashurst had witnessed the attack, she would be
too mortified to face them again.

Please, God, give me the strength to see this through. Venetia was beginning to feel overwhelmed by too many things to
balance, too many truths that had to be hidden. She felt like a
mule struggling to pull a load up a steep mountain while the
forces of gravity worked harder and harder against her.

Deciding to speak with Ashurst while her sister could not
hear them, she emerged from under the trees and found the
two men armed with huge bunches of flowers. Cranford presented his to her with a bow.

"Lady Venetia. We thought picking flowers an exemplary
reason for coming ashore. Since you stayed with your sister
while she was resting, we did the picking for you both."

Unexpected tears of gratitude sprang into her eyes. So simply he had smoothed it all over! Excuses enough to cover for
everyone, from her sister to the marquess even to the rest of
the guests. She felt a lump form in her throat. What woman
could not want such a man! He had been calm and supportive
in her crisis, yet had acted with quick efficiency. He was kind
and aware and more handsome than an archangel—how foolish he was to think he could ever have a marriage without
love!

But Ashurst was looking at her questioningly, and she knew
she must tell him something. She swallowed with difficulty.
"My sister will be fine—she needs a few more minutes." This
was difficult, and she looked down at the flowers clutched in
her hands. "This doesn't happen very often. It was coming into
the bright sunlight that set it off. She had one that day we went
into the long barrow, too. I should have known."

"How could you have known? Do you expect to be omniscient?" Cranford protested, but she ignored him.

"Has she always been like this?" asked Lord Ashurst.

Venetia shook her head. "There was a carriage accident six years ago. Our mother was killed. Vivian's head was injured but she recovered almost fully." She lifted her head. "Please, do not say anything to her about it. And I must beg you to say nothing to anyone else."

Ashurst gave his word and Venetia returned to Vivian's side. A few minutes later both twins rejoined the gentlemen.

"They have been picking the flowers we wanted, Vivi, while you rested," Venetia told her. She saw the lines of concern ease in her sister's face.

"Of course, now we must hurry back to the house, must we not?" Cranford said. "I assume you will want to put these into water."

She nodded, unable to speak past the lump that had reformed in her throat. As the four of them returned to their boats, she heard Vivian exclaim over the flowers and Ashurst ask, "Are you feeling more rested now, Lady Vivian?"

Vivi's reply was too soft for Venetia to hear, but there was no mistaking the questioning look she shot at her afterward as she settled herself in Ashurst's punt. Venetia was thankful that she would have a little time to decide just what she should tell her sister.

Chapter Eighteen

Sunday's events left Venetia more determined than ever to match Cranford with Vivian, despite troublesome doubts that occasionally assailed her. What could make more sense than joining together two people whom she loved? She had come to accept that she did love Cranford, but dwelling on that truth brought her nothing but heartache.

He had proved how well suited he was temperamentally to be a husband for her sister by the marvelous way he had smoothed over Vivian's problem on Sunday afternoon. His assertion that he didn't want a marriage based on love gave her hope that he might agree to such a marriage. Perhaps he would come to love Vivian in time.

How she would convince him to agree to such a marriage still escaped her. He was handsome and in all ways wonderful—he could marry anyone he wished. He was young—ten years from now he would still be considered prime marriage material. How unfair it was that women did not have that advantage! But he was not likely to have another chance to wed a duke's daughter, or any other woman with so large a dowry. And surely Vivian could make him happy. Such a future would be better than the kind of uncaring union he apparently envisioned for himself.

Venetia accepted that Vivian did not love him. Her twin at least liked and admired him, and that was enough. Love might come later. With such a foundation, love had a better chance to grow than if Vivian were forced to marry someone for whom she felt nothing. Why should they both have to suffer that fate?

However, determination was one thing, success quite another. Neither the viscount nor Vivian cooperated with Venetia's aim over the next several days. Despite her assurances to her sister that no one had witnessed anything more than the beginning signs of her seizure on Sunday, Vivian renewed old habits, blaming her nerves or her need to rest as a frequent excuse to withdraw from company or refrain from activities. Cranford now seemed determined to avoid both of the twins, and Venetia was lucky if she caught sight of him, never mind having a chance to speak with him.

She thought about him constantly. She could not keep her mind on anything else, for she was always watching in case he should appear. When she complained of his neglect to Nicholas, her brother shrugged and replied that he and Cranford were still working hard to unmask the blackmailer.

She learned from Nicholas that the gentlemen had begun to lay wagers on whom she and her sister would choose as mates by the end of the week. She was not pleased to discover through her maid that a similar betting book had been opened among the men servants. How could any of them guess what she might do when she herself had no idea? She decided to devote her attention to someone different on each of the remaining days, and wondered maliciously what effect that would have on the betting odds.

The party rolled on regardless of Venetia's emotional state. There was a boxing match on Monday, and on Tuesday the ladies went on a shopping expedition into Cheltenham while the gentlemen hunted hares in the hills around Rivington. Aunt Alice had decreed that on Wednesday evening there was to be a grand extravaganza—a show that would feature the many talents of the guests—and that had set them all in more of a stir than anything else that had happened since their arrival. Most of the purchases in Cheltenham were fabrics and paints for costumes and other decorations required for the performances.

Nicholas and Gilbey continued to dig for information about the suspect guests. They held quiet conversations with servants and asked what they hoped were unobtrusive questions. Reluctant to discuss their employers, the servants were more forthcoming about their fellows, but little useful information was revealed. Gilbey hoped that he would have a reply to his letter to London very soon since he had made clear the urgent need for speed.

On Wednesday morning Rivington was all abuzz with preparations for the evening's entertainment. Servants scurried to and fro, some busy helping the guests while others were assigned to transform the grand salon into what could pass for a small theater with separate areas for the stage and audience. With no plan as to how he would participate, Gilbey sought to escape the hubbub by slipping out to the stables and arranging to go riding.

One of the Rivington grooms approached him as soon as he appeared in the stable entrance.

"Thomas, isn't it?" Gilbey greeted him. "Good morning."

The man respectfully doffed his hat. "Morning, milord. Beggin' pardon, if I might have a word?" He hesitated until Gilbey nodded. "I remember you were asking some questions t'other day. Might be I've thought of something."

Gilbey gave the man his full attention. "Of course. Here, let us step out of the way. There's a shilling in it, or maybe more, if the information is useful."

"One of the guests, Lord Munslow—we were noting that he didn't bring his own groom with him, though many of the others did. Somebody wondered at it—said as how he had a groom that used to work here and wouldn't you think the fellow'd want to come back to see his old friends."

Gilbey felt his pulse leap. "Anyone remember how long ago the fellow left here?" If it was more than six years, the coincidence would still signify nothing.

"Don't know, milord. I can ask."

"Here's for your trouble so far," Gilbey said, giving Thomas the shilling. "I want to know if it was before or after your mistress died."

Gilbey decided that he would search out Nicholas to share this development instead of riding. He returned to the house, but as luck would have it, ran into his dinner partner, the baroness, Lady FitzHarris.

"Oo-ooh, Lord Cranford," she exclaimed, sounding rather as if someone were squeezing the air out of her. "You could be just the man we need! Pray tell me, what are you doing for the extravaganza tonight? Have you something marvelous all planned and ready?"

Gilbey felt a bit uneasy about where this was leading, but what could he say? "To tell the truth, Lady FitzHarris, I plan to do what I do best, namely to show my talent for observation by sitting in the audience and watching everyone else."

Lady FitzHarris chortled. "Oh dear, no, sir, that will never do! I'm certain that is not allowed."

"Why, someone has to be in the audience," he answered reasonably.

The plump baroness chuckled again. He didn't remember her being so prone to giggling on his other occasions in her company. "We will all be in the audience, silly!" she said. "We will only go up when it is our turn to perform."

She took his arm and began to propel him along the corridor. "This is too perfect, it is no doubt meant to be. We just needed one more man for our ensemble piece, and here you are. There is still time to have you fitted for a costume."

Gilbey prayed that Nicholas or someone might appear to rescue him from this situation as he journeyed through Rivington in the clutches of Lady FitzHarris, but he was not so lucky. The first St. Aldwyn he laid eyes on was Venetia when they arrived in the blue drawing room. Unfortunately, he clearly could not appeal to her for help, for she was the exact person to whom he was being delivered.

"Lady Venetia has very kindly gathered all of us who had not the slightest idea what to do and has organized our transformation into a group of dancing cards. Is that not clever? Instead of dance cards! We'll be dancing playing cards, you see?"

Gilbey's gaze had locked with Venetia's and he barely heard Lady FitzHarris at all. He had worked so hard to stay away from Venetia for the past two days, hoping that among other things his ardor would cool without the constant stimulus of her presence. Now in the space of an instant he was cast back into the fire. *Devil and damnation!* Would he never break free of her spell?

Venetia colored under his gaze and was the first to pull her eyes away. "Lady FitzHarris, please!" she said in a rather strangled tone. "I do not think we can force Lord Cranford against his will. He looks quite angry enough to scatter our cards to kingdom come."

"O-oh," responded the baroness, no longer giggling. "Come now, Lord Cranford, do say you will help us. You are not angry, are you? How could you possibly decline the honor of assisting your two hostesses and the Duchess of Brancaster, not to mention Lady Caroline Sainsberry, Lady Sibbingham, and myself? You will be in fine company with our other gentlemen!"

How could he decline indeed? He glanced up at the fancifully decorated ceiling, but found no answer there. *Dancing playing cards. In company with both twins.* Nicholas would owe him some new favors by the time this gathering was over—that is, if he survived.

An hour later Gilbey was released, all measured and rehearsed and assigned the role of the ace of clubs. He resumed his original errand, searching for Nicholas. He found him in the tapestry room, where a luncheon buffet of cold food had been set out for any who wished midday refreshment.

"I have news," he said without preamble, taking the empty chair beside his friend.

"So have I," Nicholas answered. "Where have you been? I have been looking for you.

Gilbey groaned. "Would that you had found me! Some shred of my dignity might have been saved. Instead I am sentenced to perform this evening as a playing card—the ace of clubs, no less—in your sister's dance performance."

Nicholas laughed. "Blame my aunt—the show was her idea. I have mail for you—from London, and franked by the new Marquess of Radclyffe. Reaching inside his coat, he produced the thin paper packet.

All else dropped from Gilbey's attention as he broke the seal and removed the cover. Inside he found two letters, one the awaited answer from his brother-in-law, and the other a note from his sister Gillian.

He scanned the first letter eagerly. "This is it," he said excitedly, lowering his voice. His brother-in-law had reported various bits of information, some of it irrelevant, but the passage that caught his eye read:

What I have learned about Lord Munslow is not generally known and in fact quite surprised me. He is
renowned as a gamester and is generally assumed to be
plump in the pockets, for he lives well, pays his vowels
promptly, and never blinks an eye at his losses. Discreet
inquiries in some unorthodox avenues known to me
have revealed that his pockets are in fact quite to let—he
hasn't a feather to fly with. How he manages to go on I
can't begin to imagine.

I can, thought Gilbey, clenching his jaw. *At least, I can
now*. Wordlessly he handed the letter to Nicholas. He folded
Gillian's letter and put it in his pocket to be read later.

Nicholas whistled. "Munslow! I never thought it. Why, I'd
like to—"

"Nicholas," Gilbey said. "We must continue to be unobtrusive. Come with me—we must go to the stables."

"What was your news?"

"You'll see. I think we're about to receive more."

They hurried to the stableyard and were fortunate not to run
into anyone on their way there. Gilbey inquired for Thomas
and quickly located the young man.

"I'm certain you have been busy with your duties," he said,
"but have you had any time to look into that other question for
me? The answer has become more important than ever."

The groom looked surprised. "Why, yes, milord. I sent a
message up to the house asking a word with you."

Gilbey smiled ruefully. "Of course. You see, Nicholas?
Even the servants couldn't find me in the clutches of those
confounded women."

The groom's face remained perfectly unexpressive except
for a slight twitch at the corner of his mouth.

"Go ahead, Thomas, tell us what you learned."

He looked apologetically at Nicholas. "Beggin' pardon, my
lord, to have to speak of this. Seems the fellow that works for
Lord Munslow left just a month or so after Her Grace was
killed in that accident . . ." He wrung his cap as if he would
say more.

"It's all right, Thomas," Nicholas reassured him. "Lord
Cranford knows about Lady Vivian. Was it then that the fel-

low left? There were a few who quit us at that time—you were not here then, were you?"

"That's right, my lord."

"There's the link then," Gilbey said with satisfaction. "We've nearly got him. Thank you, Thomas." He flipped the man a half crown. "Share that as seems fitting, will you?"

"Well done, Thomas," Nicholas added.

They headed for the gardens rather than the house. When they were far enough from the stable block for privacy, Nicholas slowed his steps. "What did you mean, 'nearly got him'? We've got a foolproof motive and the opportunity for him to come by the information. We haven't got that for any of the others. It has to be him."

"Oh, I don't question that, my friend. What we don't have is proof. I've got to go to London. The only other question I have now is, do we tell your sisters? If Munslow catches a hint that we're on to him before I can get back, there's no saying what may happen."

"Venetia is a better actress than Vivian."

How well Gilbey knew that! He gave Nicholas a funny look, but his friend did not notice.

"We cannot tell one and not the other. I'd say we should wait until Saturday," the duke's son concluded.

"Your sister and the other ladies will be lined up to kill me if I leave for London before this evening's performance," Gilbey said. "You've no idea how much I would like to do so, nonetheless. I hate to lose the time, but it might also seem suspicious. I will have to leave in the morning as soon as it gets light."

Nicholas nodded. "I'll see to all the arrangements."

That night the usual after-dinner rituals were given over to readying the show. Gilbey stood in the blue drawing room wearing a long black-and-white tunic over his clothes, a tabard of heavy, starched cotton painted to look like the ace of clubs hanging down from his shoulders. Petite Lady Caroline stood on a chair positioning a pasteboard crown adorned with black painted trefoils on his head.

"My goodness but you are tall," she said. "You do look splendid!"

"I feel like I'm wearing a dress," Gilbey said irritably, plucking at his long tunic. Lord Newcroft and Lord Lindell, similarly dressed, were conversing in another corner of the room and apparently heard this remark, for they chuckled sympathetically.

He forgot his annoyance a moment later when Venetia came into the room. She wore a stunning gown of black, white, and silver with black velvet spades stitched on around the hem. A dramatic headdress in the same colors concealed all but a few wisps of her golden hair and was topped by a crown covered in silver foil and ornamented with more spades.

"Lady Caroline, allow me to do that," she said, coming toward him. "You must have time to finish dressing yourself. You will look so lovely."

The other young woman relinquished the chair and Venetia climbed up on it carefully. "It won't do to treat these costumes as ordinary clothing," she said. "They have been basted together so quickly, they will fall apart at the slightest excuse."

"That would be a shame," Gilbey couldn't help saying. "You make an exquisite queen of spades."

He could not see her face from where he stood, but he felt her hands hesitate. She was only inches from him and her delicate scent invaded his senses. He forced himself to stand perfectly still.

She made one more adjustment to his crown and for a fleeting second placed her hand on his shoulder. "I am sorry that you had to do this," she said in a low voice close to his ear. "When we needed one more man I had no idea he would turn out to be you. I am sorry about a number of things."

She moved her hand to the chairback and carefully climbed down. He stopped her before she could turn away, catching her hand in his. "Are you sorry that we met?" His voice was a low whisper, the words out before he could think.

She wouldn't look at him. She hesitated for a long moment before she answered. "No. But other things."

He knew it would be folly to press her further. "I have to go to London in the morning," he said quickly, while there was still no one near enough to hear. "We have gained some information, but we have no proof. I will return by Saturday."

Startled, she turned to look at him then, the full force of her blue-violet eyes resting upon him. "You know who it is, then?"

"Shh." He put his finger against her lips. "You will do better not knowing for these next two days, and so will Vivian. How else will you be able to act the same as you have been? It is especially important now that we do not arouse suspicion." He could not help tracing his fingertip across her cheek before he withdrew it. "The nightmare is almost over. Have faith."

The Duchess of Brancaster swept in at that moment, accompanied by Lady Sibbingham and trailed by Lady FitzHarris. The duchess was resplendent in a pure white gown trimmed with silver tissue, its revealing *décolletage* nearly filled with a magnificent necklace of diamonds. From the sparkling tiara nestled on her powdered hair to the silver slippers on her feet, she was the perfect queen of diamonds. The two ladies behind her were dressed more like the gentlemen, in long tunics with tabards over them. Lady Sibbingham was a tall and rather spindly seven of diamonds, and Lady FitzHarris was a pleasantly round four of spades.

"Are we all ready?" the duchess inquired. "I am told it is time we took our seats."

"Where are Vivian and Lady Caroline? Oh, I know Caroline will be back in a moment, she was nearly ready before. And I thought Vivian was almost finished when I left our rooms to come here," Venetia moaned. "I did think it would help if we all could sit together."

"We'll save seats for them," counseled Gilbey. "Everything will work out, you'll see."

Chapter Nineteen

Lady Colney's extravaganza surprised everyone except her. The entire production showed a high level of skill and imagination.

"But I *knew* we were all supremely talented," she cooed modestly in response to the compliments that poured in the following day. "Just think what we could have done with more notice!"

One of the greatest surprises had been the revelation of the twins' secret poet. Dressed in a doublet with a large Elizabethan ruff around his neck, Lord Munslow had begun his performance by reciting one of Shakespeare's sonnets. That completed, he had gone on to another poem which the astonished twins had recognized instantly.

"That is one of *our* poems!" Vivian had whispered.

"Lord Munslow? I would never have thought it!" Venetia had exclaimed. "Do you suppose he could have memorized it when we showed it last Monday night?" She had heard tales of gamblers who owed their success to remarkable memories. "Imagine a gamester with the heart of a poet."

When she confronted him during the interval, he had smiled charmingly and kissed her hand.

"I confess, I am your man. Competing with so many other fine gentlemen, I thought to claim your attention by a different method."

"I am more than a little surprised," she said. "We thought it might be Lord Lindell. But how did you manage to deliver the poems without being discovered?"

"Ah, that is my secret. You'll find I am a man of many talents."

Venetia wondered briefly if those talents included black-mail, but she thought he lacked a motive.

All of the performances, dancing cards included, were well received by the admittedly prejudiced audience. Most of the guests were so busy congratulating one another the next morning, few besides Venetia noticed Lord Cranford's absence.

Even Vivian took little note of it, although the viscount was indeed on her mind. She found her twin in the secluded rose garden, sitting by the fountain after a late breakfast.

"Netia, I must speak with you," she began earnestly. "'Tis about Lord Cranford. Y-you must stop this trying to throw us together. Last night was just too much."

"Last night?"

"You do not know how it felt to hurry in at the last minute dressed as the queen of clubs and discover that he was my ace. I almost walked right back out, Netia. How could you?"

"Why, Vivi, I made Lord Newcroft the king of clubs. I wasn't thinking of that at all."

"You have been throwing Lord Cranford at me all week, ever since Friday morning when we went sketching down by the river. But did you ever stop to ask me what I thought about your plan, or to tell me why you thought it was a good idea? No, you just carried on by yourself. Do you expect me to believe you now that last night was not more of the same?"

Venetia was astounded by this outburst from her quiet sister. "Truly, Vivi. I admit that I have been trying to do that, but not last night. I—I had other things on my mind."

"I wish you had heard Lord Newcroft and Lord Cranford during the interval. I don't believe they knew I could hear them. Lord Newcroft said he supposed Lord Cranford had won me since he was chosen to be the ace. Lord Cranford answered that it all depended upon the game being played, whether the ace ranked high or low. They were not talking about cards at all, I am quite certain."

"I am sorry, Vivi. Do you not care for Lord Cranford even a little bit? He seems to me ideally suited to you—he is patient and kind, calm and very capable. I know he would be good to you. You find him handsome—you thought so before

I did. I had an idea that, well, if I agreed to marry the Duke of Thornborough, perhaps Father would overlook Lord Cranford's rank and lack of fortune and agree to let you marry him."

"Well, that explains that! I could not understand why you were suddenly showing interest in the duke." Vivian sat down on the fountain edge beside her sister. "I like Lord Cranford well enough, Netia, but I think you are the one who has become most taken with him." The uncharacteristically stubborn set of Vivian's chin challenged Venetia to deny it.

Venetia dipped her hand into the pool and splashed water at the bronze figure of the burdened woman in the center. "I promise you needn't worry that I will 'throw him' at you anymore. He left for London this morning."

"London! No wonder you were sitting out here looking so dejected. Oh, I am sorry."

Venetia sighed. "I suppose I should look happier. He and Nicholas think they have discovered the blackmailer, and Lord Cranford has gone to London to try to get proof."

"Who is it, then? How could you not tell me?"

"Truly, I do not know who it is." She explained why Nicholas and Cranford had decided not to tell them.

"Then Lord Cranford is coming back?"

"By Saturday, he promised. He said we must have faith."

"I see," Vivian answered. She had a very thoughtful look in her eyes.

"I don't know what we are going to do. Saturday is the day after tomorrow. How can we make a choice until we know the blackmailer? Even once we know, I am uncertain what to do. I wish we had been born peasants. No one would care whom we married. Never have I dreaded an event so much as I do the ball on Saturday."

Vivian had a very good idea of what she should do when she left her sister. Lord Cranford did not make her feel special, excited, and alive, but Lord Ashurst did. In addition, Ashurst was wealthy and obviously eligible in her father's eyes. If he might be willing to marry her—and that was a very large and frightening "if"—perhaps her father would allow Venetia to marry Lord Cranford. Vivian was convinced that her twin was in love with the viscount. She might be able to take Venetia's plan and turn it around, if *she* were to make the superlative match.

There were possible obstacles in the plan, she knew. One was that her father might not be willing to settle for a less than exemplary husband for Venetia, since she was the healthy twin. Although he did not acknowledge Vivian's epilepsy, he was not so blind as to pretend she was perfectly normal. There was a better chance that he would accept someone like Lord Cranford for the twin who was flawed.

Then there was Lord Ashurst. She had hardly been near him since Sunday. Venetia had assured her that he had not seen her seizure, but she was certain he must know that something was wrong. He had seen the beginning of it, during those nightmarish moments when the buzzing and the dizziness had begun, warning her that she was about to disgrace herself. There had been no escape, no hope of hiding what was going to happen from the one man she most wished not to see it.

Could she face him again? Even harder, could she tell him the truth? Could she face his rejection? The price of avoiding it would be never knowing if he might have accepted her.

Thursday afternoon she pondered how she could have a private word with him, and she tried to find the courage to pursue it. She and Venetia were busy, for they had much to prepare for Saturday's ball, despite all the arrangements that had been made prior to the start of the house party. Thursday evening was devoted as usual to card games and other entertainments, and Vivian begged to retire, claiming that she was tired.

On Friday morning Lord Ashurst himself forced her hand. A small party of guests had decided to go punting on the lake again, and the marquess particularly sought her out in the grand salon where she and Venetia were supervising the hanging of decorations for the ball.

"Our time was regrettably foreshortened when we went out on Sunday," he said, his gray eyes intent. "Would you not honor me with another opportunity?"

She hesitated, glancing at Venetia. Her sister bit her lip and turned away, obviously concerned, but for this once wise enough not to interfere. *Thank you, Netia,* Vivian thought. *I need to make my own mistakes.*

Dare she go? It was not the same time of day as Sunday, and the sun would not be reflecting off the water in the same way. It might be her only chance to speak with him. She nodded, committing herself quickly before she could change her mind. "Y-you don't mind waiting while I get my shawl and bonnet?"

Venetia watched Vivian leave the room with her hand tucked tentatively into the crook of Lord Ashurst's elbow. A dozen feelings buffeted her at once. Hope whispered possibilities she had not considered—perhaps Lord Cranford was not the only man who could be a good husband for Vivian; perhaps Vivian knew it and had gone with Lord Ashurst to face her future. Fear called up images of what had nearly happened Sunday and every other time Vivian had come close to danger—only this time if Vivian had a seizure, there would be no one but Ashurst to help her—Ashurst, who knew not what to expect or what to do. Venetia had almost begged her not to go, and then she had battled the urge to call her back. She did not want Vivian to let fear rule her life.

A sense of loneliness and loss stabbed her as she turned back to watch the servants arrange drapes of gold tissue over the French windows. She would be very happy if at least Vivian could make a successful match, but her own days would become long indeed. How much she would miss her sister's companionship! She thought again that her solace in a loveless marriage would have to be children. Was there one among the suitors who might make a good father? There was none among them but Cranford she could love.

She closed her eyes, fighting the sadness that washed over her. This would never do! Where was the backbone that she could always rely on? She was no milk-and-water miss. She would tell her father that she refused to choose, and that she would not abide by his choosing, either.

"Are you all right, my lady?" asked one of the maids.

No, in truth I am not. If she rebelled against her father this time, the consequences might mean she would never marry, and those imaginary children would never be born. She would have to consider some more.

She forced a smile. "Sorry, I am just tired, I think. Let us proceed with our work here."

The decorations in the salon were finished and Venetia was checking some other details with her father's steward some time later when Vivian returned. One look at her sister's flushed face and sparkling eyes told Venetia that her twin had good news.

"Thank you, Mr. Dobson. I'll speak with you again later," she said, dismissing the man. She turned to Vivian and began to walk toward the door with her. "Let us go to our rooms, Vivi. You can tell me everything."

"Oh, Netia! Everything is going to be all right, I can feel it. I have such news!"

Everything will be all right. Cranford had said something like that, too. If only she believed it!

Vivian was almost skipping. She could not wait until they reached the privacy of their sitting room. "Netia, Lord Ashurst wishes to marry me!" she blurted out as they hurried through the corridor leading to the south wing.

Ashurst. Would he be as good for Vivian as Cranford? Happiness glowed in Vivian's face and Venetia finally pushed aside her doubts. She hugged her sister. "Oh, Vivi, I am happy for you. Tell me everything he said."

"I was so afraid to talk to him. I had decided I must explain to him about Sunday. I was sure he would be horrified once he knew. But listen, he knew already! He said he has been thinking about nothing else since Sunday, and he wanted to ask me some questions, and would I mind? Would I mind! He made it so easy for me, the way he asked. He was so gentle and concerned. He asked things like how often I have the seizures, and if there are things I cannot do because of it . . ."

She colored and dropped her voice to a mere whisper. "He wanted to know if I thought having epilepsy would make being a mother difficult for me! Can you imagine that we talked of such a thing? He told me that I should not be ashamed—that what happens to me is just a natural function that sometimes goes wrong. . . . He is so intelligent! He reads a great deal, and he has no taste for an active social life. It is almost too perfect. Netia, I must be in love with him. He makes me feel so . . . well, I can't describe it."

I know, Venetia thought. *The way Cranford makes me feel.* She hugged her twin again. "Whoever would have thought it! It is more than we ever hoped for. It is wonderful. And Father could not possibly object."

The last comment slipped out unwittingly and brought her sister back to earth in an instant. "Netia. Perhaps Father would allow you to wed Lord Cranford. That is what you really wish, is it not?"

Venetia shook her head. "Even if Father approved, which I doubt, Lord Cranford has no wish to marry now. Let us just rejoice over your good fortune." The joy and sorrow mixing in her heart pushed tears into her eyes. It was Vivian's turn to hug her.

"Maybe we can do something to make it work out," she said hopefully. "I want you to be as happy as I am."

"No, Vivi. Some things cannot be fixed or finagled, despite our best efforts. God knows we would have cured your epilepsy if we could, and there is no cure for this, either. You deserve this happiness, more than anyone, and much more than I. Perhaps in some small measure it can help to make up for the suffering you have had to and will always have to face because of the accident."

She paused and looked intently into her sister's face. The tears had overflowed and trickled unheeded down her face. "Do you know how many times I have asked God in the last six years why it happened the way it did? If we had not been sitting where we were, I could have been the one who was injured and became epileptic."

"I know, Netia. Shh. Either you or I could have been sitting where Mother was, and might have been killed. There is no use thinking like that."

"But, Vivi, I was the one who switched places with you just before we started off. Do you not remember that? No matter what happens to me now, you must think of this happiness as a precious gift that you deserve. I will thank God for it every day that we live."

They had finally reached their chambers, and Vivian opened

the door to the sitting room to usher her tearful sister inside. On the floor was a folded, sealed bit of paper.

"It won't be a poem this time," Venetia said as Vivian picked it up and broke the seal.

"No, you are right," she said, scanning it quickly. "These are instructions, for you."

Chapter Twenty

The twins were not able to get a moment alone with Nicholas until after they had broken their fast on Saturday morning. As soon as they had finished eating, they convened for a war council in one of the small anterooms. There they presented the blackmailer's note to him along with Vivian's news. She and Ashurst had obtained her father's blessing with no difficulty, but the official announcement was to be held until the ball.

Venetia watched the emotions play across her brother's face. His joy over Vivian's betrothal was tempered by the seriousness of the situation they faced this morning. After congratulating Vivian and wishing her happy with a brotherly hug, he suggested that the twins sit down.

"I would give anything to be able to celebrate this good news freely," he said, standing by the fireplace and tapping the blackmailer's note repeatedly against his palm. "Unfortunately we still must deal with this other matter. There is even more at stake now than ever. I suppose it is time for me to tell you that Lord Munslow is our villain."

"Lord Munslow!" The twins exchanged a glance, both much chagrined.

"I did wonder about him, but he seemed to have no motive. I was certain that our poet and our villain could not be one and the same," Venetia said. "Yet, I suppose it makes sense. He clearly had a way to deliver the notes to our room, and if anyone had seen him, he could have claimed they were merely more poems. And blackmail is a gamble. The scheme probably even had a certain appeal to as dedicated a gamester as he appears to be."

She shivered, thinking back to the charming way he had

kissed her hand during the show Wednesday evening. "I think I would have preferred it to be the Duke of Thornborough, old as he is. It made him seem more human, somehow, to think that his pride might cover such desperation about his fleeing years. Or even Lord Newcroft, with his ambitions. Both of their reasons draw more sympathy than Lord Munslow's. I assume he needs my dowry?"

Nicholas nodded, his mouth set in a grim line. "Cranford learned that he is deeply in debt. I'm sure our family looked like a bottomless honey pot when he realized the value of the secret he had learned."

"How did he know?" Vivian asked softly, her fists and her voice tight.

"Do you remember a young groom named Joseph? He was one of the ones who left after you developed the epilepsy. I'm sure he never meant any harm—it probably just slipped out one day, perhaps when Munslow said he'd been invited to come here."

Venetia glanced anxiously at the longcase clock that stood in one corner. "What shall we do if Lord Cranford has not returned before eleven o'clock, Nicholas? He would have had to leave London by early last evening to arrive by then!"

"Do not underestimate my friend Cranford, ladies," Nicholas said, not for the first time. "It is perfectly possible that he might have done that, if he found the proof he was seeking."

"I will have to go ahead and meet with Lord Munslow as he instructed," Venetia said soberly. "Alone."

"Do you think I could tell Ashurst what is happening?" Vivian asked. "I don't know how he could fail to notice that something is going on. Perhaps we might need his help."

"He is obviously both honorable and discreet. Yes, Vivi, I think that another ally might be a wise idea at this point. We really don't know how Munslow is going to react when he learns he has been thwarted. I don't like the idea of you going to meet him alone, Netia, but I also hope it won't be necessary. What I will suggest is that we position ourselves to keep an eye on him until then. I do not trust the man, and I don't want to risk that he has set any kind of trap for you."

"Where is he now?"

"He was in the room eating breakfast when we were. Perhaps he had it in mind to keep an eye on us! If that is so, we should have no difficulty finding him. Some of the guests were going to set up a game of ninepins on the lawn. Perhaps we could set up a few other games as well, and get him involved in one."

Vivian went off to find Ashurst and enlist his help, and Venetia and Nicholas went off to find Lord Munslow. It seemed Nicholas's theory might have been correct, for Lord Munslow was easy to find and seemed more than willing to take part in some games. Ashurst and Vivian joined them a few minutes later, and they played trap-ball and ninepins until it was nearly eleven. There had been no sign of Cranford.

"Oh, this is certainly fatiguing," Venetia exclaimed, hiding the fact that her heart was in her throat. "I think I shall go in and try to find a cold drink. Shall I have some refreshments sent out to the rest of you?"

Clearly Lord Cranford was not going to be there in time, despite Nicholas's faith in him. After all, Cranford had no way of knowing that he needed to be back at any particular time as long as he returned before the ball.

Lord Munslow's expression betrayed nothing at all. He declined her offer along with the others, but made no move to leave off playing. Venetia had half expected him to offer to accompany her. She took her leave, heading to the house for appearance's sake before she went out again through the garden.

The crafty earl had chosen his site well, suggesting they meet in the gazebo at the far end of the garden. Screened by topiary, it was remote and very private. Reluctant and nervous, Venetia tried to appear casual as she strolled through the paths. A number of guests were scattered about in the various terraced levels of the garden, but there was no one near the end where the gazebo stood.

Fully expecting to have to sit and wait for Lord Munslow, Venetia was disconcerted to smell lilacs as she pushed past the huge bushes and went up the steps of the entrance. *Now what shall I do?* she thought. Someone else was sitting on the bench inside the gazebo.

* * *

Gilbey had dozed on and off as Nicholas's carriage hurtled along the Gloucester Road from London. He and Nicholas's coachman had set out from town Friday night as soon as he knew there was nothing more he could do there. He had promised a lavish reward to compensate the man for his loss of sleep and the best speed he could make.

Awake since their last stop to change horses, Gilbey stared out the window and tried to shake off the strange feeling left by the dreams that had plagued his sleep. In the dreams he had felt lost, like a man who had taken a wrong turn without knowing it. He had checked with the coachman twice to be certain they were on the right road to reach Rivington. He knew the man must think him mad, since Nicholas traveled the route often enough.

He blamed the letter he had received from Gillian in part for the dreams. He had read it Thursday on his way to London, and several times since then. She had written once again of her blissful life with her husband and family and had criticized him again for his solitary ways. It was her comparing him to his father that bothered him most. Why could she not see that he had chosen his path precisely to avoid ending up like their father? Yet in his dreams he had been in his father's study at Cliffcombe instead of in his own back at Cambridge. Everywhere he looked he saw Venetia—poised on the desk, putting books on the shelves, even spinning his father's globe with a sinful smile.

It was natural that he should feel uneasy, he reasoned. He did not know what might have been happening at Rivington in his absence. He needed to be there. Any man who could coolly gamble the amounts that Munslow owed in London while keeping the entire *ton* in the dark had a dangerously devious mind. That Venetia should be at his mercy for any time at all was unthinkable—unbearable. *Hurry*. It was all he could do not to add his shouts to the snap of the coachman's whip over the horses' heads.

He was out of the carriage almost before it stopped when they finally reached Rivington, pausing only to snatch some papers off the seat at the last moment. Racing into the hall as he stuffed them under his arm, he almost ran over Blaine, the steward's assistant. He quickly learned that the twins had been playing games out on the lawn and he hastened back outside.

Nicholas, Vivian, Lord Ashurst, and a few others were engaged in trap-ball as he came hurrying around the corner of the house. He slowed down as he realized that Lord Munslow was also among them. He saw no sign of Venetia. Why wasn't she with them? He did not wish to precipitate a confrontation with Munslow prematurely, so he headed toward the terrace outside the grand salon. He would find a footman to bring Nicholas to him.

"Where is Venetia?" he demanded as soon as his friend appeared. "Why is she not with you?"

"Thank God you are back!" Nicholas said, the worry on his face now very apparent. "She is supposed to be meeting with Munslow even as we are speaking, but he has made no move at all to keep the tryst. We don't know what to think. Could we have been wrong? But how can we suddenly break off now and go haring off to investigate? What if he is testing us to see if she told anyone?"

Gilbey's fears rose like bile in his throat, but he choked them back. Clear thinking had never been so essential. "I can go," he said. "No one knows I have returned—I'm sure I turned off before any of the guests saw me. Where is she?"

He formed a plan. "You must end the game and bring Munslow to the gazebo in a few minutes," he said tersely. "I will go now. If we are wrong about him he can help us apprehend the real villain. If not, it will no longer matter if he learns the jig is up. Don't wait too long."

Lady Norbridge looked at Venetia with what could only be called a sly smile.

"Meeting someone, my dear? Funny, I was beginning to think of this little shelter as my own personal *boudoir*. Much more private than the house, don't you agree?"

Dear God, what can I say to get rid of her, Venetia thought desperately.

"I never would have taken you for the type, actually, but then after running into you the other day in the garden, I'd have to say appearances can be deceiving. Aren't they?" She began to laugh, and Venetia nearly panicked over the thought that Lord Munslow might be approaching and would hear her.

"Please, Lady Norbridge," she began, but the countess cut her off.

"Oh, am I making you nervous? Is your friend due any moment? I can put your mind at ease. It is actually you I have been waiting for." She clicked open the watch that hung from her belt. "You are a minute or two late, are you not? Ah, I see that we have surprised you."

Venetia opened her mouth and closed it again, remembering just in time that she still was not supposed to know who she was meeting.

"So touching, your concern for your sister's privacy. Such a tragedy that a beautiful girl like her should be saddled with a hideous, incurable malady. But then, many people's tragedies make profitable secrets. You are ready to meet our terms, I take it? Perhaps you will not be totally averse to marriage with my partner. He is not really such a bad sort, at least not to look at. It is unfortunate that he cannot hold on to a single farthing that comes his way."

"Your partner?"

"Lord Munslow. Surprised you again, haven't I? We became a team soon after my husband died. We discovered we both had appetites that far exceed our capacity to satisfy them. Few people are aware of the connection. We find it more profitable to keep it that way."

Venetia realized with growing horror that Lady Norbridge meant she had victimized others before the St. Aldwyns, and apparently intended to continue.

"H-how much money do you need?" she asked. "Would it not be better if I married someone wealthy? I could still pay you for your silence."

"I thought that, but Lord Munslow actually desires to wed you, my dear. He does need to produce an heir, after all. Being connected by marriage to one of the highest-ranked families short of royalty rather appeals to him."

Venetia thought of the poems he had written and felt a little sick to her stomach. The idea of carrying the child of such a villain repelled her thoroughly.

"I suppose no amount of money would be sufficient to equal that." It was Cranford's voice.

Venetia whirled around to see him standing between the huge yews at the entrance to the gazebo.

"Lord Cranford!" uttered Lady Norbridge in surprise.

"Yes, quite." He advanced up the few steps to join them. "Pray, do not let me interrupt you, Lady Norbridge. I was finding your discussion most enlightening. Although I admit that I was already aware of some parts of it." He patted the folded papers under his arm.

Lady Norbridge blanched. "Wh-what is that?"

"Oh, you'll learn that momentarily. Let us just wait for the others to arrive, shall we?"

"Others?"

"Yes. Your partner is coming with Lord Edmonton and Lord Ashurst, I believe. I wouldn't advise you to try to leave before they get here."

Venetia was amazed by the tone of menace in his voice.

"I'm curious to know how a pair like you and Lord Munslow managed to be included in a select gathering like this one," Cranford continued.

Lady Norbridge looked at him with a venomous expression, her eyes narrowed. "We are welcomed in all the best circles, Lord Cranford. Lord Munslow is thought to be exceedingly plump in the pockets because of his extravagant ways. People like Lady Colney are easy to fool. All I had to do was drop a hint that he might be interested in her nieces and—*voilà*—we were put on the list."

Within another minute, the other three men arrived. Vivian was with them. Wordlessly she went to Venetia and hugged her, taking hold of her hand protectively.

Cranford studied Lord Munslow and Lady Norbridge for a moment before he spoke. "I have just returned from London," he then announced, "where I went in search of a groom employed by Lord Munslow, one Joseph Stone, for the purpose of obtaining a deposition." He patted the papers under his arm. "Shall I read these to you?"

Lady Norbridge turned to Lord Munslow. "I didn't think Joseph knew about our plans. You fool! How could you have let him know?"

"I never let on to him," the earl hissed at her. "He must have overheard you. You should have been more careful!"

"I'm afraid we know a good deal about your scheme, Lord Munslow, and also about certain parties in London who have been quite discreet about monies you owe to them."

"Wh-what are you going to do?" Lord Munslow asked. He was trembling.

"I suggest a nice trip abroad for you and Lady Norbridge, if you can scrape together enough for your passage. Those certain parties are not likely to be pleased with you should they realize you won't be making more payments. And we'll see to it that you won't. In addition I strongly suggest that you continue to keep to yourselves any and all of the secrets you have been trading on, including Lady Vivian's." He gestured to the little group around him. "You can see that it is not such a deep and terrible secret as you suppose. In return, we will maintain these"—and here he patted the papers again—"as our own little secret. You will have to accept our word on it, I'm afraid. It is fortunate for you that we are gentlemen."

The two villains stood still, as if quite uncertain how to proceed.

"An abject apology would be suitable," Nicholas prompted.

"Followed by a hasty departure, I would think," Ashurst added, "before we forget that we are gentlemen."

Lord Munslow and Lady Norbridge took the hint. As soon as they had departed, Nicholas and Ashurst clapped Cranford on the back and began to congratulate him. Venetia slipped the folded papers out from under his arm so he wouldn't drop them.

Curious, she opened them, only to discover that the top page was blank. She peeked underneath and found that the second page was blank as well. She checked them all, and every single page was blank. Astonished, she rounded on Cranford.

"Lord Cranford, what does this mean? All of these papers you brought from London are blank."

Cranford grinned sheepishly, in an endearing way that nearly made her heart crack. How was she supposed to live without him?

"Well, I never actually was able to find Joseph Stone, or get his deposition. Did I say that I did? I'm afraid I returned from

London with no more actual proof than we had when I left. But my brother-in-law does know the parties to whom Munslow owes money—knows *of* them, I should say."

Venetia could hardly believe her ears. "That was a splendid finesse! What would you have done if they had looked at the papers?"

Cranford chuckled. "I assumed that they would not. Their own guilt was enough to condemn them. I'm guessing it was Lady Norbridge who delivered the notes and the poems. Her room was near yours, and as a woman she was far less likely to be noticed going to and from that section of the house. We never once thought to consider a woman."

Nicholas was laughing now. "You *are* a gambler, old man, or you have become one since coming here. What have we done? Is there any risk now that you will not venture?"

"I seem to have hit a streak of luck, but I would not say I am a changed man," Cranford answered, sobering.

No, I suppose not, Venetia thought. The conversation had started to go in an uncomfortable direction. "We have news," she said abruptly, realizing that he did not yet know of Vivian's betrothal.

"Indeed," said Ashurst, beaming as he told the viscount of the betrothal. "You must wish us happy."

After congratulating him and Vivian, Cranford turned to Venetia. "And you, Lady Venetia? May I wish you happy as well? I know the betrothals are to be announced at the ball, but I am afraid I may not be there. I am exceedingly tired from my hectic night on the road, and hope you will forgive me if I need to sleep more than dance. Is it to be the Duke of Thornborough? Or has someone else become the favorite since I left?"

Venetia thought she would have liked to kick him. Or worse. The urge to pummel him with her fists made her fingers itch, but then she realized that those fingers would have quickly slid up his shoulders to tangle in his hair, and they would not have been pulling on it. Such warm thoughts! She surprised herself.

"No," she said coldly. "You may not wish me happy. And I have no intention of telling you my choice if you intend to miss the ball. There is still half the day left for you to rest before it starts."

"Venetia, you have not even thanked Lord Cranford for all his trouble," Vivian remonstrated softly. "Sir, we are deeply in your debt for what you have done. I thank you from the bottom of my heart. We all do."

Gilbey did try to sleep in his room that afternoon. He lay in his bed in torment while his mind tried to match Venetia with the various suitors that were left. The Duke of Thornborough was too old, Lord Lindell was too young. Lord Amberton was too foolish. The thought of Lord Wistowe touching her in between his other *amours* nearly got Gilbey out of his bed in anger.

That left Lord Chesdale, Lord Newcroft, and Colonel Hatherwick. *Wasted, she would be wasted, on any of them.* The good-natured colonel would always be off fishing and Venetia would die of boredom married to him. Lord Newcroft would show her off like a newly purchased horse and trot her around to every place that might advance his position. Lord Chesdale—well, perhaps Venetia could influence him to drop some of his affected posing and peering through his quizzing glass, but she would always play second to his cattle. Gilbey groaned and rolled onto his stomach.

Eventually he slept but he dreamed restlessly. He awoke hours later in a dark room, convinced that Gillian had just been there, pointing a finger at him and calling him a fool. He fumbled in the darkness until he found the tinderbox and matches so he could light a candle to look at his watch. He had missed dinner. He knew he could not miss the ball as well. *He had to know.*

Some time later Gilbey, dressed in his best dark blue evening coat and white pantaloons, walked quietly through the corridor leading to the main part of the house. All was very still, leading him to suspect that the other guests were already assembled in the grand salon, now pressed into use as a ballroom. He hated to make an entrance, especially if he was late. He did not really wish his presence to be noted at all—he just wanted to know who Venetia would marry. *So I can spend my years hating him.* The thought caught him by surprise. He decided to slip outside and watch unnoticed from the terrace. He did not think of it as cowardly, just unobtrusive.

The salon was ablaze with light spilling out into the darkness of the terrace along with the sweet strains of music. The French windows stood open, allowing a fine view of the kaleidoscopic scene within. Gilbey stood in the shadows and watched for a few minutes, picking out the Duke of Roxley in black evening clothes, looking proud and authoritarian, and the twins' aunt in bright yellow, looking flushed and pleased with life and the world.

The twins were dancing, moving through the figures of the new quadrille they had learned from the French dance master just last week. They both wore white gowns, but each had a different color for accent. Venetia's had silver trimming and a bodice inset and underskirt of blue satin. Silver gleamed in her hair as well. She looked more beautiful than ever. Vivian's gown featured lavender.

The dance ended and he lost sight of the twins. Maybe he was a fool standing out here in the dark like some sort of *voyeur*. Maybe he should go back to his room. The betrothals might not be announced for hours yet. Before he made up his mind to leave, someone stepped onto the terrace and it was suddenly too late.

"Lord Cranford. What are you doing skulking about in the darkness?" It was Venetia.

Of course. It would be. "Uh, spying? Pretending I am still in my room? Uh, obviously nothing very heroic."

She laughed, and he wanted to hug the sound and commit it to memory. He would be leaving in only a matter of hours, as soon as morning came. If he ever saw her again, they would be strangers.

"I think you have already proven yourself heroic enough for one day. I still need to thank you."

"Only for one day?"

"A day, a week, a month, a lifetime." She put her hand over her mouth when the last word came out.

He moved closer to her. He wanted to touch her, to remember that she was real. After tonight, this would all seem like a dream. "Venetia. Tell me who you have chosen. I have to know."

"Why? What does it matter to you? It is really none of your business, is it?" She was like quicksilver, she changed moods so rapidly. Now she sounded angry. She stared up at him. "If you want to know so badly, I'll tell you. Nobody. I've decided to marry no one."

He was shocked. "What about your father?"

"Hang my father. I have already told him. Oh, he was not pleased, but there it is. No announcement for me. I am certain the gossip will go on for weeks or months, maybe years."

"Why no one, after all this?"

She stamped her foot. "You just won't leave it alone, will you?" She narrowed her eyes, which glittered a little in the darkness with what might have been tears. "Maybe you deserve to know. Maybe you'll take the guilt home with you and lock it up in your study with your books. It's because I am in love with you! I cannot marry anyone else. I thought I might, but I can't."

"Venetia." He took her into his arms and felt her rigid indignation melt away almost instantly. "I love you, too," he whispered into her hair. "I tried to fight it, and then I thought I could run away from it. But I can't, God help me. I must be just like my father after all."

She pulled away a little bit, enough so she could look up at him. "No, you are not. You suffered from his mistakes, and you also learned from them. I don't believe that you would repeat those mistakes, no matter what happened."

Was she right? Was he simply afraid to take the chance? She felt so right in his arms, as if she belonged there. "I promised your father . . ." Well, no, he hadn't actually promised. She was looking up at him, completely irresistible. He reached down for her, touching his lips to hers, lost in the moment and completely forgetting where they were.

Nicholas was the one who discovered them. "And what have we here?" he said softly as he stepped onto the terrace.

Gilbey and Venetia sprang apart, then Gilbey reached for her hand and brought it to his lips. He turned to face Nicholas.

"What we have is two people who love each other. I want to marry your sister, Nicholas. How angry will your father be?"

Nicholas whistled. "We really have turned you into a gambler, old man. My sister had better keep a tight rein on you."

Venetia put her arms around Gilbey. "Are you certain?" she whispered.

When he nodded she thought her heart would soar right out of her breast. Instead it seemed to have caught in her throat. "If you come inside with me now, you can see for yourself," she said through tears of happiness. "I told him I loved you, and how you helped us. He may have felt sure that you would not offer for me, but nevertheless he did say that if you had offered, he would have had to accept you in view of how you protected our family."

"Oh, foolish father," quipped Gilbey.

Nicholas was still standing there. "He would have to agree now, anyway, old man. Seems to me you have just compromised my sister's reputation. At her own betrothal ball! Well, I never thought there was anything wrong with your sense of timing. If you take her in right now, you'll be just in time for the waltz."

Gilbey and Venetia looked at each other wonderingly and then smiled. "I never have met such a family of manipulative schemers," Gilbey said. "From now on I think the only one I can trust is your father."

Nicholas put up his hands in a gesture of innocence. "All I did was get you to come here." But neither Gilbey nor Venetia had ever seen Nicholas with quite such a satisfied grin.

Author's Note

Epilepsy is a common problem. According to one source I consulted, one in two hundred people in the United States and three in two hundred in Europe struggle with this affliction in its many different forms. The real numbers could be much higher, for many epileptics don't report their disability.

Researching this story, I was struck by how social attitudes toward epilepsy have changed only in degree since the early nineteenth century. Fear, ignorance, and suspicion are still common attitudes toward those who suffer with it today. Many epileptics hide their condition to protect their jobs, while others face chronic unemployment, sometimes simply for the lack of a driver's license. Some face a lack of understanding and support even among their own family.

I hope meeting Vivian will make my readers more aware of those who must cope with epilepsy every day. Epileptics are among us everywhere, not just in the newspaper or in the local homeless shelter. Social attitudes take time to change, but that change begins in one heart and mind at a time.

Information is available from the Epilepsy Foundation of America, 4351 Garden City Drive, Landover, MD 20785, or from your local Epilepsy Society.

P.S. The story of Gilbey's sister Gillian was told in my first novel, *A Perilous Journey* (Signet, 1994).